OLD DARK HOUSES

HOUSES

A Halloween Novel

OLD DARK HOUSES

A HALLOWEEN NOVEL

BY TYLOR JAMES

WEIRD HOUSE

First Trade Paperback Edition

ISBN: 978-1-957121-59-8

Editor & Publisher, Joe Morey
Copy editing and book design by F. J. Bergmann

Weird House Press
Central Point, OR 97502
www.weirdhousepress.com
Join the Weird House mailing list at our website!

Old dark houses creaking, groaning, moaning with the twitching of new life.

LIST OF ILLUSTRATIONS

TABLE OF CONTENTS

OLD DARK HOUSES: A HALLOWEEN NOVEL

*This novel is a love letter
to Halloween.
As such,
it is dedicated to
the true scholars of our macabre holiday:
Lisa Morton
and
Leslie Bannatyne.*

Part 1:

Save the Old Dark Houses!

CHAPTER ONE

Something is going to happen.

Everyone felt it—that unnatural chill in the air.

Leaves scurrying across the black ribbon of Main Street.

Jack-o'-lanterns glowing brilliant orange in the shuddering nights.

Old dark houses creaking, groaning, moaning with the twitching of new life.

It was one week till Halloween, just one! Everyone could feel it—that chill autumn air!

Every man, woman, and child in Sweet Hollow knew—something was going to happen.

They just couldn't say *what.*

"What?" said Harry Thanatos.

"I need them destroyed." Elise swiped away a strand of gray hair which had blown into her eyes. "Haven't you been *listening?*"

Harry and Elise lived on a hill overlooking the town. Twilight settled like a velvet blanket over the land. First stars twinkled. A thousand tiny lights, many of them sherbet orange, glimmered below. They sat in rocking chairs upon the front porch, bundled in blankets. Harry smoked a pipe. Elise sat scowling, eyes scrunched, hands knitted together.

"I've been listening all my life," answered Harry. "God knows I have. It's just I've listened so much, my ears have gone numb."

Elise ignored this remark.

Harry smoked his pipe.

"Ms. Keepwell is campaigning to preserve them," said Elise. "Did you know that?"

"Preserve what?"

"The houses, you fool! Those old dark houses."

"Fair enough." Harry shrugged, his cherry-scented smoke curling up into the dark air and fading like a ghost.

"Don't you care?" Elise frowned.

"Of course I care," he replied. "I love those old houses. Always have, ever since I was a young boy on his paper route."

"Oh, Harry, you old fool."

"Love the look of 'em. The Victorians knew what they were doing when they built those houses, let me tell you."

"I think they're stuffy and awful." Elise rolled her eyes. "I can see them from here, can't you? Hideous dark blotches upon an otherwise pristine town. Besides, they lower property value, invite squatters and vandals, increase the overall crime rate ..."

Elise went on—and on and on.

Harry sat in the dark with numbed ears, smoking his pipe.

How gorgeous was the view from up here on the hill! All those glimmering lights below, like a colony of fireflies in the vast dark. Often, on nights like this, Harry wished he were a firefly.

Elise Thanatos, a member of Sweet Hollow City Council, clutched a little harder to her plans—with the assistance of the town wrecking crew, the old dark houses would be demolished no later than November first.

There exist three silent players in this story, and they stand in crooked darkened heights. Fractured roofs brush the October sky; weathervanes screech in sudden gales; windows cracked and doors paintless; front yards overgrown into miniature jungles.

Aching and groaning in whispers of wind: *The Dark Three!*

Morton Manor loomed on the east side of town.

The Bannatyne House stood sentinel in the west.

Then, the Vallancy Estate, a sprawling abandoned mansion on the outskirts of Sweet Hollow, lurked in the Northwoods—the oldest and darkest of the old dark houses. It was also the biggest—one could easily get lost if foolish enough to enter.

Something stirred within Vallancy that twilight, as if it'd heard a cruel woman's voice on the wind: "*I need them destroyed....*"

The crumbling walls stood a little taller.

The cracked windows refracted the moon, like gleaming insect eyes.

A flurry of bats flew out the tall brick chimneys, screeching and flapping into the night. Their shadows flitted across a yellow moon, whirled over the fields and into town, then swooped and dived into the respective chimneys of Morton Manor and Bannatyne House.

As if the Vallancy were communicating with others of its kind, and the bats were its loyal messengers.

A community of old dark houses.

A community of preservationists and destroyers.

A community of children, all raring to go trick-or-treating on Halloween. Just one week away—one only!

Leaves scurried in the scandalous night. Bats skittered. Secrets stirred.

Patty Keepwell reposed beside the front window of Ellie's Café, sipping coffee, and typing feverishly on her laptop. The clicking keys sounded pleasant to her ears, and she smiled.

Her preservation essay was nearly finished. Tomorrow, she'd present it to Mayor Edmundson, and have him pass it along to City Council.

Morton Manor was built in 1851.

Bannatyne in 1842.

The Vallancy in 1798.

Two houses, one mansion, all of them old and dark and, presumably, haunted.

Patty adored these houses. Whenever walking past them on the street, she'd stop to gaze up in admiration—for they were a snapshot of a bygone century, a physical and architectural representation of the mysterious past. Curiously, she always felt as if they were somehow aware of her presence. As if all that wood, brick, stone, and glass could see and acknowledge her.

Patty drank the last of her coffee, hit Save, then closed the laptop.

"Are you going to save those old houses, Ms. Keepwell?" asked Cambria Balustrade, picking up Patty's empty mug and creamer cups and setting them on a platter.

"I'm going to try." Patty sighed. "Do you like the houses?"

"Oh, yes," Cambria beamed. "I love looking at them, particularly at night. They're so eerie and mysterious!"

"In that case," said Patty, reaching into her leather portfolio, "perhaps you wouldn't mind signing this petition?"

She handed the form to Cambria.

The barista set down her platter to sign. Her doe-like eyes scrolled down the names on the list. Only nineteen signatures. Cambria Balustrade added her own, making it twenty.

"There," she said, handing the petition back to Ms. Keepwell.

"Marvelous!" Patty tucked the page into her portfolio. After shrugging into her turquoise wool coat, she clamped her laptop and portfolio under one arm, then nodded to Cambria. "Good night, young lady. Please spread the word far and wide—we've just got to keep these old houses! They're historic landmarks. Sweet Hollow should be proud and honored to have them."

Patty stepped out onto the chilly street. The night wind nipped at her skin like icy razors, flushing her cheeks raw. She wondered with some hopelessness if her efforts were in vain. Despite her title as President of the Sweet Hollow Preservation Society, her group was small, possessing minimal influence on town affairs.

The sidewalks felt solid beneath her boots. She shivered, thinking of Mrs. Thanatos—a city councilwoman so deranged, dogmatic, and determined, what would a petition of twenty signatures accomplish?

The houses were scheduled for demolishment on All Saints Day.

Her heart broke, envisioning dump trucks and wrecking balls

destroying such precious buildings. It was akin to artistic blasphemy, like taking a bomb to the Mona Lisa. Crash! Boom! Thunder! And a wintery wind to take the ashes ...

She walked alone, frowning in daydreams of doom. Yet when passing Morton Manor, she looked up and smiled. The house, it seemed, smiled back—the blackened clapboards, the crooked rain gutter, the moonlit windows—a knowing presence stirred within. Bats pinwheeled the chimney, their tiny voices seeming to squeak: "Save us! Save us!"

Patty Keepwell had her friends in this town, by God; and although those friends were old, dark, and brooding, she intended to keep them.

The Vallancy Mansion loomed in the dark.

Despite a *NO TRESPASSING* sign nailed to the front doors, a man lived inside. Dirt smudged his face and hands. His smile was yellow and gap-toothed, and grubby rags fulfilled their pitiful duty as clothes.

During the long cool days, he'd stroll the alleys of Sweet Hollow, raiding dumpsters and garbage bins. Pushing a shopping cart he'd stolen from H. Philip's Grocery Mart, he'd collect a hodgepodge of items: half-eaten food, recycled newspapers, old toys, glass bottles, anything he could get his hands on.

The rich had everything—expensive cars, big houses, swimming pools, and influence.

This man had only what he collected in his cart.

But he also had the Vallancy. A big sprawling mansion out in the country, all to himself! Or, he wondered, did the Vallancy have *him*?

Thorn was the man's name. An odd name, a stubborn, sharp-sounding name his parents had gifted him fifty-seven years ago. It was a fitting moniker all the same, for Thorn couldn't help but feel he'd been a sharp object in society's side all his life.

Shuffled from foster home to foster home, from rehab to rehab, from street to street—until the Vallancy ushered him in.

Dark and foreboding, the old mansion had drawn Thorn like moth to flame. Thorn burned here within its crumbling walls, drowning merrily in intangible flames. For it was a break from the cold night winds, and there were plenty of old blankets to curl up in.

Always, he wore a coat of emerald fringed with golden embroidery ...

There was also company here—a man far older and wiser than Thorn, by the name of Charles Vallancy. This was his mansion, built in 1798. Charles was tall and slim and wore fanciful clothes and a powdered wig and always stared at you with sharp beady eyes and an upturned nose.

Thorn glimpsed him on occasion. Charles, rarely, stood before the great staircase, or sometimes haunted the library, flipping through the pages of a dusty book. Always, he wore a coat of emerald fringed with golden embroidery, a frilly white cravat at the neck, green ornamental vest, knee breeches, and leather shoes with stacked heels.

Thorn and Vallancy.

Vallancy and Thorn.

Despite exchanging hardly any words, they remained inseparable. For the oscillating moods of Vallancy seemed to course through Thorn's blood, so that he knew, always, what the old ghost was thinking.

Charles Vallancy thought horrible things.

Horrible, dreadful, ghastly, cruel things—the things he longed to do to the people of Sweet Hollow, particularly the children.

"The children," muttered Thorn, wrapped in blankets beneath a large foyer window. A shaft of moonlight fell upon his face, lighting it pale blue. "Those poor little children."

Thorn heard a sound and turned toward the staircase.

Charles Vallancy, eyes hard and glassy, nose upturned as if smelling something foul, stood in a semi-opaque glaze, his pallid form slightly transparent, for you could see the stairs behind him as if gazing through a fog. Now his lips twitched, quivered, and stretched into a hideous jackal smile.

And he laughed.

Chapter Two

ouses are living bodies.

Subsequently, we may postulate that a house contains a heart, brain, and soul.

A heart thumps in the attic.

A brain reflects in the basement.

As for the soul, the ghost, the spirit—such a phantasmal essence must linger throughout the wood, stone, and glass. A strange sort of smoke, swirling about the halls, corridors, and barren rooms.

A rare thing indeed, for a decrepit house to withstand the pressures of time and age! Still, the Vallancy mansion retains its vital organs, and there is little doubt that Charles is its soul.

Charles laughed, and cried, and groaned, and did all the things ghosts are wont to do. For it takes much horror, pain, and agony, to create a ghost—an adamantine personality cemented firmly in this earthly realm, writhing with too much audacity to move on to the next world.

Revenge! Greed! Pride! *The ingredients of a ghost.*

Charles Vallancy refused to witness his manse's demolishment. It was what the councilwoman desired, he knew—that miserable hag Elise Thanatos. So he'd gifted a bit of his spirit to the bats and sent them flying for the two abandoned houses in town. There, they would assemble a brain and heart for each abode.

A heart knitted and nested in the attic.

A brain bequeathed and burrowed in the basement.

Come All Hallow's Eve, those old dark houses would awaken, creaking wide their splintered doors....

Leaves of vermillion, chestnut, and gold whistled their crackly voices in the branches. Plucked by the breeze, foliage fluttered down to obscure lawns, sidewalks, and boulevards in autumnal blankets. Patty scooped up a pile of leaves and held them to her nose. Dead leaves smelled like trapped sunshine, like ancient Egypt, or an archaic book with pages of sweetest dust.

Patty traipsed down the sidewalk, her portfolio clasped to her chest. She wore a yellow scarf, denim jacket, a white skirt with pink floral brocade at the hem, and shiny black boots. Hoop earrings nestled within her coffee-colored hair. Her freckled cheeks burned pleasantly in the chill air, though a vague nervousness upset her stomach. Would Mayor Edmundson so much as glance at the petition? He was perennially busy, not to mention narrow-minded. She imagined her papers nonchalantly tossed into the recycling bin beside his desk.

Then the bulldozers and wrecking balls and beasts with yellow hardhats would arrive.

The fate of those fine Victorian houses hangs in the balance.

Jaw set, eyes gazing forward, Patty walked a little taller. Leaves crunched under her boots. Sunshine streamed through the barren poplars. She imbibed her surroundings: a jack-o'-lantern leered from every porch. Lawns bloomed strange new flowers: zombie arms stretching up from the dirt, Styrofoam tombstones that toppled in every mild wind, scarecrows reposed in lawn chairs, and the grotesque ornaments of plastic bats, skeletons, and noosed-up ghouls hung from trees.

Every house was festooned with Halloween garb—including her own.

It was said Anoka, Minnesota, was the Halloween Capital of the World, but truly, it did not compare with the annual fall festivities of Sweet Hollow.

In a few days, the Summer's End Parade would commence—a

harvest celebration with dunking for apples and costume contests, spooky floats sponsored by local businesses, and all the chestnuts, corn-on-the-cob, and chocolate candy one could desire.

Then came the night every child of Sweet Hollow pined for—not the first day of summer vacation, not their birthday, and certainly not Christmas.

Halloween. Always, and forever—that ethereal night of monsters would prolong and outlast every other holiday, custom, and tradition, grinning triumphantly at the end of the world with a smile of jagged orange teeth and glowing triangle eyes.

Patty turned the corner onto Main Street, where black-orange streamers curled about every streetlight and bench. Shop windows sported thick spiderwebs, paper skeletons, and black cats. Now, she stood before the Civic Center's old-fashioned brick façade. Inhaling a deep breath, she opened the glass door with feigned confidence.

The reception room was small and stuffy. The scuffed orange carpet beneath her shoes was a '70s relic, though quite appropriate for the town's perpetual autumn mood. The secretary sat behind the front desk. "Good morning." Patty smiled politely. "May I speak with Mayor Edmundson? I've petition signatures to deliver." Observing the secretary's nametag, Patty added, "That is, if you'd be so kind, Ms. Beauregard."

The secretary's cat-like eyes matched her green dress. She smiled prettily. Her eyelashes, long and black, blinked.

"Sure thing, Miss…?"

"I'm Ms. Keepwell," she replied. "President of the City Preservation Society."

"Ah, yes! One moment please, Ms. Keepwell." The attractive secretary pressed Line 2 for the mayor's office. After exchanging a few brief words, she placed the phone in its cradle. "You may see Mayor Edmundson now. Just down the hallway there, second door on the left."

Patty's boots clicked on the shiny linoleum. Vibrant paper jack-o'-lanterns hung from the ceiling, constructed by second-graders from Sweet Hollow Elementary. How charming they were, with their orange construction paper bodies, cockeyed yellow mouths, and green accordion arms dangling down! She reached up and tapped one appreciably, observing it jostle on its string.

At the end of the hall, she turned to the door on her left. Beside it, a tombstone-like plaque:

Mr. Arnold Edmundson,
Mayor of Sweet Hollow.

Patty rapped her knuckles against the cheap laminate door.

"Come in!" a muffled voice hollered.

Patty strode inside, shutting the door gently. Mr. Edmundson, dressed in a dark blue suit, black tie, and with excessive pomade slicking back his hair, gestured at one of two chairs in front of his desk.

"Have a seat, Ms. Keepwell."

"Thanks." She sat down.

Edmundson looked at her, not quite smiling.

"You've brought some sort of petition?" he said, finally.

"Indeed," she nodded, handing him the form. "Thirty-two signatures."

"I see." The petition lay face down on his desk. He frowned.

"I've also included an essay, which you'll want to read," Patty continued. "You see, there're numerous fiscal benefits for small towns who repair historic houses, thereby turning them into tourist destinations. It'd be a legitimate income, Mr. Edmundson, if we could repair the Bannatyne, Morton Manor, and the Vallancy instead of destroying them...."

Edmundson smiled, though it lacked warmth—a cold, thin, wintry grin.

"Ms. Keepwell," he spoke slowly, "I realize you have the best intentions. I really do. But you ought to know this humble town of ours doesn't possess the budget to fix up *one* of these houses, not to mention *three*. The Vallancy alone would cost a fortune."

"I understand that money is the biggest factor in this decision." Patty took a breath, then went on. "However, let me make this perfectly clear. My proposal is *not* to renovate these houses to utmost perfection. Not in the least, Mayor. I'm merely suggesting we repair them to the point of making them *safe*. We can pick up the detritus both inside and outside the houses, repair some windows—"

Edmundson's hand swiped at the air.

"No, no," he groaned. "Listen, Patty. Do you know how much it'd cost to replace *one single window* in one of those houses? And are you going to lend us your wallet to pay for it? Or will you be placing this burden on the taxpayers?"

"I realize these will be costly repairs, Mayor." Patty's cheeks flushed, her tone on the cusp of wavering. It took everything in her power to stifle her anger at Edmundson's condescension, yet she pushed on. "However, these repairs are an *investment*. By funneling a modest percentage of the town budget into renovating these historical landmarks, we can then make that money back *three times over* by transforming them into locations people all around the country will want to visit."

"*Those* old Victorian eyesores?" Edmundson's mouth hung open, astounded. "Who the hell would come to our town to see *that*? No, no! People come here for the Halloween *parade*, Ms. Keepwell. No one comes here for the houses. Nobody."

"Not yet," Patty persisted, smiling despite the fact she felt like crying. "But fix them up a little, create pamphlets and online literature, organize a tour, and you've got yourself a bold new tourist industry in the heart of Sweet Hollow."

Edmundson sighed, leaning back in his chair. He rubbed his chin.

He's a genuine idiot, Patty reflected. *I can smell his brains smoldering from the sheer effort to think....*

Suddenly he had both elbows on the desk, leaning drastically forward. "All right, Ms. Keepwell. You make a fair point regarding a possible tourist industry. Still, I can't say I'm sold."

"Read my essay." Patty nodded at the papers on his desk. "Then consider the petition signatures. Give me a call back at your earliest convenience. I believe you'll be surprised by my research. Very surprised, and very *pleased* to learn the financial viability of this proposal. Those old houses should be *museums*, Mayor Edmundson ... not piles of rubble."

Edmundson chewed his inner cheek.

Patty closed her eyes a moment. Discussing money was the only way to get through to this man. That was just the sort of person he was.

"I propose we hold a town hall meeting this Sunday night, Mayor," she added, cooly. "This way everyone can weigh in and have their voices heard. Now, that doesn't sound *unfair*, does it?"

A slight sliver of hope shimmered in the deep well of Patty's heart.

Kenny Vandermeer held his girlfriend's hand.

They stood on the empty street, gazing up at Morton Manor.

Last Halloween, they'd explored the decrepit old house together. It'd been the most exhilarating experience of their young lives, for the house had tested them, and they'd proved themselves brave—wandering two stories of barren rooms, exploring a library chock full of musty, water-damaged books, even climbing up into the dark, mysterious attic. Ever since that night, a kinship had formed between them.

All the houses lining the street were modern, modest, and painted in near-identical pallid colors. Kenny's house stood to the Manor's immediate left, while Anna's was on the right. Morton Manor, therefore, stuck out like a thorn among lilies—its crooked rain gutters like skeletal arms with dead leaves bunched between ulna and radius, the dusty and opaque windows like catatonic eyes, while the façade's paint had peeled away in curlicues of stripped flesh.

At night, bats swirled round the crumbling brick chimney, and their tiny shrieks almost sounded human....

"You think Patty will save it?" Anna Hardy nestled against Kenny's shoulder.

"I doubt it," Kenny frowned, squinting up at the gothic abode. "There's been talk of demolishing these houses for a long time. Plus, with Mrs. Thanatos on City Council this year, there hardly seems to be any question. It's just a matter of time."

"What a crapshoot." Anna said.

"Yep."

"There anything we can do?"

"Like what?" Kenny asked. "Throw our bodies in front of the wrecking ball?"

"Well, I mean ... I don't know! We could protest. Make some signs, have a sit-in at City Hall?"

"This isn't the 1960s, Anna."

"We have to do *something*. Remember the Halloween we spent in this house? That was the night I fell in love with you."

Kenny turned from the house and looked at her—truly looked at her, and his heart swelled within his chest. She was lovely, particularly when she smiled. Her jade eyes shone brilliantly, accentuated by black eyeliner. Her cheeks were flushed, likely due to the late October chill. Her cardigan fluttered in the breeze, and her black knee-length skirt swayed. Kenny held her close, and leaned forward. They kissed—their mouths soft and warm, counteracting the frosty wind swiping their faces.

Something lingered inside the Manor.

Not merely rats, or bats, or squatters.

A presence.

The presence had a name—Charles Vallancy.

His connection had grown stronger; the messenger bats he had sent flapping out of his Estate for Morton Manor and Bannatyne House had accomplished their mission—for their beady red eyes carried *his* eyes, and now he could see out the top of the chimneys, and through every dusty window.

Vallancy stared down at the two kissing teenagers.

How charming they were! How deeply, irrevocably in love!

A love they had first discovered within Morton Manor's yellowed, paper-stripped walls. Would they find themselves inside the Manor once again? Perhaps on a Halloween midnight?

Vallancy hoped so.

Within every splinter of wood, every fragment of brick and windowpane; within every rodent that scrabbled the creaking floors, Vallancy *knew* so.

In the blink of an eye, the fragment of a millisecond, the instant snap of a spider's silk thread, Vallancy blinked *out* of existence....

Then blinked *into* existence—this time, inside the Bannatyne House.

The Bannatyne greatly resembled Morton Manor, save for an altogether different floorplan. Charles now inhabited the rusty weathervane atop the roof; he felt the chill wind swirl about his metallic form, the orange corrosion of his flesh, and the incredible screech as he spun toward the street, and, staring down, discovered Patty Keepwell gazing up at him.

The weathervane screeched—*he* screeched.

Patty's face creased with curiosity. Did she recognize him? Or was she merely reacting to his turning in the *opposite* direction of the wind?

Vallancy admired the woman, for she intended to preserve his Estate. At the very least, she might prove useful. He doubted, however, that she would prove independently successful.

Indeed, Ms. Keepwell and those two amorous children would require more than a mere petition, essay, or town hall meeting to accomplish his purposes.

Charles Vallancy knew with steadfast certainty that, like all things in this weary, wanton world, everything must inevitably come to *life,* or *death.*

CHAPTER THREE

"**M**ake it right!" Elise Thanatos barked. She sat in the corner booth of Ellie's Café, gruffly handing her fourth vanilla latte back to the barista.

Too much sugar.

Too little!

Not frothed correctly.

Too hot, *way* too hot!

Cambria Balustrade, busily remaking Elise's latte while single-handedly attempting to serve a full house, gritted her teeth with curses. Turning up the pressure dial on the steam wand, she frothed yet another cup of skim milk.

She'd have her revenge on Elise Thanatos—somehow, someway.

The temperature not exceeding a hair over 155 degrees Fahrenheit, Cambria added two espresso shots, one pump of sugar-free vanilla syrup, then capped the cup, circumnavigated the counter, and placed it on Elise's table.

She thought, *If you turn this one away, I'm going to throw it in your face!*

The crowd of customers, all waiting in line, gazed across the room at Mrs. Thanatos. They, too, were awaiting the verdict.

Elise lifted the cup, suspicion brimming in her icy blue eyes.

In a prim poise of pretend propriety, she sipped.

She set the cup down, licking froth from her dry lips—the way her tongue darted out reminded Cambria of an iguana.

"At long last," Elise smiled, "a decent cup of coffee for a loyal customer."

"Glad you're happy," Cambria muttered, then raced back behind the counter. Thanking each customer for their patience, she speedily produced cappuccinos, hot chocolates, triple-shot Americanos, and varieties of hot tea, nearly every beverage served with a muffin, scone, or oven-toasted pastry. Occasionally, she glanced over her shoulder at Mrs. Thanatos.

How cruel that old woman was!

How she hated, despised, loathed her!

Mrs. Thanatos, belly warmed by delicious coffee, tapped away at her laptop. She regarded herself as an important woman and considered it salient that others knew she was important too. She tapped at the keys ostentatiously.

There were a dozen fresh emails in her inbox—early preparations for the spring election, allocations related to the upcoming town parade, and, of course, decisions regarding the destruction of those stupid old houses on November first.

She smiled, enjoying the noise and bustle of the morning crowd. She enjoyed the café setting, liked to think all those people going about their lives occasionally glanced over at her, more than a little awed by the crucial work she was doing—doing for *them,* as their Number One Public Servant.

Around eleven o'clock, the café emptied. Cambria busied herself with wiping down tables with a wet towel. Elise nearly closed her laptop, but an email notification pinged on the screen's bottom right.

With an aggravated sigh, she opened her gmail once more. She had grown tired of this cramped café, but really, what was one more email?

From Mayor Edmundson, no less. She clicked on it.

Within seconds, rage contorted her brow and her every pale wrinkle flushed to deep red.

Her eyes darted around the room. No one else in here—save for Cambria, busily scrubbing tables and chairs. Normally, Elise would never allow a single member of the public to glimpse this side of her, but she couldn't help it.

She began to scream. Snatching up her empty cup, she threw it across the room. It plunked against the back of Cambria's head.

"Hey, you old hag!" Cambria shouted, rubbing the back of her head. "Take a chill pill or else get *out!*"

Elise pinched the bridge of her nose. She closed her eyes. Opened them. Reread the email. She couldn't *believe* this.

It was all the fault of Patty Keepwell, that idiotic historian with a fetish for crumbling relics....

Edmundson had sent out a group email, scheduling a town hall meeting for six o'clock *tonight*. All the stupid plebians, every crazy troglodyte, Cro-Magnon, and yokel—everyone who wanted their voices heard on the matter would attend. Many of the town's older residents, Elise suspected, would *support* renovating the houses.

Undoubtedly, she knew she must attend tonight's meeting. If further arguments needed to be made in favor of demolishment, she would be there to supply them.

Elise snapped her laptop closed and gathered up her purse. At the door, she turned toward Cambria, who stood behind the counter as if it were a shield. "I'm sorry I threw the cup, young lady. Admittedly, I've lost my temper. But those old houses—don't you see—they *must* go!"

She shoved her palm against the door and left.

"I'll get you for that, Mrs. Thanatos." Cambria whispered, glaring at her through the front window. "You bet I will, bitch. You bet, you bet, you *bet!*"

Elise Thanatos' beige-colored Buick thundered into life, pulled onto Main Street, then glided out of sight.

Plaster crunched beneath Thorn's shoes. Dust and decay proliferated in the air. Tranquilly, he wandered the dim hallways of Vallancy Mansion.

His master, as he'd come to call him, had gone away.

Where to? Thorn hadn't an inkling. He only knew, on occasion, Charles disappeared to places unknown—ethereal realms unseen, plains of pain, perhaps of pleasure, although most palpably that of phantom!

21

Thorn stroked his long gray beard. He had not eaten in two days. Soon, he would search for food from the dumpsters. The receptacle outside Ellie's Café, for instance, was a fine place to rifle. Dozens of pastries often surpassed their sale date and had to be thrown out, and Thorn would gleefully gobble them up.

A slow and steady *thump ... thump ... thump* resounded from upstairs.

Thorn longed to see it again—the organ, the creature, the *pump* intrigued him.

He climbed the elegant staircase up to the second floor. The boards creaked beneath his weight, light as he was. At the end of a great hall—a door.

He opened it, then ascended the steps up into the attic.

Once inside the spacious loft, he skillfully weaved around musty trunks, suitcases, antique lamps, coatracks, and random furniture.

Placed upon a teak desk coated with dust—a wine box.

Inside was a fine vintage, the finest Thorn had ever seen, and it *thumped, thumped, thumped.*

Surreptitiously, Thorn slid open the box.

He stared at it.

Dark red, like a dead rose or a fine Merlot.

The organ pumped its music, its aortal valves piping tremulously, with thin purple veins crisscrossing the crimson surface.

A heart lay in the wine box.

Charles Vallancy's heart.

Thorn reached down to touch it, as he always did, though never truly intending to lay his hands upon it. As his dirty finger quivered a mere half-inch away—the music ceased.

Silence. Dust floated about the room; tiny, microscopic worlds spinning randomly.

Now, all Thorn could hear was the heart inside *his own* chest.

Thump! Thump! Thump! Thump!

Instinctively, he knew Master Vallancy had returned—and yet he stood in the Forbidden Place! What would happen to him, should he be found out? Thorn wheeled around, dashed across the loft, then slammed the door behind him.

Vallancy's heart started up again, a muffled *thumping* beyond the door.

As Thorn made haste down the twisting hallways, passing room after room, he halted at the top of the main staircase.

Charles Vallancy stared up from the bottom of the stairs.

"Naughty child you are, Thorn." Vallancy smiled with wooden teeth. "What shall I do with ye?"

Thorn smiled now too—a nervous, appeasing grin.

In a sudden panic, Thorn rushed feverishly down the stairs. He took three at a time, then lowered his head and passed straight *through* Master Vallancy. A terrible wintry chill washed through him; an arctic ice in his veins, a brittle frost in his marrow, a crystal solidification in his brain! Thorn didn't stop running until he was well beyond the front doors, awash in warm autumn sunlight. At the cast-iron entrance gates, he leaned against the bars, panting.

He glanced back at the dark, towering mansion.

Although Thorn spotted no movement in any of the windows, he heard the echoes of his Master laughing, laughing, laughing....

A house is a living body.
Its heart palpitates in the attic.
Its brain cogitates in the basement.

As six o'clock approached, Patty attempted a mood of serenity. She meditated inside her Volkswagen, parked in the modest lot outside

Town Hall. Her eyes were closed, counting down from one hundred. She continually lost count, interrupted by some number or statistic she planned on sharing with the townspeople.

Tonight she intended to convince the citizens of Sweet Hollow to save and preserve the old houses. She would do it with facts and logic, coupled with her gift for passionate oration. If she did not succeed, those beacons of history and heritage would be erased forever. Such a thought was anathema to her very soul.

Patty sighed, restarting her count.

Save and preserve ...

History and heritage ...

When Patty opened her eyes, she flinched.

A woman stared through her driver's side window, mere inches away. She loomed with a scowl, thick mascara accentuating her cold blue eyes.

Reluctantly, Patty rolled down the window.

"Hello, Elise," she attempted to smile, anticipating only hostility.

"You're going to fail tonight," Elise blurted, cutting to the chase. "The demolishment will continue as scheduled, and those nasty old shacks you call 'houses' will be nothing but heaps of wood and glass by November first. Mark my words."

Elise stalked off across the parking lot, then pushed through the Town Hall's mahogany double-doors.

"Always a pleasure, Elise."

Patty grabbed her portfolio and a thermos of black tea from the passenger seat. She opened her door and got out. The parking lot was suddenly crowded. Car doors opened and slammed. Voices floated on the air.

Patty studied her surroundings in mild surprise. The meeting had been scheduled on such short notice, yet the turnout was incredible.

Slowly, the people flowed toward Town Hall—an old building featuring a simple, church-like structure. A scarecrow lay slumped in a lawn chair on the front porch; a raggedy farmer's hat lay cockeyed on its head, and its black button smile gleamed in the twilight. Beside its straw legs were an assemblage of pumpkins, both large and small—soon to be carved for Halloween night.

"Hey, Patty!" Anna Hardy, a senior at Sweet Hollow High, shouted for her attention. Kenny Vandermeer, her boyfriend, stood beside her. They waved from the strip of dead yellow grass beside the porch steps.

"Hey, you two!" Patty cheered as she approached. "Will you be lending your voices on tonight's topic?"

"We're doing what we can." Kenny pushed up his glasses, although they never ran the risk of slipping off his nose. It appeared, at least to Patty, to be a charming, yet nervous tic.

"So get this," Anna said, leaning against the porch railing. "We noticed there wasn't much press for tonight's meeting. So we took the liberty of creating some posts online. We sent out invites. As for all the folks who aren't on social media, we handed out fliers. Show her, Kenny."

Kenny reached into his jacket pocket, then unfolded a vibrant flier with the words *SAVE THE OLD DARK HOUSES!* stretched boldly across the top.

Patty studied the crowd for a moment, reeling with gratitude. A sea of familiar faces swelled all around her, and, like a tide, rolled up the porch steps and entered the building.

"My God! You kids ..." Patty laughed, shaking her head in astonishment. "Thank you both *so much* for ratcheting up the publicity. Let's join the party, shall we?"

Smiles.

Slivers of hope.

Glimmers of possibility.

The three stepped inside.

CHAPTER FOUR

T he endless rows of metal folding chairs filled up quickly. One had to weave, duck, and dive merely to claim one.

Ceaseless chatter. Pungency of armpit sweat.

Elbow to elbow, knee to knee, and ear to ear.

Patty threaded her slender figure through the jostling crowd. Upon reaching the stage, she placed her papers upon the dais where two microphones were arranged. Mayor Edmundson hovered nearby like a fly over a sugar cube.

"Patty." He nodded curtly. "Quite a crowd we've got, no?"

She gazed at the congregation as if they formed a vast sea; and, in a sense, they did, for the roar of that human ocean was immense; voices of a continual tide; children's cries like seagulls circling; the occasional whisper or breathy laugh blowing like a maritime wind.

Mothers and fathers discussed trivialities.

Children squirmed in their chairs.

Babies gurgled—one positively shrieked.

Teachers, truck drivers, bank tellers, librarians, police officers— everyone was here. Everyone!

Two folding tables stood on either side of the podium. One was designated for members of City Council. The other awaited Patty and her ilk from the Preservation Society.

Patty sat down, soon joined by Robert and Therese—veteran preservationists who'd occupied positions on the board even longer than she had.

"What a ruckus!" Robert, an eighty-year-old man, grinned mischievously. "Look at these folks, each one of them here for the old houses!"

"I've never *seen* such a turnout." Therese's green eyes scanned the room while her hands busied themselves with a crochet blanket. Therese was never without a craft, just as Robert was never lacking his impish smile.

Lyle Close, Susan Chambers, and Elise Thanatos—three out of eight members of City Council—sat down at the opposite table. They dressed in black and gray attire as if fresh from a funeral, and their faces resembled grim portraits. Gradually, the room quieted; the sea tide receding into itself.

Everyone faced forward, like a hundred compass needles pointing north. Whispers, jitters, breathy talk! Patty examined the cramped hall. Not one empty chair in sight—all thanks to Kenny and Anna's impromptu promotional campaign. They leaned against the far back wall, waving at her with carefree grins. She smiled back, discovering tears in her eyes which she quickly blinked away—her heart was thankful.

Mayor Edmundson tested the microphones with a sharp tap of his index finger.

"Good evening, everyone," he announced, straightening his orange polyester tie. "Thank you all for coming! We'll be discussing our plan to demolish the old dark houses, seeing as they are untenanted and unsafe. Our City Council members are in unanimous agreement. Our Preservation Society, however, is disputing that opinion. We'll begin tonight with our speakers, then move on to comments and opinions from everyone. Rest assured, all your voices will be given ample time. Our first speaker of tonight, *against* the motion of demolishment, is our Preservation Society President. Ms. Keepwell, will you please make your case?"

Patty scooted back her chair. It screeched obscenely. She winced.

Therese lent her a reassuring wink—a cat's green eye glinting in the dark.

Robert flashed both a smile and a thumbs-up.

The podium was positioned beneath a modest spotlight. Every rustle of clothes, every whisper, pop, and creak in the floor—each note arose in the otherwise silent air. Patty clutched onto her papers as if they were a buoy, and faced the crowd.

She glanced at the Council's table. Elise sat in the middle with vacuous eyes, her nose upturned like a priggish aristocrat.

Patty began, *"'Untenanted and unsafe.'* You heard it, folks. Those are the mayor's words regarding Morton Manor, Bannatyne House, and the Vallancy Mansion. For the moment, I'd have to agree. They *are* untenanted, and *quite* unsafe. However, I argue that we can restore these old structures, make them safe, and present them as educational tours." She took a moment to sip from the thermos she'd placed beside the podium, then continued. "These three houses are the oldest relics of our town—*our town*—built by our forefathers. They are an honorable heritage, indeed, and we must preserve and protect them. Will this be a costly project? Certainly. I don't pretend such expenses will be slight. But just imagine—people *love* historic houses, as many of you here today will testify. Did you know the younger generation, too, is fascinated with them? Go on Instagram or Pinterest, and you'll find thousands of young people taking glorious pictures of houses not unlike those we plan to destroy this November first. The revenue potential for historic tours is not only significant, but exciting! Therefore I ask: *what are we doing* with all this talk of demolishment?"

A rippling murmur.

Nods of agreement.

Patty had been clutching her papers for dear life, yet now laid her hands flat on the podium. Her shoulders relaxed. The sweat on her brow cooled. Behind her, Elise Thanatos audibly scoffed—yet even this did not bother her.

A plump woman with two children on her knee shouted from the front row, "Those houses are beyond repair, ma'am. I mean, they're absolutely decrepit! You can't *restore* houses like that. Better to knock them down and start over."

A laugh.

A chorus of agreement.

"On that note," Patty smiled dryly. "I'd like to bring something to your attention."

Patty unclipped a black-and-white photograph from her papers and held it out to Edmundson. "Sir, will you please hand this to the lady?"

The mayor grimaced. "This really isn't part of protocol, Miss—"

Patty raised her eyebrows in a 'do you dare challenge me?' fashion, insistently holding out the photograph. Edmundson sighed, lumbered down the narrow aisle, then handed the picture to the woman.

"Now," said Patty. "Tell us, what do you see in this picture?"

"It's an old church, I guess," the woman replied, pushing her children's curious hands away.

"A rather crumbling, destitute church, wouldn't you say?"

"Like a haunted house."

"One which should be demolished, rather than preserved?"

"Absolutely." She nodded.

"Delightful! Now, I'd like to point out, *that* church is the same one you're sitting in *right now*."

The woman frowned at the picture. Even her two children, too young to speak in full sentences, cocked their heads as if they understood. Then, gradually, a smile inched across the mother's lips. "Oh good heavens! It *is*, isn't it?" She held up the picture, waving it with exasperation. "Our town hall used to be a *church!*"

A few old-timers nodded agreement—a Presbyterian church, they were proud to point out. Several in the crowd had attended Sunday service here, prior to relocating to the newer church near Sweet Hollow Cemetery.

"That photograph was taken in the late eighties," Patty continued. "Back when I first joined the Preservation Society. I and my loyal colleagues, Robert, and Therese, organized its complete renovation. Those refurbished oak floorboards beneath your feet? Imagine old, damp, rotting wood. The glass panes in these tall arched windows? Once broken stained glass. This very stage upon which I stand? A crumbling altar. Point in fact, ladies and gentlemen, the building we're meeting in presently, was once an *old dark house*. Just thirty years ago, our town decided to preserve and protect it. I argue we can do the same for Morton Manor, Bannatyne House, and the Vallancy. Thank you."

Patty took up her papers, rejoining her table to boisterous applause. The crowd whistled, cheered, hollered.

Anna and Kenny chanted from the shadowy back row: "*Save-the-old-dark-houses!*"

The chant was taken up by half the crowd, despite Mayor Edmundson's shouts of opprobrium. Elise Thanatos stood straight up, fists clenched, rapacious for her turn to speak.

After several entreaties, Edmundson managed to quiet the crowd. At last, he announced: "And now, speaking for the motion to *continue* our plans to demolish the houses, is our City Council President, Elise Thanatos."

Elise attempted a smile; her lips cold and hard as moonlit marble; her narrowed eyes chiseled from stone. She began to speak; her voice surprisingly pleasant, the sing-song of a wild thrush; all ears bent in her direction.

The town was empty.

Not one police cruiser glided through the streets.

Not one watchful parent peeked from behind a living room curtain.

With such a lack of witnesses, *this* was the perfect moment to commit a crime. Cambria Balustrade, a pretty girl of just nineteen years, closed the café early. Riding her bicycle down Main Street, she soon took a right on King Avenue for Town Hall.

A large, hefty pocketknife weighed in her jean pocket.

It'd been a birthday gift from her father, who'd used it to sever line and earthworms while fishing. She never knew quite what to do with it, as her hobbies were not outdoorsy. Consequently, it'd collected dust upon her closet shelf. Now, however, she'd discovered a use.

Cambria Balustrade smiled.

Elise Thanatos was a gifted orator.

The crowd, despite their enthusiastic applause for Patty Keepwell, grew riveted upon Elise's every word. Like a Bible-thumping evangelist, her voice carried high and low, sweeping and diving about the room like a vulture. Every hair on every arm and neck stood straight up, as if statically charged.

Elise pointed to the mother with two toddlers on her knee, and shouted, "Your children! God knows, you'd do anything to keep them safe ... *wouldn't you?*"

"Obviously, I would." The mother glowered. "What's your point?"

"My point, ma'am, is simple," Elise spoke sharply. "Those old houses, with their rotting floors and decrepit staircases and broken glass and rodent infestations ... are they safe for your children? Would you let your two darlings wander into a place like that?"

"How can I even dignify that with a *response?*" A look of disgust crossed the mother's face, and the two children perched on her knees began to fuss.

"Quite right!" shouted Elise, ignoring the woman's reply. "Although I don't have a child of my own, *if I did,* I would keep them as far away from the Morton, Bannatyne, and Vallancy as possible. But you know, people? Children disobey their parents all the time. Sad, but true. Children *will* trespass into these houses. All it takes is a dare, and they'll want to prove their courage. Now, as for the teenagers, they enter these old houses to do a bit *more* than that. Under the cover of such derelict roofs, teenagers often resort to addictive drugs, among *other* nefarious activities, whose perverse nature I need not specify."

A long, slow gasp from the crowd—their imaginations, sparked by Elise's vaguely threatening allusions, were now piqued with panic.

Patty groaned, performing a face-palm. Had Elise any statistics or academic reports to support her notions? Were teenagers truly using old houses for drugs and orgies? Patty doubted it. And yet the fear had been stoked. Elise, as it turned out, was an expert at stoking fear.

Elise continued on—and on and on.

All eyes were glued to the stage.

Cambria leaned her bike against the tailgate of Mrs. Thanatos' car.

The parking lot was jam-packed. Elise's rusty brown Buick remained parked near the back of the lot, only five spaces down from Patty Keepwell's purple Volkswagen.

Cambria thought Patty's car looked like a cute phosphorescent bug. Elise's vehicle, meanwhile, resembled a prodigious brown turd.

Cambria retrieved the knife from her pocket. Flicked it open. Tested the blade with her thumb. She hissed, a fresh trickle of blood slipping down her palm. She'd resharpened the blade before leaving the house, something her father had shown her how to do.

Kneeling on the gravel lot, she felt every sharp stone and pebble imbed into her shins. A wave of guilt and trepidation gave her pause, though she held fast to the knife. She recalled Elise's aggressive complaints, her incessant scowl; and, finally, the coffee cup so rudely flung across the room. Cambria rubbed the back of her head, remembering the offense.

Elise deserves this, she thought. *If anyone deserves this, it's her.*

Poising the blade over the front driver's side tire, she counted:

"One ...

"Two ...

"*Three!*"

She thrust in the knife.

A dry *whooshhh* from the tire.

She laughed, surprising herself. That smelly whoosh escaping the big brown Buick struck her as hilarious—like flatulence from an inanimate object. She stood up, surveying the parking lot and the street beyond. No one to catch her, to call her out, to shout at her. Ravens croaked in barren poplars lining the town hall's front lawn, uninterested in petty human affairs.

She kneeled again, this time beside the rear tire.

Whooshhhh ...

Cambria Balustrade giggled.

Her knife thrust in and out—the act repeated on each tire. The vehicle shrunk down onto its rims. Cambria looked about once again. Still alone, save for the ravens in the trees and the faint stars in the darkening sky.

Using the now slightly dulled tip of her knife, she scrawled six words into Elise's hood:

I AM A

WICKED

OLD HAG.

"Down with the houses!"

"Not safe! We have our *children* to think about!"

"Don't cheat the taxpayer over such foolishness!"

Three-hundred-sixty degrees. A full and complete pinwheel. No one applauded Elise Thanatos, no—they *screamed* for her.

Fear. Hatred. Sweat.

The crowd called for destruction.

Elise preached, her voice rising, descending, then soaring to zenith pitch: "Property values lower *drastically* with these flophouses around! Happens *all the time* in this country. Knock them down, I say, and build safe, modern homes for families to live in!

"Think of the vandals, too! The bums, the squatters! Did you know, ladies and gentlemen, there is a *homeless man* residing in the Vallancy? It's true! I've seen him wheeling a stolen grocery cart of trash all the way out there. Now, is that someone you want your children around? *Is it?!*"

Anna Hardy folded her arms. "God, she's horrible!" she shouted over the din, shaking her head in disgust.

"A true tyrant." Kenny agreed, adjusting his glasses. "But what can we do? Let's get out of here."

They'd entered Town Hall with soaring spirits, now they started for home in despair.

"We'll make a stop at the Manor," Kenny mumbled, his arm around Anna's shoulder. "The Bannatyne, too. Let's say our goodbyes."

Patty sat at the table, chin resting in the cradle of her hands, gazing solemnly at a crowd she no longer recognized.

Fear is a powerful motivator. More powerful than love, sometimes.

It was sad to think, but by evening's end, Patty found the conclusion inescapable. She gathered up her papers and tea thermos, gave Charles and Therese a tight hug, then strolled hopelessly down the aisle toward the doors.

Seven-thirty p.m.

Voices floated, hovered, shouted in the gathering darkness. Car doors slammed. Engines fluttered to life. Wheels churned the gravel.

The parking lot emptied and the sun dipped behind the western hills.

Patty froze with one foot inside her vehicle—a shriek pierced the night. She turned in surprise, frowning at the sight of Elise Thanatos encircling her broken down Buick. A small crowd gathered, murmuring conspiracies.

"Who did this?!" The veins in Elise's neck bulged. "I'll sue! Hear me, goddamn it? I'll—"

Her eyes now focused on Patty Keepwell.

Elise bared her teeth like an angry dog. She broke into a run.

Patty stood petrified with fear and uncertainty. Should she climb into her car, lock the door? Maybe, but she did nothing. Her eyes were transfixed upon Elise's fast-approaching form.

Elise's tight fist raised, then reeled back for a punch.

She struck hard at Patty's cheek—yet before it landed, her wrist was caught mid-air. Sheriff Bradley had observed the situation from across the lot and sped over in the nick of time.

"Now, now, Miss." The large, good-natured man chuckled. "Let's not escalate the situation."

Elise jerked her hand out of the sheriff's grip. "Escalate?" she shrieked. "Look at my car! Is that not *escalation?* This woman," she pointed at Patty with a crooked, quivering finger, "this evil, vindictive woman *did this!* Just look at my tires! My hood!"

Elise broke into a sob, covering her face. Her shoulders drooped like snow-laden branches.

"I had nothing to do with this, Elise," Patty spoke gently, overcome with pity for the woman. "Honest. I was in that meeting with you the *entire time.*"

"It was someone else, Elise." Sheriff Bradley affirmed. "Likely someone who didn't attend tonight's forum."

"But if not her, then *who,* Sheriff?" Elise jabbed a finger dangerously close to Patty's face. "Tell me! If not Keepwell, my opponent in this preservation debacle, then *who?*"

She stamped the ground, demanding justice where none was to be found.

"Ms. Keepwell?" The sheriff spoke firmly. "I think it's best you drive home. Mrs. Thanatos has had quite a day."

Patty didn't need to be told twice. She climbed into her vehicle, shut her door, then reversed out of the spot. Before pulling onto King Avenue, she glanced in the rearview mirror. Elise Thanatos stood beside Bradley with her arms crossed, glaring defiantly at Patty's taillights. She resembled a distressed bird with ruffled plumage—both sad and absurd. *No one deserved to have their car vandalized tonight,* Patty reflected, stomach churning as if she'd truly been guilty of the crime. *All the same, if Elise didn't consider me an enemy before, she certainly does now....*

Chapter Five

At one in the morning, Patty descended the stairs into her kitchen. After preparing a cup of cinnamon tea, she claimed a stool at the polished counter. The last few nights were spent restlessly, and tonight was no exception.

A dozen framed photographs hung upon one wall; snapshots of an amateur life. On the left, a picture of Patty's smiling young face upon receiving a first-place trophy. She'd been the fastest swimmer on her college team, though never took athleticism very seriously—whenever presented with opportunities for prestigious competitions outside the state, she'd turned them down flat. Another photograph captured a charming pose of her wise, lovable parents—now deceased, thanks to diabetes and lung cancer. Next, a photo of herself crowned in academic regalia, the tassel of her cap hanging comically between her excited eyes, while in her right hand she clutched a diploma; a master's degree in history she'd used to land a job at the Sweet Hollow Preservation Society, which, when all was said and done, did not quite lend the satisfaction she'd fervently pined for.

Her eyes drifted away from this wall of bittersweet memories, and settled on the sliding glass door which looked out on the backyard. Two gnarled apple trees stood sentry outside. A pile of wet leaves stirred beneath their barren branches.

A cruel wind blew.

Dead leaves swirled in the air, and the wind seemed to whisper its wanton dissatisfactions. The tree branches fluttered like human arms and hands, waving frantically for help. Patty inhaled the aroma of her cinnamon tea, wishing she could help the old dark houses. Save them. Protect them.

Tomorrow night was Halloween.

Demolishment was scheduled the morning after.

Yay for property values, I guess. Patty rolled her eyes, wondering if all people ever cared about was money. Didn't they ever see past the ends of their noses and wonder at the ancientness of life? The intricate history of a street, a house, a flower? Or did such mystery and beauty elude them, their minds forever stultified with tepid and terrestrial matters? With a sigh, Patty poured another steaming cup of tea. She gazed out the glass door as the wind made panicked creatures of the trees.

She was reminded of *The Wizard of Oz,* and wondered if a storm wasn't on the rise, if a tornado wouldn't wipe her and her house away, so she'd wake up in a land that was novel, magical, and threaded with a yellow brick road. Her little townhouse, of course, would've landed directly on top of Elise Thanatos.

Wishful thinking, Patty. As usual. But what the hell, where would the world be without wishes? Hopes? Dreams?

If only I could do a bit of good for once! Forty-two years on this planet, and I've yet to accomplish anything. God knows I've been spinning, directionless and dizzy, unable to succeed in anything ... but when I think about it, have I even tried?

The night winds groaned like hungry panthers.

Patty sipped her tea; wishing, hoping, dreaming.

Lightning flashed.

Wind howled.

Rain pummeled.

Trees bent.

The town was soaked to its bare bones. Even the moldering dead in their graves surely complained of being wet. For it was Halloween morning, and such thunderous crashes and ghostly winds provided a proper soundtrack.

Elise Thanatos stood beneath the shelter of her front porch, cloaked in a blanket. She gazed through a curtain of drizzling rain. Distantly, she spied the old dark houses. Soon they would be no more.

Soon, she would look Patty Keepwell in the face and laugh.

She laughed now, a wicked witch cackling in the wind.

Harry snored in the upstairs bedroom. Completely oblivious. He always was, with his incessant reading, pipe-smoking, and numbed ears.

The wind blew ice cold; a warning of the shuddering winter to come.

Elise returned into the house, where the wind could not reach. The blankets still wrapped around her, she plopped down on the living room couch, flicked on the lamp, and pretended to read a magazine. The fine print on glossy pages could not capture her attention, however. Her eyes roved the words, but inside she obsessed over that ridiculous Patty Keepwell.

That woman thought she could slash her tires, scratch cruel words into her hood, and *get away with it!* Truly, that woman thought she could do anything—*that* was the problem. There were plenty of people in this world who thought they could do anything they wished, desired, or dreamed. Hell, that was Patty in a nutshell—idle dreamer, unsatisfied wisher, hopeful enthusiast.

Meanwhile, more sensible women like Elise knew to get what you want, you must play the game of society. Flash a smile. Get people to trust and vote for you. Get elected to City Council. Then narrow in on those dark eyesores that've haunted you all your life and, with the assistance of a few important men, knock them down.

The wind, rain, and thunder lashed at the house in a chant: *knock them down, knock them down, knock them down!*

In less than forty-eight hours, Elise's dream would come true—not because she was a dreamer, but because she was a pragmatist.

She had worked hard for this day.

On November first, she would reap the benefits.

As for Patty, well … fate had something in store for her, too.

Fate, Elise smiled, *has* plenty *in store for Patty Keepwell.*

39

Elise grew tired, tossing aside her magazine. She flicked off the lamp and sat in the dark. A sorrow, like a rose, bloomed inside her belly. She could not identify the cause of this feeling, yet was certain of its presence. Sluggishly, Elise climbed the stairs to her bedroom. Harry lay on his side, snoring like the old man that he was.

She climbed into bed and faced the window.

Through thin ivory curtains, she glimpsed a flash of purple lightning. The house rattled in its foundations. Wind rip-lashed the siding. Tree branches broke and skittered across the roof.

Harry snored.

Elise closed her eyes, remembering the reason she hated those old dark houses in the first place. It wasn't the lowered property values, and it wasn't the sheer ugly sight of them, and it wasn't any of the things she'd ranted about at Town Hall.

No.

She hated old dark houses because of *the man.*

The man she'd met just a few months before Harry, and who brought her to Vallancy Mansion when she was just a young lady. The structure was crumbling and ruined even then, a veritable haunted house. The man, handsome in his raffish way, promised her an evening of lighthearted adventure. Alas, after they were behind closed and paintless doors, their adventure transformed into a nightmare—for the man's kisses were not innocent, and his callused hands were not gentle. She lay helpless upon the splintery floor while the man violated her. She thought things couldn't get any worse—then, they did.

On Halloween morning, Anna and Kenny lay naked in the Manor's darkened parlor. A storm raged outside. They lay on a blanket, breathless, clutching each other.

Anna smiled serenely, holding her boyfriend's face to her chest. Lightning glared against the dusky windows, briefly rendering them as lavender silhouettes.

"I love you." Kenny's voice muffled against her breast.

He'd affirmed this many times before, but tonight was different.

Sex wasn't much like they'd thought it'd be. It'd been awkward, but at least they'd had the grace to laugh at each other's fumbling attempts. Yet their laughter had faded into gasps, feeling parts of themselves they'd never felt before, parts within and without, and their hearts surged with new life like flowers blooming—unidentifiable, alien flowers of the most sublime colors, their fragile aromatic petals unfolding in multiple layers, the stems lush green and threading deep into each other's souls.

Yes, tonight had been *different.*

Tonight, they were saying goodbye to Morton Manor, where they'd fallen in love.

Tonight, they'd committed what seemed an ancient and sacred rite; a ritual never to be forgotten, one that bound them, blood to blood, soul to soul.

Eventually, they put on clothes, deciding to return home before their parents discovered their absence. Each garment was pulled on with a sense of longing, a desire never to leave each other's sight. Anna reached for the door with great sorrow—and found it locked.

"I can't open it." She laughed.

"The frame is probably swollen," Kenny said. "Humidity from the weather and whatnot. Let me try."

He pulled. Yanked. Clenched his teeth.

Locked.

Kenny shivered, his entire body caught in a dance of nerves.

"What's wrong?" Anna frowned.

"I don't know. It feels like ..."

"Yes?"

"Well, it feels like something doesn't want us to leave. Like we've said goodbye, but the house isn't ready to do the same."

"That's absurd." Anna scoffed, thinking, *but is it?*

"Come on." Kenny grabbed her hand. "We'll find another way out."

The young lovers moved through the Manor with flashlights. The windows did not budge an inch, no matter how hard they tugged at the sashes.

The Vallancy's basement flooded. Rainwater oozed through stone walls, lapped the dirt floor, then crept inch by inch up the stairwell.

Spiders ascended webs.

Rats scurried up the stairs, abandoning their nests.

Snakes took to the rising tide and glided across dark waters.

Thorn, meanwhile, reclined upon the parlor's divan. He heard the sloshing, trickling sounds from beneath, and the rain hammering above.

He shivered, despite his cocoon of blankets. He'd long run out of wood to burn, as well. His teeth chattered—what few teeth he had left.

Thoughts of the future—a future dark and dreadful—swirled in his consciousness like the first ominous flakes of winter. For it was Halloween, and the Mansion would soon be destroyed. His own home—obliterated!

The storm, it seemed, signaled some horrid harbinger of Things to Come.

Rain! Thunder! Lightning!

Somewhere in the basement, Charles Vallancy's brain deliberated in the flood.

Connived. Calculated. Conceived.

Pondered. Plotted. Philosophized.

A mysterious three-pound organ secreted in a shadowy corner, pulsating like some strange alien organism—an organism called Vallancy.

Houses are living bodies, Thorn reflected. *A heart in the attic, a brain in the basement, and a soul in between.*

Thorn sat bolt upright with a scream.

Charles Vallancy stood before him; a lambent silhouette of dim white radiance. He smiled, clutching something within his right hand.

"Get up, worthless vagabond." A voice of smoke, immaterial yet plainly present. "Stand steadfast, I say! I've something to reveal to thee."

"But why, Master?" Thorn got up from the divan, blinking sleepy eyes. "Why reveal anything to me?"

"Because you are a tool," Vallancy replied, his nose upturned. His wig writhed, as if nasty insects inhabited the yellowed curls. "Now, what is a tool for, Thorn?"

"To be used, Master."

"*Precisely.*"

Vallancy held out his clutched fist, then unfurled his fingers.

Two flies lay sedate on his palm.

"First they mated. Then I caught them, and here they'll remain. One is named Anna. The other, Kenneth."

He brought his palm to his lips, swallowing the two flies in a gulp.

Thorn grimaced. No matter how hungry he got, he'd never once thought to devour a fly. Half-eaten food from a dumpster seemed a better alternative.

"Two itsy bitsy flies!" Vallancy nodded with satisfaction. "Such can hardly be considered a meal, Thorn, can it?"

"Surely not, Master. No meal at all...."

"It is an appetizer, then." The old ghost's eyes now roved the warped and damaged walls, lost in his depraved ruminations. Thorn thought, *if a ghost is immaterial, then a ghost's thoughts must be close to nothing....*

"Come tonight," spoke the Ghost, "I shall catch *many* flies. They each shall give of their life and soul and youth. I shall catch them in my spider's web of houses, and keep them as prisoners, until my humble mansion is no longer at risk of demolishment. Do you understand, Thorn?"

"Yes, Master."

"You are to assist me in this endeavor?"

Thorn replied tremblingly, "If you ... wish it so."

Charles Vallancy's smile sank into a troubled glower. His dark eyes shone with torment. A moon-like gleam radiated out from every wrinkle and crevice of his dead face, and that gleam was called sorrow.

"I cannot truly die, Thorn," he said, shaking his head with melancholy. "You must understand. For if I die, *you* die. After all, where shall you go if my mansion is reduced to a pile of rubble? The street? The dumpster? No, Thorn. No, no, no! *That* would not do."

Vallancy paced the room, though there were no footsteps to be heard. "You are better than the common vagabond, Thorn. There is a bit of pluck in you yet! A bit of vibrancy within that lugubrious soul of yours, just as there is in mine. Thus, tonight, when all the little witches and goblins and devils are begging for candy, you shall provide succor. Now, if you should refuse my demands—"

Charles spun on his heels. His corpse-like face, cadaverous and pale, twitched as he whispered, "Then I shall turn *you* into a fly, Thorn. And you know perfectly well what I do with flies ... don't you?"

43

Thorn nodded, slowly.

"Remember," Charles' ethereal form began to fade, a moon-shadow dimming into the background of night, "one who assists the spider shall not become the fly...."

The old ghost vanished—a candle flame snuffed by unseen fingers.

Thorn stood alone in the ash-gray parlor.

And the mansion was old, cold, and dark.

CHAPTER SIX

The sun rose like a flaming pumpkin into the October sky. Dead leaves glimmered with wetness. Toppled Styrofoam tombstones trundled and scraped along the sidewalks, pushed by a chill wind. Kenny snored upon the blanket in the parlor.

Anna leaned against a window sill, gazing vacantly through the glass. The front door still would not budge, and using a kitchen chair to batter the windows proffered no results. The windows were more solid than they appeared—unbreakable, in fact.

Unbreakable.

Unbelievable.

Unnatural.

Anna studied the windowpane six inches from her nose. She could've sworn there'd been cracks in the glass last night—now there weren't any.

Impossible. She half-laughed, half-cried from exhaustion. Houses didn't heal themselves of their fractures, their spiderweb cracks, their wounds. She must've just imagined there'd been cracks in the first place.

Placing her fingertips to the smooth glass, she traced a word in dust:

HELP

Then she roused Kenny out of his sleep.

"There'll be people out and about soon," she said, shaking his shoulder. "We'll need to get their attention."

Kenny sat up, squinting at the vermillion light gleaming in the windows.

He looks odd this morning, Anna thought. *Older somehow. Slightly worn and wiser.*

"Last night was wonderful," Kenny yawned, putting on his glasses. "You know, other than the being trapped part."

"I'd rather be trapped with you," Anna smiled, "than anyone else in the world."

"Well, that makes two of us."

They kissed.

Kenny gazed at Anna's loving face. She looked different than yesterday, he thought. Her beauty had matured; the blush of her cheeks no longer a spring blossom, but a midsummer flower. It perplexed him. Was he seeing things?

If there truly was a difference in their appearances, it was as subtle as a singular fracture in a windowpane and as imperceptible as a one-degree change in temperature. They shivered that morning, holding each other, waiting for someone to walk down the street.

Someone they could scream for.

Harry Thanatos strolled down Sowin Street. An apple lay inside his jacket pocket.

The apple was a gift, and his wife demanded he deliver to Patty Keepwell.

"Why don't *you* gift it to her?" he'd grumbled. "I'd rather do some porch sittin'. Enjoy the fall colors, maybe."

Elise had told him he was a fool.

"An apology, Ms. Keepwell," Harry muttered, practicing his lines. "A sincere apology from my wife. Wasn't no way you could've wrecked her car, you bein' in the Town Hall with her and all. So, here's a shiny red apple. Dunno why she don't just give it to you herself ... but she bein' so busy and all, why ..."

Harry sighed.

He felt a fool, indeed.

He walked and smoked his pipe, telling himself it was good exercise.

The apple bulked up his right pocket.

The sun rose higher in the sky.

A car zipped past, stirring leaves of tangerine, banana-yellow, and tarnished gold. His squinted eyes studied the houses on both sides of the residential street—each house brimming with skeletons, bats, vampires, zombies, and leering jack-o'-lanterns.

Harry grinned, remembering one Halloween night from sixty years ago. His mother had dressed him up as a mummy. All that toilet paper! Head to toe! With just holes for eyes and a slit to breathe—and if he needed to use the bathroom, he had better pray. His four-year-old sister, Angelina, had been a ghost that year—a bedsheet draped over her bulky physique.

Back then, you couldn't buy costumes.

Back then, you had to make them yourself.

Harry thought the costumes he'd made with his mother and sister were far scarier than the ones they sold in stores these days—though the rubber masks, in all their artistry, had come a long way.

He shook his head, memories weaving through his mind like a thousand spiders spinning soft silky webs. He laughed, slapped his thigh, feeling radiant in all that memory and morning sunshine.

Then, he halted in the middle of the sidewalk.

Turned to his right.

The Bannatyne House towered above him.

The glorious gothic giant loomed with the sun at its back; a vampire turned away from the light.

"Huh…," Harry Thanatos mumbled. "I done walked past Ms. Keepwell's place and never knowed it."

Indeed, Patty Keepwell's modest townhouse remained two blocks back. His childhood memories had both possessed and distracted him. Now, he stood somewhat dazed, gazing up at the garish, architectural monstrosity that was Bannatyne House. A smashed jack-o'-lantern lay in scattered fragments at his feet, the pieces rotting and collecting flies. These he absentmindedly kicked away. *Kids will be kids,* he thought, taking in the house's façade.

47

He, too, sometimes felt indolent, dreamy, and half-asleep.

The two windows on the second floor resembled lazy eyes.

The door was a long thin nose.

The front porch like a slackened jaw, with stairs (*lips*) puddled onto the front yard.

The Bannatyne resembled an indolent patient; dreamy, and half-asleep.

Harry laughed.

He, too, sometimes felt indolent, dreamy, and half-asleep. All those days and nights with Elise made him feel that way, ashamed as he was to admit it. She could be so sharp, so cruel sometimes! It was better to shut her out.

Numbed ears.

Smoked pipe.

Closed heart.

These were his means of silencing the pain. Silencing the constant cutting of his wife's serrating voice. It hadn't always been this way.

Once, they'd been happy. Once, they'd loved each other.

Once, thought Harry. *Once upon a time …*

Sometimes it takes a fool to do something audacious. This morning, Harry felt a fool.

Dare I disturb the universe? He recalled the line from an old poem whose author he couldn't remember. Neglecting the apple in his pocket, and the mission his wife had sent him on, he climbed the groaning front steps (puddled, wrinkled, drooling lips!), walked across the porch, and rapped his bony knuckles against the front door.

To his amazement, the door creaked open—just an inch.

He pushed it wide.

A darkened hall stretched before him.

A coat tree stood to his left. To his right, a reception room with a ratty couch.

Harry stepped inside, shutting the door.

It was dark, but his eyes adjusted. He laughed, amazed to find himself here. He hadn't been inside the Bannatyne since he was a teenager, egged on by a dare from his pals. How many years ago had that been?

Harry Thanatos was seventy now.

"Which means," he said, his voice booming throughout the empty rooms, "I haven't stepped foot in this house in over half a century."

He hung his jacket on the coat tree. After tucking his pipe into the front pocket of his shirt, he went exploring.

It's Halloween, for God's sake. Everyone is entitled to a little fun, a little scare, a little mischief! I've just got to see if this old house is like I remember it, all those years ago....

Room by room, Harry explored.

Harry felt watched, the white hairs on his arms stiffening. Soon, he climbed the rickety staircase. He was compelled to visit the second floor. Something drew him up the stairs. Something intangible, inexplicable, like a ghost pulling on his arm.

Why not, for God's sake?

It's Halloween.

Everyone's entitled to a little fun, a little scare....

Thorn walked free at last.

All it took was a single step out the front door. Free as a leaf on the wind, blown hither and thither across rolling auburn fields. Thorn's shoes dampened as he trampled through forest brush, then fields of tall grass. With a dirty quilt thrown over his shoulders, he put miles between himself and the Mansion.

Nothing could touch him here, in the clear light of morning. He felt, perhaps, that if he struck the sun—he could get away with it.

The Vallancy was a prison; a cage of wood, stone, and glass.

He would never return.

"Never, never!" he shouted to the grass rustling against his pants, to the tawny fields that flowed like a harvest sea; an ocean of grain and grass, flooding the countryside and undulating with the wind—these waves of October smelling of corn and wheat and earthen dew.

Thorn had spent many nights inside the Mansion. He'd had nowhere else to go. No alley was warm, no forest provided adequate shelter from the rain, and God knew if he squatted in one of the town's abandoned houses he'd soon be discovered, arrested, and taken away to some horrible institution.

Now, where would he go? Where to spend his nights?

Maybe he'd hop a train. Sleep in a boxcar.

Maybe he'd jump off the Sweet Hollow bridge—a high, ramshackle structure on the southside of town. He'd sink into the chilling river, never coming up for air.

Better to die than be a slave!

But there were the children to think about—all those dear children of Sweet Hollow would be out tonight, and what was it Vallancy had told him?

That Thorn should help turn them into flies.

Flies for the big old spider named Charles Vallancy. A wicked web would be spun, and they'd all be gulped down like common food; their youthful blood to sustain him.

Thorn would have none of this.

Thorn had lived a long, weary life. He'd done much he wasn't proud of. Still, he would never stoop so low as to harm a child. No, indeed! He'd never so much as harm a fly....

The way Thorn saw it, humankind was a world of flies, all buzzing and zipping around, attempting to avoid those sticky webs of fate. The supreme goal was to land on a delicious picnic sandwich, or a child's abandoned mango popsicle on the beach, or the grisly remains of some creature fit for consumption. Innocent, ignorant, just trying to get along—that was Thorn. And if Thorn was no better than a fly, what reason had he to capture any for Charles Vallancy?

"To hell with you, Master." He grinned. "Master-bastard! That's your name, Vallancy-Schmallency! Master of the Bastards!"

Thorn stomped and muttered through the fields until arriving at an extreme slope. Losing his footing, he tumbled down a wet grassy hill.

At bottom, the land plateaued, and before him were the buildings and houses and streets of Sweet Hollow.

A fine place to live—if you had an income.

Thorn stood, picking strands of grass from his beard. He began his long trudge into town, hoping Good Fortune had not abandoned him yet.

Elise Thanatos laid heavily in bed; depression gripping her soul with iron pincers.

Exhaustion wore her thin; the anticipation of the November first demolition, the spiteful defacement of her Buick (which, humiliatingly, had been towed all the way to Sam's Automotive before the entire town) and her obsessive plotting against Ms. Keepwell had compounded her emotions to make her feel ugly inside.

Perhaps I am *ugly inside,* she reflected.

There was a ring of truth to this suggestion; a doomful tolling that was not in the least flattering. Additionally, she'd freshly awakened from a nightmare. With great effort, she sat upright. Panting. Dampened with sweat.

She'd dreamed about the man who'd taken her inside the mansion all those years ago—where he'd touched her, tortured her, *branded* her.

She lifted her nightshirt, where a *V* was carved just below her belly button. Her fingers now traced the slight bulge of that distinctly shaped scar—a constant reminder of the man's first name. She closed her eyes, attempting to steady her breathing. The nightmare remained fresh in her mind—an exact replay of that fateful night he'd promised her kind affections yet delivered torture.

A pain that lasts a lifetime.

A wound that never heals.

A scar; tattoo of humiliation.

After the man had forced her onto the dirty floor and stolen her innocence, he'd smiled hideously, teasing her with a long, shimmering blade. His teeth were white, his smile wolfish; to think she'd once found him charming! He'd laughed at her bulging, panicked eyes. He'd laughed at her pain, her raw and seething cries for him to *stop, please stop.* Then, with the tip of his blade, he'd carved the first letter of his name into her stomach, her navel filling with warm blood....

Elise covered her mouth, sobbing uncontrollably. Tears slid off her chin. She couldn't remember the last time she'd cried. How long had it been, *exactly?* Months? Years?

A tsunami of grief, pain, and regret swept through her heart.

Worse than everything, however, was that nagging, loathsome feeling that she'd somehow deserved it. And such hurt, such guilt, forced her to remember—*The apple! I gave it to Harry. I never should have thought of doing that—what's wrong with me? If Patty should bite into it, finding the blade inside ... Harry will take the blame. He'll be taken to jail. I'll never see my husband again, save for behind bars. God, what have I done?!*

She jumped out of bed, all prior lethargy vanquished.

Is it too late? Maybe Patty hasn't touched the apple. Maybe she never even accepted the gift!

She imagined Harry standing on Patty's front porch, holding out the apple. Patty's trusting hand reached out to claim it, then lifted the shiny red fruit (with one small defect, one sliver-thin line of imperfection) toward her open mouth....

Elise dressed quickly, then ran downstairs. Snatching her keys from the kitchen table, she raced out of the house without bothering to shut the door. The Buick awaited her in the driveway. It featured all new tires, yet the hood still sported that degrading carving: *I AM A WICKED OLD HAG.*

Elise remembered nothing of her humiliations now, for her attention was riveted to her hand on the car door, her keys jamming into the ignition, her foot hammering down on the gas pedal as she peeled out of the gravel drive.

She gripped the steering wheel, fervently praying: *Please don't let Patty bite into that apple. I don't know what I was thinking. I'm wrong, I'm evil, I don't know why! Oh, Harry, you old fool, I love you, but I've lost my mind. Please, don't let it be too late....*

CHAPTER SEVEN

Patty Keepwell went for a walk.

The storm had kept her up most of the night. Still, she'd managed four hours of uninterrupted sleep. The sun fell like warm, rejuvenating balm upon her shoulders. Now was perhaps her last chance to visit each house—*the dark three*—for the final time.

Come tomorrow, everyone in town would be privy to a continual, cacophonous crumbling and crash.

Ashes to ashes, dust to dust.

Patty's bittersweet smile met with the sun, and an icy breeze brushed her cheeks. Petitions, essays, and a town hall meeting hadn't been enough. She did not brood, however—merely opened her heart and breathed deep the last air of October. The earth moved solidly beneath her boots. Everything seemed ancient—the sun, the soaked earth, the twittering sparrows in the barren birch trees lining the street.

She'd done every reasonable thing she could to save the old dark houses; in this fact alone, she found solace. Without resignation, nor ill will for Elise Thanatos, she strolled down Lieber Street toward Morton Manor, content to say goodbye.

It was a beautiful morning.

It was a terrible morning.

The gray hairs on the back of Elise's neck dampened with sweat. Her face flushed red as a crabapple—*What have I done what have I done what have I done*—she parked on the street, directly behind Patty's Volkswagen. Two children riding bicycles down the sidewalk pointed at her hood and laughed.

They're right to laugh. I am a wicked old hag. No different from that evil witch in the fairy tales, giving the poison apple to the princess....

Elise ignored the kids' aspersive jeers, tapping her knuckles against Patty's front door. She jabbed the doorbell incessantly. Its distant, pleasant chime resounded within the house. She knocked. Waited. Knocked thrice more times.

A bead of sweat dripped down her forehead, tickling the bridge of her nose. She wiped it away. Trembling. Heart seizing up in her chest, threatening to explode. A singular image flashed in her mind, delivering a vicious punch to her stomach: Patty lay dead inside the house, face down on the living room rug, blood oozing thick from her mouth, the partially-eaten apple having rolled out of her hand....

Elise began to cry.

She battered her palms against the door. Rang the bell a dozen times in quick succession.

"Open up, *please*," she cried.

She glanced behind her then. The two kids on bikes watched, snickering.

They stared at her. Their whispers floated on the air, and Elise caught them just right in her ears:

Wicked ...

Old ...

Hag!

"Get away from my car!" Elise spun around, her face hot-red with rage. "Don't make me tell you twice. Now *get!*"

Grumbles. A rolling of eyes. Blithe curses. They pedaled down the street.

Elise inhaled deeply, facing Patty's door.

She placed her hand upon the doorknob.

Turned it—she pushed the door inward.

Warily, she entered.

THUDTHUDTHUDTHUDTHUD!

Anna pounded her fists against the parlor windows.

"Patty!" she screamed. "We're locked in!"

Ms. Keepwell stood on the street, smiling up at the house.

"Hey!" Kenny shouted, likewise slamming his palms on the windowpane. "C'mon, Patty. We mean it!"

After much exertion, now tired and out of breath, they froze.

Patty strode toward the porch—at last, they'd captured her attention! She climbed the sagging steps, ran her left palm over the door's flaking yellow paint, then stepped before one of the windows. Cupping hands around her eyes, she peered into the dusty glass.

Staring directly into Patty's face, Kenny tapped the pane.

Patty's eyes roved curiously, observing the parlor with its ripped-up divan, scuffed floorboards, and the decrepit grandfather clock against the far wall. Kenny's face hovered inches away. Patty did not see him—she saw *through* him.

"She's gone insane," Kenny concluded.

"No." Anna shook her head. "It's the Manor. It won't allow her to see us."

"Now *you've* gone insane."

"How else would you explain this?" Anna pushed him aside and placed her nose against the glass, flush with Patty's, then screamed at the top of her lungs.

"Please, shut up!" Kenny grimaced, covering his ears. "I can't handle that."

"Don't call me insane, then."

"Fine," Kenny huffed. "How's *slightly deranged* for a euphemism?"

"You're not funny. We've been hearing weird sounds in this house all night. All those pops, creaks, groans in the wood? It's like this place is waking up. Becoming aware of itself, or something...."

Kenny sighed. Anna's notions grew crazier. Sure, the noises had been odd—yet he chalked this up to the house settling into its foundation, or perhaps rats scurrying beneath the floorboards. He gazed about the cobwebbed ceiling, the cracked plaster walls, the abraded gray floors. It was a dead old house—not alive, not conscious.

Houses, after all, did not possess nervous systems. They felt nothing. They were nothing.

Still, he thought, *this is the house where we fell in love. In a way, haven't we also fallen in love with the Manor itself? It's like it refuses to let us go ... bunkum, of course. Mindless superstition. Crazy-talk.*

He thought of his scientific heroes—Richard Dawkins, Carl Sagan, Neil deGrasse Tyson—knowing they'd never approve of such supernatural hokum. Anna was making extraordinary claims, sure, but where was the evidence?

Patty withdrew her face from the glass, blew a kiss, then made for the street. They watched her stroll away, hardly believing it.

Now, they stared at each other.

"You look tired," Anna frowned.

"So do you."

"I think we're changing, Kenny."

"Changing?"

"Growing older." Anna nodded grimly.

"In the course of a single night?"

"Every minute, in fact. Every *second,* another line, another wrinkle! I can see creases around your eyes, your mouth ..."

"Oh, Jesus." Kenny groaned. "You have them too!"

"What the hell is happening to us?" Anna's voice quivered.

"How the hell should I know?" His arms shot up in exasperation. None of this made any sense. What scientific explanation could he possibly ascribe to their bizarre situation? His mind either drew blanks or suggested yet further impossibilities. The physical deformity of their faces were undeniable, and thereby constituted as evidence—but of what, exactly?

"Wait a minute." Anna froze. "Let's think about this. What do we have that this old house doesn't?"

Kenny paced the room, rubbing his chin with quivering fingers. He adjusted his glasses. Fidgeted nervously with the hem of his button-down sweater.

Anna observed him. Her boyfriend resembled a professor, contemplating an operose equation. He halted in the middle of the room, visibly shivering.

"What?" Anna grabbed his shoulders. "You've an idea. Go ahead, spill it."

"Youth," he whispered. "It's the one thing we have which The Manor doesn't. That's why we look older, Anna. More tired, and weary …" He laughed, shaking his head. "Crazy as this notion is, I think this house is stealing our youth."

"The crack in the glass." Anna faced the window. "It was there last night; it isn't this morning."

"The front door!" Kenny pointed at it.

Anna gasped. The door was painted a vibrant yellow, like a spring daisy freshened by an overnight rain.

Thorn sloshed through alleyway rain puddles, his stomach grumbling with hunger. Despite rifling through the dumpsters behind Ellie's Café and the Summer's End Restaurant, he'd discovered only soggy pastries and rotten meat burrowed with maggots.

The morning was soft, calm, quiet.

He slunk along the sunny street like a cat.

Where to go? Where to stay? An alley won't do. None of the empty houses will do—Vallancy will find me there, no question. He'll find me and, this time, never let me leave.… Master-Bastard, he is!

Thorn stomped on the sidewalk. Cursed and muttered. Oh, the things he'd do to Charles Vallancy—if only that ghost were a living man!

All the anger, disappointments, and sorrows of life flooded through him. Frustration played tricks with his mind. He howled at the sun and took offense at the very air he breathed.

He went on in this way—muttering, cursing, stomping his feet.

Street threaded into street, each one nameless to his mind.

Suddenly, he halted.

An old Buick idled on the street, its driver's seat empty.

Thorn smiled and reached out, touching the windshield with his grubby fingers, then tracing the words *WICKED OLD HAG*, carved into the hood. He slunk toward the driver's door.

Where to go? Where to stay? An alley will not do....
Thorn tried the handle.
To his delighted surprise, it was unlocked.

Vallancy Mansion remained the remotest of the *dark three;* a hideous, sprawling structure located on the highest hill in all Sweet Hollow.

Patty strolled through rolling fields of damp grass, then began climbing the northern slope. Despite being well into middle age, she was in exceptional shape. She ate healthily and exercised, and always looked eagerly toward Sundays, when she swam laps in the community pool.

A forest of gold, russet, and auburn soon lay before her—a brilliant conflagration, these kaleidoscopic flames of autumn! For Patty Keepwell, the fall season possessed a grandeur and richness comparable to a second spring. She breathed in the air, and it smelled of sunshine, earth, and rain.

After a steady uphill climb through fifty acres of forest, she arrived at the iron gates.

A dirt drive threaded through yet another field of tall grass—what had once been a well-manicured lawn. The Mansion loomed solemnly; an ominous sentinel of wood, stone, and glass.

The fluted columns seemed fit to topple; the pedimented entry a withered, paint-chipped, doomful affair; the cracked bay and oriel windows darkly gleaming like a hideous smile in the dark; and the old-fashioned carriage porch on the southern end had sadly caved in, its Tudor arches worn away by rain-damp wood, lichen, and termites.

Patty's smile faltered, her hands resting upon the gate's cold iron bars.

How does one articulate the ineffable? she wondered, ruminating upon the Mansion's peculiarities. *That silent, dark presence which inhabits the Mansion ... something, or someone waiting in the shadows, poisoned by a heart both cruel and vainglorious ...*

She didn't understand these ghostly intimations, yet felt them intimately. Indeed, the very notion of ghosts sometimes upset her to the point of tears. Such restless spirits were undoubtedly the inventions of tragedy. An unsettled soul not fit to leave the earth; tied, and shackled to their former life; their adamantine chains composed of guilt, hatred, and sorrow.

If ghosts exist, they must surely roam the Mansion's shadowy halls.

Maybe even Charles Vallancy himself.

Patty's knowledge concerning the man was prodigious. She had, after all, researched his life with no little academic professionalism. Born April 6th, 1731, Charles Vallancy had been raised by aristocratic parents who'd sent him to one of the best colleges in London. In his twenties, he began his career as a British military surveyor. During an expedition to Ireland, he grew enamored with the country, and called it home for many years. Consequently, he'd written multiple volumes concerning the history, philology, and antiquity of that mythic green land. His reason for abandoning his bosom-country for America remained, to this day, an utter mystery.

Here, Charles had built his mansion.

Here, Charles had remained until his death in 1812.

Sweet Hollow possessed a strange, dark history, and Patty loved nothing more than to ruminate over its facts and legends. Now, quite suddenly, she gasped.

She stood mere inches away from the Vallancy's towering front doors—her hand lay upon the rusty brass knob!

She jerked her hand away.

A moment ago, she'd been standing before the wrought iron gate. Now, she'd caught herself a second away from entering the derelict Mansion....

"What am I doing?" she asked aloud, wondering if she'd lost her mind.

Like a distant answer, a low creaking resounded from inside.

The weight of some rodent scuttling across the floorboards ... or someone's footsteps.

She shivered.

Patty retreated from the ugly, paintless doors. Quickly, she returned to the gates. Her stomach curdled with sickness—as if she'd narrowly escaped some unspeakable fate! How deeply absent-minded she'd been—and who knew for exactly how long? Inexplicably odd to suddenly awake, hand on the doorknob, unthinkingly entering that ghastly, haunting abode....

The Mansion's eerie presence spread like an intoxicating fog across the land—that moth-to-flame attractiveness, those invisible eyes which stared from darkened windows—Patty almost considered returning to the doors.

"Goodbye, Mr. Vallancy." Patty clanged the gates resolutely shut behind her. "May you rest in peace, at long last."

She walked swiftly through the forest, down the slope, then crossed the fields for town. Behind her, the Mansion loomed darkly atop its hill—staring straight and steadfast like some spooky sentinel.

Elise leaned against the kitchen counter, sighing with relief.

Patty's house was empty. No dead body. No apple.

Where is Harry then? she wondered. *If Harry wasn't home when she knocked, where has he wandered to? Could be sitting on a bench in the park, perhaps, having a smoke. Or maybe he's gone down to Carl's Barbershop for a cut. Lord knows he needs one. If only Harry had a cell phone....*

Then her eyes shot wide.

That familiar, heart-pounding terror returned. *What if Harry gets hungry on his walk, and eats the apple? A few bites are all it would take—*

The obnoxious revving of an engine sounded from the street—so loud she could hardly hear herself think. Her fists bunched. How she loathed those jackass teenagers and their cheap cars. Always revving, speeding, racing up and down the streets, music pounding through their speakers.

She frowned and listened. Peculiar. The engine sounded ... familiar. The revving died down now, the engine idling with a soft, rapid *click-click-click-click*—her Buick's signature sound.

She rushed to Patty's front door. Swung it wide.

Someone sat inside her car! A gross, filthy-looking man in ratty clothes. He revved the engine a final time, then the Buick darted violently forward—as if the driver hadn't operated a vehicle in years and had forgotten how a shifter worked—just barely clipping the bumper of Patty's Volkswagen.

Elise's mouth gaped. Her car's new tires peeled up black smoke as they spun on the asphalt. Gaining traction, the Buick swerved down the street until disappearing around the corner.

"Why, you son of a *bitch!*" she screamed, shaking her fist. She felt ridiculous, yet this was her instinctive reaction—like an old woman hollering at kids to get the hell out of her yard.

The entire neighborhood watched. Children paused from jumping into wet leaf piles. Old ladies peeked from behind curtains. Two teenagers pointed, cracking smiles. A man walking his Border collie frowned at the scene—even the dog sniffed the air with greater curiosity.

Elise retrieved her cell from her pocket and dialed 911.

Thorn grinned, ignoring stop signs and crosswalks.

Power! Freedom!

It'd been twenty years since he'd sat behind the wheel.

Twenty!

He stepped on the gas, zipping down Main Street. Several cars screeched to a stop at the intersection, frantically honking their horns.

"Freedom!" Thorn laughed. "No boxcar for Thorn! No bridge, no alleyway! Take that, Master-Bastard!"

A police cruiser flashed its lights behind him, pulling out from one of the wide alleys between commercial buildings. The siren wailed and lights flashed.

Thorn stomped on the accelerator, racing out of Sweet Hollow at ninety-three miles per hour.

Chapter Eight

Harry Thanatos had been ten years old the last time he'd set foot in Bannatyne House. It'd seemed like an immense mansion then. Now, at seventy-one years of age, every room appeared tiny and claustrophobic. More like walk-in closets than rooms. The hallways were narrow, and a tunnel-like stairwell led up to the second floor.

At least it ain't too dark in here, Harry thought, squinting at the sunlight splashing through the windows. He roamed the second-floor hallway, opening the door of each room and gazing in.

The floorboards were scuffed black from the weight and movement of previous occupants. Wallpaper hung in peeled strips like filleted flesh. A silty dust floated through the air in golden specks.

Damaged portraits and idyllic landscapes still hung in the old bedrooms. Each room contained a divan, an armoire, or an armchair, though not much else. A four-poster bed took up most of the space in what must've been the master bedroom. Its crimson tapestry lay in tatters upon the posts, like destroyed battle flags. Harry went in and lay down, laughing as the dust puffed up from the sheets.

He sneezed, then coughed into his fist.

How many years since someone slept in this bed? Made love? Died?

How many ghosts lingered about these dusty old rooms?

None that he could sense, anyway.

Harry considered heading downstairs, lighting a new pipe, and having a smoke on the sitting room divan. How delicious, to smoke his cherry-flavored tobacco in an ancient room full of dust! He would dream and meditate, watch the smoke mingle with the silty air, and bask in the sunshine streaming through the window.

But ... no. Now wasn't the time. He sat upright.

He *must* get going—there was the apple to deliver to Ms. Keepwell. A gift of forgiveness, according to Elise. A strange gesture, Harry thought. Why didn't his wife simply apologize?

Then again, his wife was a strange bird. Women, in general, were strange birds. He and his numbed ears did not understand them. And they, in turn, did not understand him. Only his pipe and books and the sun and these old dark houses seemed to understand Harry Thanatos.

Now, Harry was hungry for a smoke.

No, no. Better not smoke in here. What if an ember should fall on the dry wood, and catch fire? Lord, how embarrassing! Though I suppose it would save the damned demolition crew some work....

Harry got out of bed.

He headed for the staircase. He'd grab his jacket from the coat tree, light up his pipe, and head out for Patty Keepwell's house.

At the top of the stairs, he paused.

I haven't seen the attic yet.

As a child, he'd been too afraid to go up there. Afraid there'd be monsters awaiting him with groaning bellies and angry teeth, salivating with the horrible desire to rip his body to shreds and gulp him down.

He was seventy now.

Seventy, by God! If seventy years wasn't enough time to get over one's fear of monsters, then surely one never would. Harry ambled to the end of the hall, where a string dangled from the ceiling. He pulled it, unfolded the accordion steps, then climbed up into the attic.

His head popped up from the rectangle in the floor, resembling a curious gopher. He looked around, blinking.

Dark up here, but not terribly so.

A single window faced the street, a round cupola with a bullseye frame. The sun winked against the glass. Beneath the window, placed upon a straight-back chair—a delicately carved wooden box. A music box, perhaps.

A lot of things up in this attic.

No monsters. Just things.

Ratty couches, tables laid on their tops, and rickety brown chairs loaded with wooden crates full of junk. Large trunks with broken locks. Moldering cardboard boxes; daddy longlegs scrabbling across their sides.

Harry pulled himself up into the attic, stooping to avoid banging his head on the rafters.

Cobwebs hung thickly. Spiders the size of half-dollar coins lay motionless at the center of their sticky gray nests. Harry ducked low, avoiding them at all costs. The daddy longlegs, however, did not bother him. He brushed them from boxes and crates and peered inside.

Clothes, mostly. Blouses, jackets, hats, mittens, suspenders, and leather shoes. It all smelled like dead moths and mildewed lint.

Harry coughed, hacked, sneezed, then blew his nose into his pocket handkerchief.

He opened a few trunks now, and found still yet more clothes, shoes, and hats. He reached inside, nabbing a gray fedora. Shaking it free of dust, he placed it atop his head.

The hat fit.

"Think I'll keep it." He closed the trunk, the lid making a loud SNAP as it closed on the frame. Harry jumped up a few inches—if not for his new apparel, he damn near would've scalped himself on the rafters.

He thought of himself then, wandering around the attic with a bleeding head.

I've got to be careful. I'm an old man. I could die up here.

Yes. He very well could die up here. Anything can happen if you're alone in an old dark house—especially when you're seventy years old.

Harry tensed. He heard his heart *buh-thump, buh-thump, buh-thump* in his chest. He placed a hand over his heart, as if reciting the Pledge of Allegiance.

His heart never sounded so loud; its noise filled the small space of the attic.

I'm going to have a heart attack. I've got to get out of here. Now.

He made for the entry in the floor. Just as he'd made for the stairwell a few minutes ago—but he'd turned back, hadn't he? Because he'd wanted to see the attic.

Now, he wanted to see what was inside the elegant box beneath the circular window. Its inlaid floral patterns were remarkable, and it featured a dark brown, nearly black, polish.

It'll only take a minute. Just one! If I don't go see now, I'll regret it the rest of my life. Sitting on the porch with Elise, smoking my pipe, night after night, wondering, what the hell was in that little box?

He crossed the room, ducking the cobwebs.

The spiders, as if sensing his presence, scurried to the ceiling.

With an ache in his lower back, his heart pounding in his ears, Harry crouched at the window. He looked out onto the street.

To his surprise, a woman stared up at him.

Patty Keepwell!

Harry gasped, ducking out of sight.

She couldn't know he was in here—*my God, what would she think? That he was stealing, loitering, squatting like some common hood?*

But she hadn't seemed to notice him.

Her gazed was soft, serene, sentimental.

Like she was saying goodbye.

Yes, that makes sense. After all, that's what I came in here for, wasn't it? To say goodbye to the old house?

But he was doing more than saying goodbye.

Now, he was exploring. He'd become ten years old again, infected with the spirit of adventure. This was scary, yes, his thumping heart didn't lie.

But it was *fun.*

What was inside the box? Was it, after all, only a music box?

He bent low, his heart beating louder than ever. Unclasping the tiny metal eye where a lock might've once been, he opened it.

Harry's jaw dropped.

He didn't know what it was, at first—he only knew it was disgusting, something he shouldn't possibly be seeing!

Buh-thump! Buh-thump! Buh-thump!

The rhythmic beat sounded in his ears.

Except it wasn't his own heart making the noise—it was the heart inside the antique box. A fist-sized, thumping, sanguinary organ.

Pulsing. Quivering.

Its aortic valves throbbed, faster, faster: *buh-thump!-buh-thump!-buh-thump!*

Harry Thanatos screamed.

He retreated a step, tripped, then fell hard onto his back. An intricate cobweb dangled above him. An enormous spider slid down on a single strand and hovered an inch above his nose.

Harry whacked the spider away. Turning onto his belly, he crawled across the floor. His palms collected splinters. He felt the hole in the floor with his shoes, found the ladder, and climbed down. In all his panic, he missed the last three steps and fell on his ass.

The pain in his tailbone—*excruciating!* He groaned.

Slowly, he rose to his feet. He placed a hand against his lower back and ran unevenly down the hall, the stairs, then to the sitting room. His body itched and tickled, as if a thousand spiders crawled beneath his clothes—*were they?* he wondered with terror. His heart beat hard and fast, much too fast, inside his chest—but it was not nearly as loud as the heart upstairs.

The heart in the attic.

The heart of Bannatyne House.

He nabbed his jacket from the coat tree. Didn't bother to put it on, merely threw it over his right arm. He grabbed hold of the doorknob and pulled.

His face blanched white.

I'm locked inside. But that's impossible, goddamn it! How could ...

He pulled and yanked. His chest heaved, panting, out of breath.

He pounded against the door, shouting Patty Keepwell's name, hoping she was still standing on the street. Hoping she'd hear him.

Harry shouted, cried, then began to whimper.

Nobody came to unlock the door.

It was not yet eleven a.m.

Sheriff Bradley was having one hell of a day.

"Halloween over yet?" he asked his empty office. The door was closed. A mug of black coffee steamed on his desk. Two missing person reports had just been filed; one for Kenny Vandermeer, and one for Anna Hardy. Neighborhood kids. Boyfriend, girlfriend. Good, smart kids. Likely just ran off for a bit of fun, though their parents were understandably concerned.

Still, that was the least of Bradley's problems. He reached into the bottom drawer of his desk, drew out a bottle of rum, and poured a dash into his coffee.

"That goddamned Thorn in my side," he muttered, capping the rum, and burying it back in the drawer.

Thorn, a local homeless man, had stolen Elise Thanatos' car. Just last week, Elise had four tires slashed and her hood scratched up. The woman was a nasty old bird, but he felt sorry for her all the same.

Bradley had chased Thorn in hot pursuit. The bum drove like a maniac, nearly killing several pedestrians. He'd made it ten miles into the country. Luckily, Deputy Johansen (his best officer on the force) had assembled a Jersey barricade across Clark Ashton Road.

Bradley sipped his spiked coffee.

A wonder Thorn hadn't been crazy enough to drive straight *through*. Instead, he'd slammed on the brakes, climbed out of the car, then began jumping up and down, ranting about God knew what.

Quite the spectacle. Bradley shook his head, helping himself to another cup of coffee from the Bunn machine.

Now, Thorn sat in a holding cell in the station's far back room, constantly muttering about hearts in attics, brains in basements, and a lot of strange crap about the Vallancy Mansion. The man was obviously mentally ill and destined for a trip to the Sweet Hollow Cognitive Rehabilitation Center.

Bradley sent an email and phone message to the staff supervisor, hoping to hear back shortly. Most likely, however, he'd have to keep Thorn overnight.

Elise's car had been returned unscratched (save for the carving in the hood from last week—whoever committed that deed was still to be apprehended). Then, the cherry on top of the proverbial sundae—Elise informed Bradley that her husband was missing.

Old Harry, up and vanished into thin air—like smoke from his pipe. Absent since seven a.m.

He'd gone out on an errand, Elise said, and never returned.

Thus, a *third* missing person added to his list.

"What a day." Bradley groaned, downing the rest of his coffee. "And it ain't even over yet. I've got a feeling this Halloween is gonna be a *long* one."

A knock on the door.

"Come in."

Johansen entered the cramped office.

"What's the matter, Deputy? You look piqued."

She sat in one of the two guest chairs. Johansen could laugh and joke with the best of them, but she also had a serious side. A tough-as-nails personality you didn't want to screw around with.

"We've received three unusual reports this morning, Sheriff."

"Great! Even more to worry about. The nature of the reports?"

"Loud, strange noises coming from Bannatyne House and Morton Manor."

"Noises?"

"Yes, sir. Neighbors across the street say they've heard screaming, groaning, creaking. The kind of stuff you might hear on a haunted-house soundtrack."

"Any rattling of chains?" Bradley chuckled. "Bubbling cauldrons? The screech of a black cat, perhaps?"

Johansen frowned.

"Look, Deputy." Bradley eased back in his chair. "We've got some real problems to deal with today. Two missing kids, one missing husband, and this Thorn fella. The kind of reports you're talking about we get just about *every* Halloween. Pranks, that's all."

"Pranks at eleven in the morning, sir?"

"People are serious about Halloween in this town, Deputy. You know that. Some like to start the fun before dark."

"Well, I appreciate your candor." Johansen made for the door.

"Look, Deputy, I didn't mean to dismiss—"

"I'll keep you posted on the status of these reports." The door clicked shut.

He sighed. *Excellent. I've pissed off my best deputy.*

Sheriff Bradley then did the most responsible thing he could think of—he grabbed the rum from its bottom drawer and poured himself a shot.

Happy Halloween, thought Sheriff Bradley.

Chapter Nine

Alice Vandermeer stood on the Manor's front porch, holding herself against the cold. She wore a long wool coat and a navy-blue stocking cap. The wind whipped her auburn hair into her eyes. "Kenny!" She knocked loudly on the yellow door. "You in there, hon?"

Silence.

Stillness.

A narrow view through the dusky windows proffered only barren, rotting rooms. She tried the door—locked.

Her son was missing; a fact she found difficult to accept. Undoubtedly, he'd slipped out of the house last night to be with Anna Hardy. She was no fool—Kenny snuck out at least once or twice every week. But he always came back.

This time, he hadn't.

Something's wrong, she knew with grave certainty. *What if he's hurt? In pain, somewhere, unable to call for help? What if he and Anna have been—*

No. She wouldn't think of it.

Not yet.

It was early in the day, and there was hope.

Alice scanned the streets, half-expecting the kids to jump out from a hedge or from behind one of the houses and shout, "Got ya, Alice! Happy Halloween!"

No one jumped out, except a voice: "They'll return sometime this afternoon, Alice. Don't you think?"

She gazed across the hedgerows which divided the Manor's yard from the Hardy residence. Jason Hardy leaned against one of his porch's columns; arms crossed with a handsome smile. He resembled some '50s beatnik poet, with his black sweater, long hair, and well-trimmed beard. He was quirky, perhaps a little cynical, yet was nonetheless an honest, hard-working single parent.

"You don't suppose they went out of town?" Jason frowned. A dozen silicone zombie heads hung from his porch ceiling. They swayed in the wind around him, but he paid no attention. Alice remembered the day Kenny had helped Jason and Anna hang them up, how much fun they'd had together.

"To be honest?" Alice shrugged. "I haven't a damn clue."

"Maybe they're messing around the Bannatyne House," he suggested. "Or the Vallancy, maybe. I suspect they've gone to pay their respects."

A shiver trickled across Alice's shoulders.

The Vallancy.

She hadn't considered that prospect. Morton Manor and Bannatyne House were dangerous enough—but the Vallancy Mansion sat so far up in the hills, no one could hear you if you screamed.

"Does your daughter have her cell on her?" Alice asked.

"She left it on the kitchen table."

"Perfect." Alice sighed. "Kenny left his charging on his nightstand."

What the hell? she thought. *Don't all kids carry their phones these days? Incessantly texting, snapping photos, doom-scrolling through infinite social media?*

Yes ... they do. Just not our Anna and Kenny.

Alice supposed this was a good thing—at least they weren't rotting their brains out. Today, however, she almost wished her child was one of those "average" teens. Almost. "So," she said, attempting a smile. "What the hell are we going to do?"

"Good question," Jason replied, stroking his beard. "Honestly, I'm hoping they'll come home in a few hours with their tails between their legs. In the meantime, why not join me inside? We'll have coffee. Make a plan."

Coffee. A plan.

Music to Alice Vandermeer's ears.

She stepped off the Manor's porch, walked around the hedges; then, halfway across Jason's yard, she paused.

Voices. Calling her name, calling for help.

Anna? Kenny?!

She stared over at the Manor—then, something directly above her head prompted her to look up. The overhanging branches of a sycamore tree bent in the wind, creaking, and groaning in ghostly gales ...

A case of the wind, Alice inwardly laughed. *Sure. Kid stuff. Nature's tricks.*

Nodding with a soft smile, Jason held the door open.

Alice stepped inside.

Harry Thanatos decided to have a smoke, after all.

What the hell? He was trapped inside an old dark house. Not even the windows budged. A human heart thumped two stories above—though he tried not to think about it. Maybe, he reasoned, he hadn't seen the heart at all. Senility had finally crept into his moldering brain, and he'd merely imagined it.

His own heart, however, told him that was a lie.

He sat on the divan, huddled beside the sitting room window. He fiddled with his pipe, and a mailman strolled up the street.

Dropping his pipe and fixings on the cushion between his legs, he leaned over, and slammed his fist against the glass.

The man paused on the sidewalk.

Gawked up at the Bannatyne.

"You there, sir!" Harry shouted, his voice raw and quivering. "I need help! HELLLLP!"

The mailman frowned, then walked up the street.

Gone in an instant. The fourth person this morning, in fact. All stopped, cocked their ear to the wind, then ambled away.

Harry's voice grew hoarse.

"The one way to cure that," Harry mumbled, "is to shut up."

Finally, he lit his pipe, and began to smoke.

Sweet fragrant fumes drifted and wavered in the soft light.

The sun climbed higher in the sky.

Harry checked his watch.

2 p.m.

Christ, I've been stuck in this stuffy old house for hours! Stuck in here with that thing *beating, pulsing, shivering in the attic . . .*

He groaned. The sight of it—the sheer sight of a bloody human heart, beating inside that old decaying chest!

It gave him the willies.

Elise has surely noticed I've been gone all day, he mused, shifting the direction of his thoughts. *She's probably running around everywhere, searching for me. But she wouldn't stop here, would she? No. She'd check the Sweet Hollow Pub. Carl's Barber Shop. The park. Maybe even Ellie's Café. But she wouldn't think to look here, in this old house she hates so much, which will be destroyed at dawn's first light. . . .*

A weird feeling stole over Harry Thanatos. He thought, *This house is keeping me hostage, so that my cruel wife won't knock it down.*

"Is that it, old Bannatyne?" Harry asked the cracked plaster ceiling, the landscape hanging crooked on the wall, and the ripped-up divan upon which he reclined. "Keeping me for hostage? Tit for tat? Quid pro quo? Nonsense! My wife would just as soon knock this old house down with *me in it!*"

Harry laughed.

A laugh much too loud for an empty house.

The wicked willies gripped him stronger. A sense of terror whirled in his brain, his heart thumping in unison with that heart up in the attic. *Whose heart was that, anyway, for God's sake?*

No—on second thought, I'd rather not know the answer.

My old ticker can't handle that.

So he drew from his pipe, exhaling smoke which billowed about the room like tempest clouds, like swirling fog, like dragon's breath—or some hateful and restless ghost.

Youth is an entire life of its own; a time when reaching adulthood seems impossible, a mirage, a distant dream. The spring of life is found in youth, so it's said. How effortlessly energy and vibrancy inhabit the mind! At a sufficiently early age, one's thoughts are fresh and clear as morning dew. Curiosities and concepts flutter the air like roving butterflies. Idyllic summer days trickle slow as honey, and a child calls it Forever.

But know this: Youth is a trickling battery cell—draining hour by hour, year by year, minute by minute until emptied, corroded, and dead.

Anna and Kenny wandered the rooms separately; parlor, kitchen, library, dining room, the second-floor hallways, and bedrooms. A small flight of stairs on the second floor led up to a scarred attic door....

This, they did not open.

Nor did they descend into the basement.

Old houses are notorious keepers of secrets. After all, where better to hide a secret than a cramped attic or lowly basement?

And, sometimes, secrets can be ugly.

In fact, the two youths had already discovered *one* of said secrets: *Morton Manor was a vampire.*

Yes. It must be so.

How else could they have grown old? For the Manor drained them of their youth, sucking at their souls just as a vampire imbibes blood.

The front door glowed a beautiful vibrant yellow.

The cracks in the windows and ceiling had healed, now smoothly immaculate.

The floorboards creaked without anyone stepping on them—they were beginning to un-sag, becoming straight and flat. Only a matter of time before the varnish seeped back into the wood, making the floor gleam like new.

Anna's eyes clustered with wrinkles. Deep lines furrowed her forehead.

Kenny's hair gleamed silvery gray, and a dark stubble bristled his jaw.

Neither of their bodies grew or changed in proportion to their increasing age. Only their flesh responded. Their flesh, and the weakening bones beneath.

Kenny's back hurt like hell, as if someone had repeatedly whacked the lower half of his spine with a ballpeen hammer. Anna cried at the terrible ache in her hands and fingers: the onset of arthritis.

"We'll find a way out," said Kenny, stroking Anna's silvery hair. "I promise."

Anna wasn't crying about being trapped, but about the long, slow agony in her joints. Is this what they had to look forward to in their old age? Pain, suffering, and sorrow?

"Oh, Kenny," she groaned, staring into his eyes. "You look like you're forty! Older than my dad, even!"

Kenny's brown eyes shimmered—that look he had whenever coming upon an idea. "If I look forty to you now, Anna," he blinked, thoughtfully, "how old will I look by *tonight?*"

The Sweet Hollow Police Force was operating on high alert. Deputy Johansen patrolled the residential side of town, while Officers Dalton and Landis combed the commercial streets. Three missing persons occupied every second of their time: two teenagers, and an old man.

Johansen kept photographs of Anna Hardy, Kenny Vandermeer, and Harry Thanatos in a manila folder on the passenger seat. She'd spent hours questioning residents in the suburbs—to no avail.

Everyone knew Anna, Kenny, and "old man Harry."

Everyone knew everyone in Sweet Hollow.

The three hadn't been so much as glimpsed within the past twenty-four hours.

Strange.

It was damned near impossible to disappear in a town like Sweet Hollow. Not even the naturally reclusive could remain *completely* out of sight. Local horror novelist Timothy Ravencourt, for instance, was a man as reclusive as they come. Still, it was common knowledge that he lived in Ravencourt House on the outskirts of town—one of those handful of historic houses the Preservation Society had managed to renovate years ago.

Johansen glided up Sowin Street, parking just outside Bannatyne House.

Her fingers tapped the wheel. She chewed the inside of her cheek, gazing at that derelict, deteriorating domicile. Squinting, she leaned out her open window, and the breath caught in her throat.

The front window curtain *moved.*

Just imagining things? she thought…. *No. Not a chance.*

Her walkie-talkie crackled: "Deputy Johansen? It's Dalton. Anything to report?"

She held the Motorola up to her mouth and pressed the button. "I'm about to check on Bannatyne House."

"The *Bannatyne?* What for?"

"Thought I saw movement inside. Could be those kids we're looking for. Hiding out, maybe. Playing some Halloween prank. We received reports about odd noises coming from here and the Morton, earlier. Nobody took it seriously, our humble sheriff included."

"You need backup, Deputy?"

"No, thanks. Just keep up your side of patrol."

"Will do. Over."

Johansen clipped the walkie-talkie to her belt.

Climbed out of the cruiser.

Stepped up onto the sidewalk.

Was it just her, or had the Bannatyne's front steps gotten a fresh coat of paint? The steps shone a light green in the late evening light— almost turquoise.

Why would someone paint a house about to be demolished?

She peered through the front window.

The curtain partially obscured the room. Inside was an old divan, a crooked landscape on the wall, and, angling her head just so, she glimpsed part of a coat tree in the hallway.

A *jacket* hung on it. Adult-sized, it appeared.

Could be Harry's jacket. Or somebody else entirely. A stranger in town, perhaps. Some homeless squatter.

The NO TRESPASSING sign nailed to the door accomplished next to nothing in warding off those determined to enter.

Johansen tried the door.

To her surprise, it was unlocked.

She took a deep breath, one hand resting on her service pistol.

Gingerly, she entered the house.

"This is Deputy Johansen of the Sweet Hollow Police," she called. "There anyone here? Please respond."

The hallway stretched darkly before her. Waning sunlight filtered through a window in the room just ahead, to her right.

She approached the coat tree, reaching out for the jacket.

Somebody groaned—a low, sickly sound. She spun to her right, facing the sitting room doorway. An old man lay slumped on the divan—he hadn't been there moments ago, when she'd peered through the window.

A pipe, still smoking, rested in his lap.

His mouth hung obscenely open; a face obscured with lines, wrinkles, and crevices full of dust. His faded blue eyes shone vacuous and glassy.

"Harry?" she muttered, shocked by the man's withered visage. "My God, is that *you?*"

She stepped into the room.

As she did so, the front door swung shut.

The lock *clicked.*

Darkness floated gently down the sky.

The falling of raven feathers. Sifting coal dust.

A vast ebony cloth dropped by the hand of God.

The sun grew raw, round, and rubicund, rolling down the hills like a tossed jack-o'-lantern. Crimson seeped into the horizon like an open wound. Sherbet clouds drifted, mingling like dancing couples before fleeting across the sky's stage.

A bone-chill wind blew through the trees, scattering leaves like decks of crimped cards. Finally, the sky leached black.

First glimmering stars; the moon ascending like an old pale queen to her summit-throne.

Charles Vallancy paced his moon-shadowed halls.

Nearly time.

Nearly!

Rats scurried in the attic; he saw through their red beady eyes, felt their feet as his own as they scuttled the ragged floors. A few nibbled at the wine box that held his heart—these creatures he forced away with sheer will; an invisible presence shoving them onto the floor.

The rats fed on their own children, becoming long and plump, growing enormous....

Bats emerged from tall chimneys. Charles fluttered above the night fields; hearing what they heard, sensing what they sensed, feeling what it was to be a creature of furry body and leathery wings and all-powerful sonar.

He felt the little flies in his mental web; *four* of them now, this newest one named Johansen. How quickly they added up!

"All on a Samhain night's work." Charles' laughter echoed in the dank hallways. He paced across a moldy Arabian rug, once of elegant material, now badly stained from the leaky ceiling.

His laughter drowned every hall and room of the mansion; such was the mirth of madness.

His heart thumped—*up there!*

His brain quivered—*down there!*

All Hallow's Eve—*at long last!*

Children the whole town over jumped into costumes. Unfurled their annual candy bags. Plucked black-orange buckets from beneath the kitchen sink. Ripped the cases off their biggest pillows. Soon there would be demons and devils, goblins and ghouls, witches and werewolves, pirates and princesses scouring the streets.

Frankenstein, Dracula, the Mummy!

Kruger, Voorhees, and Myers!

Monsters both old and modern, parading the streets clutching candies in their sweaty hands. Screams, shrieks, laughs! Only Halloween possessed the power to elicit such a jolts—an eerie joviality never to be felt on any other day of the year.

It was Halloween, and the moon winked its dead pale eye.

Charles Vallancy held out his hand. Four flies, growing gray in their wings, wandered the bizarre lifelines of his ghostly palm....

How many darling flies might one big spider catch in the night? Charles' smile stretched to his ears—an eerie wolfish leer. *For it all depends upon the expansiveness of one's web, the sticky allure of one's threads....*

The power within him was growing; he felt it surging in his heart, his brain, his soul. A trembling energy, a quivering elation! Soon, he would be indomitable. If only that scoundrel Thorn had stuck around, he would've experienced the single greatest thrill of his miserable life—what it felt like to be a vampire.

To feed off the vitality of youth.

To bloom and blossom in blood.

For the Blood is the Life.

For Charles Vallancy—more blood, more life!

It was a night for trick or treat, and Charles had all the tricks.

He merely had to open wide his doors, and *they* would come.

All the children of Sweet Hollow; painted faces grinning, candy bags rattling, voices cheering and whooping in the graveyard airs—*All!*

PART II:

HALLOWEEN NIGHT

Chapter Ten

The little monsters of Sweet Hollow erupted from their houses, smiling beneath rubber masks and ghoulish make-up. Capes and gowns rippled in the wind. Bat and angel wings and alien antennae bobbed as they ran up the streets. Giant trick-or-treat bags crinkled in their clenched hands.

Adults handed out candy from the comfort of their homes, or else gathered in the Sweet Hollow Pub to drink hard cider, dance to seasonal pop tunes, and parade in scanty costumes of pharaohs, witches, and Red Riding Hoods.

Elise Thanatos, meanwhile, sat bundled in blankets upon her front porch. The rocking chair beside her creaked in the wind, vacant of its good-natured occupant.

Why hasn't he returned, for God's sake? What sort of trouble has he gotten into? Elise sipped from a mug of hot cider, liberally spiked with brandy.

She frowned over the dark country.

The dark country frowned back—dark as a starless universe, save for the eerie sherbet glow of a thousand jack-o'-lanterns all lighting up the front walks, porches, shop stoops, and streets; veritable will-o'-the-wisps, these countless burning suns within a universe called "Halloween."

It beamed a brilliant blue; a cold luminescence ejecting . . .

A jack-o'-lantern glowed upon her bottom porch step. It sported an insane, buck-toothed smile, with a long green stem that curled like a pig's tail. Harry had carved it only a day prior.

"Is that a self-portrait?" Elise had joked with him. Harry replied by grinning like the jack-o'-lantern, and they'd both laughed.

"Oh, Harry," Elise sniffed. "Why haven't you come *home?*"

Had Harry gotten hungry enough to take a bite of the apple? Had he, in his gluttony, swallowed the razor blade? Was he lying in a ditch somewhere, or in some dark alley, cold and dead?

It can't be. The police searched everywhere today. They would've found him. And if not him, somebody else.

She closed her eyes, imagining Harry and his bleeding mouth, clutching his stomach, collapsing onto the Ouspenskaya riverbank. His pipe still smoking upon the ground, his blue eyes rolled up into the back of his skull, the apple bobbing down the rushing river …

She began to cry.

On that final night of October, on which she should've been rejoicing in victory, eagerly awaiting the morning of demolition crews and wrecking balls, she now felt weak, wanton, and wretched.

I'm a widow of my own making. I've killed my husband! I've—

A soft, watery light shone across town. An eerie, graveyard blue gleaming in the dark upon the northernmost hill. Elise stood up. The blanket fell to her feet. "Vallancy," she whispered, knowing the light undoubtedly emanated from the mansion.

It beamed a brilliant blue; a cold luminescence ejecting from all thirty-one windows of its façade.

Elise sensed the hush settle over town as trick-or-treaters halted on the streets, sidewalks, lawns, porches, then turned, all gawking northward.

Then, as if in answer to the Vallancy, two separate radiant colors emerged upon the landscape. One in the east, the other in the west. Elise gaped in awe, perplexed by their luminous beauty.

Here, a deep ruby red! *Bannatyne House.*

There, a glistening emerald green! *Morton Manor.*

Despite the chill air, Elise trudged in her slippers to the edge of the porch. She leaned over the railing. A wind blasted her face, blowing her hair crazily and delivering the overwhelming scent of dead leaves, wet earth, and pumpkin seeds.

She stared across the hallowed country, utterly entranced by its blazing lights.

At that moment, every man, woman, and child in Sweet Hollow fell under the spell of awe and mystery.

Harken!

Gawk!

Ogle!

Like a zombie arisen from its wormy, rain-damp grave, a mummy shambling from its sarcophagus, or a vampire emerging from its cold castle crypt, the Old Dark Houses awakened—though they were not so dark anymore.

Morton Manor glowed green.

Bannatyne House radiated rouge.

My, how heads turned!

A pirate's hands held out a pillowcase, while an old man clutched a bundle of candies above it, never to let them drop into the case, for his eyes were drawn to the same source as the pirate's own.

Vampires ceased all sanguinary pleasures.

Slashers stopped their slaughters.

Ghosts stifled groans and held still their chains.

Morton Manor in the west.

Bannatyne in the east.

Vallancy in the north.

Green. Red. Blue.

A Halloween stoplight.

Everyone, indeed, *stopped.*

"Someone's made a haunted house out of our haunted houses!" shouted Snow White, only six years old. She stood on Lieber Street, shivering in the autumn night. "There'll be candy for us, maybe the best kinds! Let's go, let's go, let's *go!*"

Snow White trundled fast toward the closest of glowing lights. In her case, it was Morton Manor—glowing greener than a witch's wart. She didn't know what she wanted more—delicious candy, or the warmth of shelter. All the children on Lieber Street followed the young girl's lead. Others zipped away in the opposite direction, toward the blood-red façade of Bannatyne House.

No one approached the Vallancy. It was much too far away. Still, a few adventurous teenagers looked upon that blue twilight with some yearning in their hearts....

Patty Keepwell placed a black plastic cauldron filled with candy on her front stoop. A sign taped to the cauldron read *Take Two!* Then she pulled the string on her light-up skeleton, a welcome beacon for trick-or-treaters. "Skelly" was its name; a series of bones barely clinging together which hung from her porch rafters—it'd been a gift from her parents on her tenth Halloween. She sighed fondly, patting Skelly on his blue-gleaming clavicle. Finally, she went inside, poured a glass of red wine, then reclined on her couch. *I Walked with a Zombie,* a Tourneur classic, remained paused on the TV.

Snuggling under a blanket, she gazed about her living room walls. A series of framed photographs lingered under her gaze—one of which featured an eleven-year-old Patty celebrating her birthday. Mom, Dad, and even Skelly sat around the table while her cheeks puffed out in the act of blowing out candles. On the opposite wall, a shelf of first-place trophies from her days as an athletic swimmer, among other artifacts of a bygone life. She sighed deeply. That old heavy feeling returned—the inescapable conclusion that she'd been capable of more. *Someday,* she thought, *I'll do something great. Something goddamned heroic. There's still time yet. Right?*

Suddenly her living room flooded with blues, reds, and greens; her windows a kaleidoscopic swirl of colors. What was *this?*

She set her glass on the coffee table, slipped on her boots and coat, then stepped outside. A moment ago there'd been a sea of trick-or-treaters, noisily shrieking, shouting, running from door to door. Now, the street was empty.

Vacant asphalt gleamed beneath the streetlights.

Patty wandered out into the street.

Three colors. Three directions.

North, east, west.

What the hell is going on?

Like everyone else, she had to see the lights up close. She buttoned up her wool coat, shivering. Curiosity tugged her like an invisible string, drawing her west toward Morton Manor, where a seaweed green spilled across the sable sky.

Anna and Kenny grew old together.

Eyes dimmed.

Skin sagged.

Backs bunched.

They'd gone from eighteen years to seventy in less than a day. Kenny made his usual science jokes about entropy, attempting to provide levity in an increasingly weird and horrible situation. "We're going to die," Anna croaked, "and you're making jokes."

"Well?" Kenny shrugged, a careless old man. "I can't very well make jokes *after* we die, can I?"

Anna ignored this. Wrinkles collected about her lips in a scowl.

Sitting cross-legged in the Manor's library, restlessly perusing a pile of musty books—they suddenly began to scream.

A thick swampy green coaxed from the plaster walls, the ceiling, the floorboards. Like gas in a chamber, the fog surrounded them. They held each other, screaming in voices no longer their own: voices rusty and ragged with age.

"Anna!" Kenny grated.

"Kenny!" Anna rasped.

The swirling green fog enveloped everything.

They did not move from the floor, for they *could not* move. A strange paralysis overtook every bone in their bodies, embedded every wrinkle and line in their flesh, every neuron of their brains and fiber of their hearts. They screamed, frozen to the floor, not understanding why.

New voices soared through the Manor: young, pleasant, cheerful voices.

High shrieks. Giggling laughter.

"Where's the candy?" shouted one.

"What a pretty fog!" exclaimed another.

"*Get out!*" Anna screamed. "Leave now, or you'll be trapped too!"

Snow White's eyes shot wide. Obeying Anna's warning, she retreated to the front door—how horrible that rasping voice! How shrill and frightening that dreadful tone; like that of an ancient witch!

A plump kid, older, dressed as Michael Myers, caught her by the shoulder. "It's all part of the haunted house, stupid," he sneered. "It's *supposed* to be scary!"

The children flooded through the door.

Snow White, carried by the wave, was thrown back into the house. She cried. She couldn't leave. The doorway was blocked with bodies.

Anna raged against the miserable sense of being chained to the floor, weighed down by oppressive gravity—she longed to stand upon her own two feet and drag Kenny out the door while it was still *open*. Alas, every attempt to move her legs proffered no result—she could speak, blink, turn her head, and this was all.

The veins in Kenny's neck strained while he gritted his teeth, attempting to merely stand up—at last, he hung his head in despair, entirely out of breath.

More kids, voices, laughter.

A Halloween party had begun.

Except this wasn't a *party*, Anna knew.

For Morton Manor, this was *prey*.

Like the oozing of a wound.

A glowing, blood-red fog seeped from the pores of Bannatyne House. Part liquid, part gas, it leaked from every seam and corner, drenching all in luminescent ruby. Deputy Johansen and Harry Thanatos became soaked in this sanguinary fog.

Harry lay on the divan; he could not move. His pipe dangled from his hand. His face had grown astonishingly ancient; a thousand wrinkles upon his shriveled lips, his face gaunt and dreadful, his eyeballs reduced to mere pockets of jelly.

A moan, like wind over the lip of a bottle, escaped his open mouth.

91

The Bannatyne had sucked the life out of him—those precious few years! He lay upon the divan, blinking, unable to move, sure to die.

The breath rattled in his chest.

He thought of his wife.

He thought, still more, of the heart thumping in the attic.

Buh-thump, buh-thump, buh-thump.

His own heart was beating much slower.

At least he was *breathing;* ragged, labored, each breath a miracle.

The front door opened wide. Children flooded in.

Painted faces with skeletal grins.

Candy bags rattled against their sides.

Their excited eyes roved the rooms, ready to spot anything that may be hiding, lingering, hulked in clotted corners of the ruby fog—anything that would jump out and scare them.

Johansen sat paralyzed at the kitchen table. She'd sat down to rest, only to discover she could not rise. Her walkie-talkie remained halfway to her lips, her finger not quite on the button.

The walkie crackled.

"Johansen?" asked Officer Dalton. "Reports about strange lights are flooding in from all over town. Can you see any lights where you are? Over."

Oh, I can see the lights just fine all right, she thought. *Especially the red one.*

She blinked, eyes roving the foggy red kitchen. Her finger could not descend the half-inch necessary to press the talk button, no matter how hard she tried. *As if a spell's been cast over me ...*

"Harry!" she shouted. "You still alive in there?!"

"Who said that?" a tiny voice asked. "That don't sound like a scary ol' monster to me!"

A four-foot-tall witch stood in the kitchen entryway, soon joined by a short-statured murderer, plastic knife held up for stabbing. Then a quarterback from the Sweet Hollow Robins. Then a groaning zombie, a unicorn, a fairy princess with a shiny tiara ...

"Get out of here, kids!" Johansen shouted, frozen at the table. "It's not safe!"

They laughed. The police officer was acting funny!

"Why don't you *move?*" giggled the Fairy Princess. "Are you supposed to be a statue?"

"I cast her under my spell!" giggled the Witch. "Now she must stay here *forever!*"

"I find neither of you very funny," Johansen replied, sternly.

Officer Dalton crackled through the walkie: "Johansen, pick up if you can hear me. Over."

"Would if I could, pal," she grunted, using all her willpower to try to press the talk button—to no avail.

"Me and Darrin are on our way to the Bannatyne," said Dalton. "If you're still doing your check-in, you'll have backup shortly. Over."

The kids laughed.

"Just press the button!" cried the quarter-back. "Don't ya know how to work a walkie-talkie?"

"Indeed I do, twerp," Johansen scolded. "Now get out, before it's too late!"

Now *that* was a riot. The quarterback fell on the floor, holding his belly, rolling with laughter. "She thinks she's scary!" he said. The witch threw back her head and cackled. The fairy with the tiara twirled exuberantly round the table. More children filed into the house, all relishing the bright bleeding fog.

Bannatyne House was a strange new world.

Like a sandbox of ruby sediment—it was simply impossible not to dip in one's hands and play.

Patty stood on the leafy lawn of Morton Manor.

Something was wrong.

Very wrong.

The door was freshly painted.

Half the shingles were brand new—slick black tiles.

The rain gutters were no longer crooked, and free of rust.

A line of children stretched down the sidewalk, up the path, the porch steps, rushing through the front door.

Every child in the neighborhood, she knew, was either on their way to Morton Manor, the Bannatyne, or the Vallancy. They *must* be, for no natural child would miss out—all the old, haunted houses, luminous in legends, famous for fables, and peculiar with pasts, had suddenly come alive.

Alive. Patty shivered in the moonlight, for she knew it was true.

CHAPTER ELEVEN

"Gin seems to slur my speech by breaking my tongue," mumbled Paul Petrie, pouring another gin and tonic. "Or is it my mind that twists first, and the crumbling mouth follows?"

Two old philosophers sat on the front porch.

Bannatyne House stood directly across the street. They watched children dance away into its crimson glow.

They didn't know the reason behind tonight's phenomenal colors; sanguine hue, ocean-sapphire, and swamp-green flooding the sky like spotlights. Nor did they much care. Despite constant speculation, every theory was postulated with levity. All attempts at certainty had been abandoned. Wisdom began in ignorance, after all, and they agreed it was better to laugh, drink, and behold spectacle—God, what else was there?

Two old college buddies. Harvard graduates, 1972. Both retired.

Drunkards they were, and fools—harmless enough.

David took up his glass. The ice clinked. He sipped. It was good. Refreshing. The lights looked more vibrant than ever. How those children clamored! Sprinting down the street, they disappeared into the Bannatyne's red glow. Peering through the open door, he could see the light was actually a swirling fog.

"Just one more, I say." Paul slurred. "I always do! Then it sneaks up on me—insidiously."

"What sneaks up?" asked David.

"The gin, old friend! A sleek black cat in the alleyway of my broken will. Then suddenly I am sucked clean of full sentences. Overtaken by my own Mr. Hyde; that jabbering fool who insists on 'just one more.'"

"Ahh," said David.

"Thus prolongs the curse. Yet still! How marvelously the tongue rejuvenates at dawn."

"Ahh," said David.

The men clinked glasses and drank.

The street emptied. Every child had disappeared into the house of red fog.

The Bannatyne's front door slammed shut—the men quickly leaned forward, nearly dropping their beverages. The children's voices were silenced. No longer could they glimpse anyone through the red-tinted windows.

They took to woolgathering.

Why could they not see the children?

What awaited in those crimson shadows?

The street was ominously silent, like a forest hiding some unseen predator.

No laughter, giggling, taunting.

No footsteps echoing on pavement.

Halloween night, and yet—no trick-or-treaters.

All had been tricked.

"Do you hear that?" David frowned, setting his glass on the small table between them.

Paul nodded. "Here comes trouble."

A distant siren grew closer, followed by the flashing lights of a police cruiser.

Two officers opened their doors and stepped out. They inspected Deputy Johansen's cruiser parked out front. Finding no worthwhile clue as to her situation, they approached the Bannatyne House.

Paul and David turned and stared at each other.

"Tonight's vicarious spectacle has only just begun." Paul smiled his white dentures, pouring them both another drink. "Let's enjoy ourselves, shall we? Here, now! Bottoms up."

Alice Vandermeer awoke with vague surprise. Her cell phone lay in her limp hands—the volume on high, so she wouldn't miss any calls. *How could I have fallen asleep? With my son God knows where?*

She sat up on the couch, planting her feet on the carpet.

She checked her phone.

No calls. No messages.

Her heart weighed heavily in her chest.

She'd spent all afternoon with Jason Hardy, scouring every locale in Sweet Hollow—especially the abandoned downtown district which lay to the south. They'd explored derelict buildings and houses, even the crumbling dance hall on Harlequin Road. The forsaken "old part of town" was an obvious place to search, as the kids loved exploring historic ruins.

All they'd discovered were overgrown weeds, piles of brick and plaster, graffitied walls, and a few roving spiders.

They'd paid a visit to Vallancy Manse and the Bannatyne as well—pounding on the locked doors and windows, calling their children's names until their voices grew hoarse.

Only the spindly leaves falling from trees had answered.

Only wind, and the odor of decaying foliage.

And has my child become wind? The silence of falling leaves? The odor of decay?

Dark thoughts crashed upon her like an ocean tide; threatening to weigh her down, drown her beneath the pressure, and thereby render her useless as a name drawn in sand. Tears stung her eyes.

Where is my son?

Her head jerked toward her front door.

Voices murmured outside.

A distant crowd.

She stepped to the narrow window set within the door. A verdant sea washed over the houses, the street, the sky. She felt as if she'd drowned, died, and awoken to an underwater world of emerald scintillations.

Strangest of all, the entire neighborhood were gathered outside Morton Manor.

97

Something is wrong, Alice ruminated. *Very wrong.* This thought had stalked her all day, returning like a dangerous, unwelcome guest.

Opening the door, she stepped out as if in a dream. She didn't bother with shoes or coat. She walked across the damp lawn, icy leaves chilling her bare feet.

A line of children filed through the Manor's open door, disappearing into a green fog. Adults, meanwhile, stood on the street. Some visibly worried. Others laughing it off as a Halloween prank.

Patty Keepwell gazed up at the Manor; anxiety and wonder passed over her face like fighting shadows.

"Patty?" Alice joined her on the frigid sidewalk. "What the hell's going on?"

The Manor towered above them; each window a beacon light of alien green. Its front door hung wide open, revealing a hungry mouth.

A Green Giant with a ravenous appetite for children ...

"I don't know."

Patty's eyes never once strayed from the Manor. She traced its façade with extreme awe, as if gazing up at satellites not of this earth. "The children are drawn to it instinctively ... like moths to flame."

Moths to flame. Alice didn't like the sound of it. In her mind, the children began screaming inside the Manor, all burning up in the flames of a witch's green fire.

Alice looked up then, catching other colors upon the sky.

Misty blood red.

Ethereal jewel blue.

The colors hung upon the stars, festooned like a luminescent banner across the cosmos.

"Who's *doing* all this?"

"The Houses." Patty replied. "They're protecting themselves."

Alice frowned. Who was protecting who? She didn't understand.

"They *know*." Patty's thoughtful blue eyes searched the Manor's tall, crooked height. "They're going to be destroyed tomorrow morning, and they know it. Now they're opening their doors, collecting our children. So long as there's kids inside, the houses won't be demolished. That's not all, however. Notice that bay window? No cracks. The front door? Fresh coat of paint. The rain gutter? Brand new."

She's crazy, thought Alice. *She thinks the houses are ... what? Alive?*

The line of children emptied into the Manor.

Only two youths remained, heading steadily for the Manor's door—one was a local barista, Cambria Balustrade. She held a skeleton's hand. The skeleton's name was Joshua—her seven-year-old brother.

"Cambria, wait!" Alice cupped hands around her mouth. "Stay out of there, honey!"

The green fog swallowed them.

Creaking on its hinges, the door swung shut—no human hand, it seemed, had been necessary to push it closed.

The silhouettes in the windows vanished.

The green fog swirled.

Eerie silence.

How perfectly spotless, Alice thought, shivering in the wind, *that daisy-yellow door!*

Jason Hardy drove north, focusing on that eerie blue glow up in the hills. His Chevy pickup handled the winding roads with ease, though he reminded himself to slow down. His fingers drummed the steering wheel. Perspiration slicked his forehead, despite the chill wind blowing through the driver's side window.

His headlights glared into the dark like the eyes of a demon cat.

He thought only of his funny, sweet, intelligent daughter. Anna had grown up fast—next year, she'd be off to Madison University. Still, she'd always be his darling little girl.

Their years together had been joyful, though not without difficulties. Being a single father wasn't easy, of course, and he was forever rueful over the fact that Anna had never met her mother.

Jason remembered the day his wife died; a nightmare in snapshots, those bright clinical snippets. Blinding fluorescent lights. Green-tiled floor. The stench of blood, sweat, and urine mingling with sour disinfectant. His wife's terrible screams.

Maryanne had squeezed his hand like an iron vise—the last time they'd touched.

A tight, sweating, nail-digging grip.

She'd howled like a werewolf; impossible to forget that spine-shuddering scream!

Then erupted the cry of a newborn infant; his daughter, Anna; flesh of his flesh, blood of his blood. Then, louder than his baby girl's first wailing cries—the silence of Maryanne. She'd died in an instant; the result of an undetected heart condition.

All that blood, strained exertion, and screaming.

Maryanne had a weak heart—no one knew until it was too late. The doctors watched it all unfold; tears in their eyes despite their clinical professionalism. Nothing they could do. Maryanne had taken her last breath.

From that moment on, it was Jason and Anna against the world.

He'd raised Anna haplessly, cluelessly, at first. He made mistakes, yet learned quickly, and the years raced past. Jason read every child-rearing book he could find, salvaging the wisest advice and discarding the rest. He was a kind, loving father, but as he drove over the narrow dirt roads, he wondered if he hadn't raised his voice a time too many.

Anna ritually snuck out at night with the neighbor boy, Kenny Vandermeer. A fine kid, really. Intelligent, good-humored, and polite. These positive qualities didn't cancel out Jason's concerns, however. Anna often arrived home in the dead of night, or in the pre-dawn hours, and he'd be waiting for her.

To scold.

To shout.

Tears burned in his eyes—was he a bad father, just as his own had been? He wiped his face with the back of his hand. Straightened in his seat. Shoved his guilt way down deep—now was not the time to cave into one's emotions. He needed stoicism; he needed to keep his head.

The dirt road threaded through a moon-shadowed forest.

Miles and miles, all uphill.

He parked outside the wrought iron gates, letting the engine idle as he slid out of his seat.

He gazed up at the Vallancy. The windows burst with azure light, as if every room were flooded by a tropical sea—a teeming ocean within the Mansion. Who knew what sort of life lingered inside? What sort of sharks, octopi, and sea urchins called it home?

"Charles Vallancy." Jason spoke aloud, hands resting on the gate's cold iron bars. "That you? Alive after all these years?"

Jason Hardy scoffed. He didn't believe in ghosts—not really. Such fictions were for the superstitious-minded. He pushed open the wrought iron gate. The rusted hinges released an elongated squeal, like an infant pterodactyl breaking out of its shell.

He strolled into the field. Wheatgrass brushed against his waist. He glanced over his shoulder, through the gates to where his truck idled. The cab's light glowed warmly in the dark.

Once more, he faced the Vallancy.

The front doors were wide open.

He'd come here with Alice earlier in the day. The doors had been locked. Now, a lazuline fog spilled out the doorway. Shadows shifted within the Mansion's cobalt interior.

"Anna?" he shouted, taking three steps forward. "For God's sake, honey, are you *in there?*"

Silence.

Odor of wet grass, dead leaves, and wind.

A live ocean inside a dead house—shadows shifted, swarmed. The foggy light teemed with unknown life; pooled within its rotting walls.

Who could've orchestrated this? Wealthy pranksters, maybe, gifted with the technological expertise to wire up an old mansion with generators and lights—thousand-dollar spotlights with blue filters, powerful enough to catch the attention of an entire town. Plus a few thousand dollars more for red spotlights, then green ones, then to wire it all up, in secret, within each of the old houses.

All this, for a Halloween spectacle? Hell, if it could happen anywhere ... it'd be here. Sweet Hollow is an obsessed town. Here, every man, woman, and child are preoccupied with thoughts of harvest-time, gothic novels, and jack-o'-lanterns. If an anthem could be ascribed to this place, it'd be "The Monster Mash."

Jason laughed at the thought, despite the fear treading his spine and prickling at the back of his neck. He approached the doors, drawn by the light much like a child is drawn toward lightning bugs.

The ground moved.

He stopped.

Stared down.

Just your imagination. Keep going. Anna might be inside, lost, afraid, crying her eyes out. It's a big place. Three floors, countless rooms, plus an attic, a basement ...

He pushed forward. Grass rustled against his jeans. Thoughts of discovering Anna and Kenny inside. He'd scold them on the drive home, the night's taxing anxieties finally put to rest.

A low, steady rumble, a groan from the dirt—the earth shifted beneath him. He jumped backward—something pressed up against the soles of his shoes. Roots and grasses tore audibly from the dirt; the shredding noise of sprouts, stems, and stalks.

A grinning face emerged from the ground.

It glowed fiery orange.

Jason screamed. He couldn't believe what he was seeing. All he could do was scream.

Again, he leapt back. The ground writhed, as if all that grass was only a lid covering a coffin of enormous writhing earthworms. More orange faces cropped out of the ground; triangle eyes, noses, and jagged teeth.

The rippling earth; the clamor of things bulbous and rotund protruding from the soil.

Jason danced crazily, as if avoiding gunshots at his feet. He leaped from spot to spot, avoiding every inch of squirming ground. An earthquake roared beneath him.

Now, he ran the dirt path that divided the field. This strip of ground acted as an oasis amongst the field of churning earth. A thousand, nay—a *million* faces now! Flickering orange peepers glaring at the heavens, some staring at the gates, others turning their heads to scowl directly at *him*.

Prodigious sherbet gourds, smudged with dirt, a candle burning solemnly at their seedy centers. The faces were alive; their mouths and eyes moved.

"Impossible." Jason whispered. "The stuff of horror films, or a Grimm's fairy tale. Not true, it can't be—"

But it was.

An infinite patch of jack-o'-lanterns glared angry flames into the depthless night.

Now, the mansion's doors opened wider; a fetid corpse-breath eked out, floating in a tendril of blue fog. It slithered across the field until, encircling Jason's skull, it whispered in the Count's voice: *I bid you welcome....*

A stunt, a prank, an illusion!

Jason Hardy shook his head, denying his senses. It was Halloween, after all; formerly known in some areas of the world as Prank Night, or Mischief Night.

Impossible for pumpkins to burst from the ground, gutted and pre-carved, fitted with burning candles!

Impossible that three dead houses should come alive in the night; their rotting facades steadily improving, like deep wounds healing at a miraculous rate.

Jason gazed at the open double doors. His heart thundered, threatening to break loose from its moorings. Did he not hear his daughter's voice on the wind?—*Help me, save me!*

No! he thought. *Not my daughter's voice at all. A high falsetto, a mocking impersonation.*

The jack-o'-lanterns, numerous and infinite as stellar grains upon a cosmic beach, winked, blinked, twisted their leering mouths—*Enter,* they communicated. *Enter at once!*

But he would not—yet.

If Anna was inside, he would rescue her. But he wouldn't do it alone. The Vallancy would only capture them both—or, more likely, the masochistic creeps behind tonight's horrific delusions would capture them.

Jason ran for his idling pickup.

He'd return shortly with backup, supplies, and a sensible plan. If there was anything Jason Hardy was good at, it was making plans. After all, he'd practiced making plans his entire life.

He'd planned a life with Anna's mother, and when that life vanished, he'd planned how to raise a daughter, how to save up money so she could attend an excellent college.

Now, he'd plan to save Anna's life.

He pushed through the rusty iron gates, then climbed into his truck. He stomped on the accelerator. A cloud of dirt and gravel flew up into the moonlight. The moment he arrived home, he'd call on Alice Vandermeer—along with anyone else brave enough to accompany them. As a team, they'd bring their children home.

The Mansion's eerie luminescence, jutting above a universe of evil, flickering faces, gleamed in his rearview mirror like the strange sun of some unholy planet.

Chapter Twelve

Harry Thanatos was going to die.

Every breath seemed a minor miracle. Any second now, he expected to drift off into eternal sleep. His heart slowed to a minute quiver; several times, it stopped altogether.

He lay slumped on the divan, too exhausted to move. He did not feel seventy years old anymore so much as a mummified relic from two thousand BC.

His heart was tired.

His body was tired.

His flesh and bones were tired.

The house had done this to him. Harry was certain. Somehow, someway, the few precious years of his life had been leached from his soul and bequeathed to Bannatyne House.

Squinting at the red fog, he counted time between the beatings of his heart. The time increased between each beat, until his only anticipation was that of death.

In the fog, children danced, jumped, paraded in the redness. This was fun to them.

At least for now.

"Wake up! Wake up!" a boy screamed, bouncing up and down on the cushion beside him.

Harry was so fatigued and docile, the kids mistook him for sleeping. One child declared he was dead.

A little girl wearing a creepy clown mask poked Harry in the stomach. When Harry's yellow eyes shot wide open, the girl shrieked and ran away.

Meanwhile, two police officers slammed their fists against the front door.

"Johansen!" they shouted. "You in there?!"

The moment that Bannatyne's door had shut on its own free will, Deputy Johansen had become unfrozen. However, her freedom from paralysis rendered no positive results. She yanked and pulled on the doorknob, which turned freely, yet did not *open*.

"I'm here!" she shouted, yanking on the door. "Get a battering ram, or something!"

She could hear them out there—shuffling across the porch, speculating, shouting her name.

Still, they couldn't hear *her*.

Even when Johansen spoke into her walkie-talkie, they didn't hear— as if a mysterious force field had enveloped the house. A malevolent bubble which allowed its occupants to see and hear everything outside; yet for those looking in, they heard nothing, and saw nothing—save for the luminescent crimson fog.

Officer Landis smashed his fist against the window. He grimaced, bringing back his hand, jumping up and down in a tantrum of pain.

"I broke my hand!" he shrieked.

Incredibly, the battering ram they'd hauled out of the cruiser did not prove effective in breaking down the door—it could not even smash in the windows.

Johansen watched from the sitting room. Tendrils of terror drifted through the labyrinth of her mind; she felt lost, so lost. She didn't understand why they couldn't break down the door, or the window— cheap, fragile glass which should've shattered upon first impact.

Harry observed everything with detached amusement; he was not frightened, for his exhaustion was too extreme. Besides, he'd witnessed that horrid human heart beating all by its lonesome up in the attic. Nothing would shock him ever again.

106

"*Officer,*" whispered Harry, using all of his breath, every ounce of energy merely to whisper.

Johansen flinched, then spun around. She'd forgotten Harry was laying on the divan, roving the room with glazed eyes.

His breaths were ragged, trembling, quivering in his throat.

"*Officer Johansen . . .*"

She laid a hand, gently, upon his shoulder.

"Is there something I can do for you, sir?"

"*The heart . . .*"

"Your heart, sir? Are you telling me you're having a heart attack?"

"No." Harry swallowed, and his tongue felt like sand in his mouth. "*The attic. That's where the heart is. Kill it, and maybe that front door will . . . that front door—*"

The light faded from his eyes, eclipsed by a dull sheen.

Harry Thanatos stared emptily into the red spaces.

His final thoughts were not of the heart up in the attic, nor the mystery of the red fog, nor even of his wife, but of the apple in his jacket pocket.

The shiny red apple he'd never delivered to Patty Keepwell.

Johansen ignored the din of the battering ram and the exasperated voices of her colleagues outside. Reaching out with two fingers, she gently closed Harry's eyes.

Hundreds of children partied in Morton Manor's green-glowing rooms.

Like an unsupervised birthday bash, Kenny thought. He stood at a second-floor oriel window, gazing at the street below. His mother, Alice, stood beside Patty on the sidewalk. Both women studied the house. Kenny was positive they couldn't see him. Nor could they see or hear any of the children.

From in here, it sounded like World War II.

From out there, silence.

Silence, and the grim jade fog.

Kenny brought a hand to his face, feeling thick lines and folds about his chin, eyes, cheeks. His neck sagged. Wiry gray eyebrows stuck out wildly, a few dangling in his vision like a cat with overgrown whiskers.

If only Mom could see me now....

All his hair had blanched white, though it was difficult to tell through all this green fog. *Where did the fog come from, anyway?*

The walls.

The floor.

The ceiling.

Not *through* them, as if from an outside source, but from the boards, bricks, and plaster itself. Kenny knelt down (despite his painfully aching back) and touched the floorboards. His fingers came away damp.

"Perspiration." He frowned. "The floor is ... sweating."

Anna traced the room's wallpaper with her wrinkled fingers.

"It's breathing, too," she said.

"It's *what?*"

"Come here," she instructed. "Put your hand against this wall."

He did so, and grimaced. The wall undulated beneath his palm; the wall *breathed.*

Steadily.

In, then out.

In, then out.

Kenny yanked his hand back, disgusted.

"Jesus, that's gross!" he scowled, his stomach curdling. "The walls are breathing, and the floor is sweating!"

Anna bent down and touched the floorboards. Then she straightened, rubbing the moisture between her thumb and index finger.

"It's become a living organism," she stated ponderously.

"That isn't possible."

"I *know.*"

"Then *why* is it happening?!" Kenny raised his hands, exasperated. "What viable theory could there be?"

"I don't know!" Anna cried out, her voice shrill and rusty with countless years. She burrowed her head into Kenny's shoulder. "All I know is, we've got to find a way *out.*"

"We will." Kenny swallowed, gathering his senses. "I promise. And once we do, we can get everyone else out too."

Anna looked up into Kenny's crinkled face.

Tears slipped down both of their cheeks, following the trail of a thousand wrinkled ravines.

"Is this how we'll look when we're eighty, Kenny?"

"Eighty? I feel more like a hundred."

"Close your eyes," she said.

"Why?"

"Just close them."

Kenny closed his eyes.

Anna kissed him deeply on the lips. Momentarily, they were their eighteen-year-old selves again. New love blossomed with all the years ahead; young, fresh souls open to spring rains and good fortune.

As their lips touched, they remembered their plans—they'd graduate from Sweet Hollow High, work various jobs, and save up money to travel the country. They'd drive all the way to California, plop their butts down on a hot sandy beach, then watch jeweled waves crash upon the shore until midnight. Then, beside a campfire, they'd make love.

Abrupt as a stabbing blade, a child's voice pierced the quiet: "Two creepy old people up in a tree! K-I-S-S-I-N-G! First comes love, then comes—"

"Little boy," Kenny shouted, waving his fist at the Grim Reaper in the doorway, "you'll be damned to hell!"

The child backed into the hall, nearly tripping on his black gown. Moments later, his feet thudded on the stairs.

Anna laughed heartily.

Kenny noticed her laugh hadn't changed—still his girlfriend's sweet giggle, and not that of a cackling old woman. For this, he was grateful.

They held each other in the swirling green fog.

"Okay," Kenny sighed, after a minute's thought. "Let's find our way out of this dump, Anna."

Hand in hand, they pushed through the crowded hall, then downstairs into the kitchen. Children chased each other through the rooms, playing ghosts-in-the-haunted-house, among other Halloween games. They paid no mind to Anna and Kenny, mistaking their severely aged faces for nothing more than exquisitely detailed latex masks.

Now they stood before the basement door.

"Maybe there's a window down there the house has forgotten to lock," Kenny suggested. "Or at least something we can use."

"Have you forgotten this house is alive? There could be *anything* down there."

Kenny looked at her with his ancient face.

"I'll protect you," he said, his eyes still young, vibrant, unwavering. "Now stop being a scaredy-cat and come on."

"Wait." Anna retrieved a flashlight from her jacket pocket, then opened the basement door. Her foot was the first on the stairs.

"I'm no damsel in distress, Mr. Vandermeer," she said. "Maybe I'll protect you."

Slowly they descended into the dark, musty basement.

Chapter Thirteen

link!

Paul Petrie and David Chambers cheered their umpteenth drink of the night. Swirl of ice cubes. Drips of condensation. Scent of gin mingled with wet pavement, moonlight, and speculative palaver.

Tonight's dramatic show had commenced with the luminescent fog beaming from the Bannatyne's doors and windows. A mediocre beginning, the men agreed, though the entertainment tremendously improved after the front door shut on the children inside.

Now, two officers worked futilely at the task of breaking into the house.

"Deputy Johnson, is that her name?" David asked, sipping his gin and tonic. He'd heard a name on the wind; one of the officers had spoken the name.

"Johansen," Peter corrected, reclining in his chair with a Montecristo cigar.

"Ah."

"Seems the deputy's been locked in that house for hours," said Peter, "even *before* the lights started up."

"Ah."

"Are you always so guilty of monosyllabic utterances, David? Wait—never mind that now. Who's *this?*"

The men grinned above their drinks; two Cheshire smiles glimmering in the shadows.

A third cruiser pulled up beside Bannatyne House, parking a few feet behind Dalton and Landis' vehicle, which remained bumper to bumper with Deputy Johansen's cruiser—a veritable parade of small-town authority.

SHERIFF OF SWEET HOLLOW was painted in bold white lettering upon the doors.

Sheriff Bradley strode confidently up to the Bannatyne's front porch.

"Evening, Sheriff." Dalton's young face smiled with embarrassment. "Landis has injured his hand, it seems."

"Just a sprain, actually," Landis said.

"I understand we've got an unresponsive officer inside," Bradley replied, cutting to the chase. "So, then? Let's get her out."

"The door won't budge." Landis wiped sweat from his brow. "We've rammed it a hundred times."

"So what's the matter? Break a goddamn window." Bradley frowned.

"*You* break a goddamn window." Using his good hand, Landis handed the sheriff a red battering ram approximately nineteen inches in length.

"You two call yourselves police officers?" Bradley shook his head. "This is ridiculous. Stand aside."

They stood aside.

They crossed their arms.

"Uh, Sheriff?" Dalton interjected, "We've already tried—"

Bradley waved him away.

He stepped to the front window. Looked inside. A red fog obscured everything. Not only could he not see Johansen, but not one child came into view. The red glow shadowed the sheriff's face. For a few eerie moments, his fellow officers thought he resembled a demon.

"I thought y'all said there were a bunch of kids in this house?"

"There are," Dalton replied.

"Why can't I see them? Or hear them, for that matter?"

Dalton shrugged.

Landis shrugged.

Bradley rolled his eyes. He drew back, then slammed the stainless-steel ram against the front window—*Ping!*

He scowled at the ram for a moment, then slammed it into the glass again.

Ping! ...

Ping! ...

Ping! ...

After the dozenth attempt, Bradley gasped, "It's not a window!"

Dalton raised an eyebrow. "It isn't?"

"Not a chance," Bradley shook his head. "It's been replaced with … I don't know. Bulletproof glass, maybe. Have you tried the other windows, or just this one?"

"Every window on the first floor." Landis scratched his graying beard. "All impenetrable."

"And the door?"

"There isn't a hope in hell of breaking down that door, Sheriff," Landis replied, gravely. "Believe me, we tried."

The sheriff retrieved a piece of spicy cinnamon gum from his pocket. He unwrapped the foil and stuck it into his mouth. A nervous habit, though healthier than the one he kept hidden in the bottom drawer of his desk.

He chewed, frowning up at the old house.

The house of red glowing fog and disappearing children.

"Listen," he sighed, chewing the red-hot gum. "I've got my best deputy in that house. Not to mention countless children. We need to get *in,* and we need to get them *out.* Then we've got to do the same over at Morton Manor—as I'm sure you've heard, the same crazy shit is happening over there. Panicking parents are phoning the station every minute. We can't afford to do nothing. So I'm calling for backup."

"Respectfully, sir," Dalton interjected with a pained smile, "How are more officers going to solve anything?"

"What the hell else should I do?" Bradley called over his shoulder. "The more brains in this scenario, the better."

The sheriff sat in his cruiser and radioed back to the station.

Backup would arrive soon.

Five officers were already present at Morton Manor.

113

Now two more would be sent to the Bannatyne.

All hands were on deck now, which meant the station would be left unattended, save for the receptionist, Maurice Wainscot. Bradley was fine with this. He needed more heads on this job, and he needed them now.

Across the black ribbon of Sowin Street, lounging beneath a porch roof, Paul Petrie raised his glass, "To the clever architect of the Bannatyne House! How cunning his genius must've been, to secretly replace every door and window with an unbreakable substance— seemingly manufactured to frustrate officers of the law...."

"Aye, to the architect!" David raised his glass now, too.

"Listen, you Ivy League creeps!" Bradley stepped out of his cruiser and slammed the door. "Shut your mouths, will you? You two may find this funny, but I sure as hell don't."

Paul and David shut up then.

They did *not*, however, cease from clinking their glasses.

Muttering obscenities, Sheriff Bradley returned to the Bannatyne's porch. He shoved another stick of cinnamon gum into his mouth.

Prank.

Witchy curse.

Godly punishment.

Reality TV experiment!

Concerned neighbors milled about the sidewalks, discussing what must *really be going on.*

A man rammed his shoulder against the Manor's front door, sobbing, and bruising his arm. Others attempted breaking windows with sledgehammers, crowbars, and random stones. All were arrested, dragged away, and instructed to sit tight in the back of a cruiser.

The air reverberated with shouts:

"Kyra! You in there, honey?!"

"Sam! Can you hear me? Mommy and Daddy are worried!"

"Elliot Voje, you come out here this *instant!*"

Not one child was glimpsed behind the Manor's eerie green windows, nor in the ruby reds of Bannatyne House—as if the luminescent fogs had entirely absorbed them. Nor was there a single trick-or-treater remaining on the street. All had fallen prey to the houses' devious attractions. The only children left were infants, supervised at home by a grandparent, or else burbling sleepily in strollers while parents cried, chattered, and panicked.

By now, Alice Vandermeer had donned thick black socks, tennis shoes, a coat, and scarf. Despite the nagging anxiety plaguing her heart, she felt comforted by Patty Keepwell's calming presence. *She has her wits about her,* Alice reflected. *Like a sturdy anchor amidst a tossing tempest.*

Patty spoke of strange, fantastic, unearthly ideas.

Alice believed her.

After all, how could she not? Before her very eyes, the Manor subtly twitched and contorted, adjusting itself into complete restoration. Every fractured shingle exchanged for a new black tile. The lichenous window sills were now smooth and dry. The rotting clapboards hung straight, clean, and freshly painted.

Only an hour ago, the Manor's renovation was considered an impossibility!

"Early this morning," Alice blurted, steeling herself against the cold, "I tried to enter the Manor. The door didn't budge, so I looked into the windows. There wasn't any green light then, nor fog. I could see straight into the living room, Patty. Wasn't much in there, save for a grandfather clock, a ripped-up couch, and some cobwebs. I called my son's name. He never answered."

"Maybe he *did* answer," Patty shrugged. "Maybe you just couldn't hear him. To tell the truth, I have a feeling these houses are capable of a great deal more than we'd expect. They're living beings now. Capable of feeling and thinking."

"As if they've got a heart and brain," Alice mused.

"Exactly. But these houses haven't come alive for no reason, Alice. Someone made them alive."

Alice opened her mouth, intent on asking just who could be capable of making houses come alive—then silenced.

Jason Hardy's pickup honked loudly, urging people to disperse from the street. He pulled into his driveway, separated from Morton Manor by a row of waist-high hedges. Soon, he stood at the perimeter of the teeming horde. He surveyed the crowd, frowning, hands on his hips.

Alice waved to get his attention.

He spotted her, making his way across the lawn.

"Alice, listen!" Jason joined them on the sidewalk. "I was just out at the Vallancy. What's happening here is happening at the mansion, too—except worse."

Worse? Alice thought. *How the hell could it be worse?*

Jason meant to tell her about the ground rupturing, splitting beneath his feet, and the thousand orange faces leering up from the ground—but he shut his mouth.

It sounded crazy.

It *was* crazy.

"*Somebody* has to be behind all this." Jason shook his head, exasperated. "Whoever they are, I think the root of our problem hides within the Vallancy. Don't ask me how I know. I just do."

"He's right," Patty nodded gravely. "This all begins with the Vallancy. I can feel it, can't you? The malevolence? It's just as real as this wind, the streetlights' wan ellipses, that green shade emanating through the windows…."

"I think we'd better go." Jason affirmed. "I say we go search for our kids. At the very least, perhaps we'll discover who the hell's responsible for tonight's shit-show."

"What makes you think we can get in?" Alice emitted a dry, humorless laugh. She hadn't intended to sound mocking, but hopelessness had edged its way into her voice. "None of the house's doors will open, Jason. None of the windows will break!"

"True, but the Vallancy's front doors are wide open."

"What if we get lost? There must be a hundred rooms!"

"One hundred and seventeen," Patty smiled demurely. "But you won't get lost. Not if I come with you. I own a blueprint of the Vallancy. We can swing by my house, grab it, then head out."

Jason and Alice gazed at their local historian with slight trepidation. A soft light gleamed in the back of Patty's eyes. Her offer to help seemed honest. Genuine. Who were they to refuse?

"A fine idea, Patty." Jason called over his shoulder, already stalking off toward his house. "I'll grab flashlights, extra batteries, anything we might need. We'll leave in five!"

Jason pushed through the crowd, ignoring the cries and curses about the toes he stepped on. Meanwhile, a female police officer slammed her stainless-steel battering ram against the Morton's daisy yellow door. Parents cheered for this futile exercise, still hopeful their children may be saved.

"You really think this is a wise idea, Patty?" Alice asked. "Searching the Vallancy Manse?"

"I don't know." Patty chewed her bottom lip, her eyes once again glued upon the Manor. "But if anything, it sure beats standing here, watching the police flail around."

CHAPTER FOURTEEN

lise Thanatos grew more humiliated by the mile. The rumble of her engine drew attention, while the crudity carved into the hood announced her presence.

People turned, stared, pointed, but this was the least of her worries.

Anger and grief molded into one hideous life and lay pregnant in her stomach—a resurrected stillborn. She cried like a widow—where in God's name was Harry?

Gliding down Sowin Street, she laid on her horn to disperse the crowd. The street resembled a raucous block party, with three police cruisers clustered outside Bannatyne House.

Elise wiped her eyes, wondering if Ms. Keepwell wasn't behind all this. Perhaps, she thought, this was her last-ditch attempt to save the old dark houses. Save them with wild glowing lights and haunted attractions—essentially, weapons of mass distraction.

Poor kids!

Trapped inside those houses like flies, suffering in the ghastly web which Patty has spun. She might not have done all this on her own—No, she's too incompetent for that!—but surely she has her accomplices. Just like she'd hired somebody to slash my tires and carve up my hood . . .

Vindictive women.

That's what we are.

In a way, I suppose, Patty and I are alike. We won't take no for an answer. And, sometimes, we go too far to get what we want.

Next: the intrusive thought of Harry lying dead somewhere, mouth gushing blood, the half-eaten apple having rolled not too far away ...

She slammed her fist on the wheel.

"*Stop!*" she demanded, with gusts of grief exploding in her chest. "Stop *thinking* that!"

Elise hated herself for her emotional outbursts; she felt angry and absurd, like some low-born creature helpless to change. It'd been this way ever since she was a little girl—with no one around to talk to, what choice was there but to berate oneself? Adroitly, she made a U-turn and headed back in the direction she'd come. She'd seen enough. She didn't care what was happening in town. She just wanted her husband back.

Like vermin, the people pooled into the street.

Shouting. Shrieking. Gossiping.

Elise honked the horn, revved the engine, and shouted for people to get the hell out of the road. Some cursed and flipped her off. Elise gave it right back to them.

She had no patience for rude and conniving people like Patty Keepwell, this entire town, nor even herself. Once the lane cleared, she sped down the street. She did not worry about being pulled over and fined, as the police were preoccupied.

What if Harry, like the kids, is trapped inside Morton Manor? Or the Bannatyne? But that wouldn't quite make sense, would it? The lights didn't start until half an hour ago ... and he's been missing all day.

At the sight of Patty's house, she eased off the accelerator, then parked behind the familiar VW Beetle. A faint golden glow shone from the living room window. Elise would give Patty a piece of her mind— perhaps. Maybe she'd simply inquire if Patty had seen her husband, or if he'd ever even showed up at her house. Truly, Elise did not know what she'd do when she saw Patty—give her a hug, cry on her shoulder, slug her in the face—everything was up in the air, a knot of undecided confusion.

Elise popped open her car door, then froze.

Patty Keepwell emerged from her house, carrying what appeared to be a rolled-up poster, or a map. Strangely, she kissed the neon blue skeleton hanging from her porch rafter, right on its toothy grin, then practically skipped down the front steps and across the street.

All that youthful energy. Where the hell does she get it? Probably from her sheer animosity—enough hatred to power three haunted houses and kidnap every child in town.

A Chevy truck idled across the street.

Patty hopped into its backseat.

Elise squinted into the truck's darkened cab. A woman sat in the passenger seat. Elise couldn't make out who. Jason Hardy, the local artist, sat before the wheel. He wore his usual black sweater and thick-framed glasses, and in the back of his pickup was the usual jumble of half-finished canvases, plastic tarps, and tripod easels.

One of Patty's accomplices, no doubt. Why else would he be driving her around? They think they can kidnap those kids and hold this town hostage— maybe even my husband—but they can't. They won't. I'll make sure of that....

The Chevy pulled out onto the street and headed North.

Elise performed another U-turn, following not thirty feet behind. All her confusion suddenly faded, replaced by a sense of angry certainty. The anger felt good; a driving force that provided her direction. Jaw clenched. Hands strangling the wheel. She would locate her husband. She would get to the bottom of tonight's Halloween catastrophe.

Come hell or high water . . .

A dark, dank dungeon.

A dirt floor, tightly packed from a century of footfalls.

Armed with flashlights, Anna and Kenny searched the Manor's basement. Their pale beams cut through the green fog. The stuff swirled, shifted, swayed in unnatural directions. No wind, breeze, or draft down here, yet it moved as if it had a mind of its own.

No windows. No gaping holes in the stone walls. No secret tunnel they could escape through.

They were looking for a way out.

There wasn't one.

"Do you think it's toxic," Anna asked, "all this green stuff?"

"Probably." Kenny shrugged, parting his silver hair from his eyes. "Though there's not much we can do about it, is there?"

Anna breathed through her nose. The mist crept into her air passages, then coiled deep inside her lungs. She felt it like a poison bulging in her throat; tasted its flavor of skunky lime; felt it soak into her brain, contaminating her thoughts with alien greenness.

She hated this. Hated being down here. Her body was frail and tired. Her joints shrieked in their silent hell, as if her bones were prodded with small needles. Her skin hung loosely on her bones.

Death had never felt so close.

"Look!" Kenny pointed at a basement corner.

Something lurked on the floor.

It quivered. Jittered. Swelled.

"What *is* that?" Anna held a hand over her mouth, afraid to breathe. She took a gulp of green fog. Held it in.

Kenny approached the creature—black, trembling, huddled.

No bigger than an infant, swaddled in ebony fur and leather.

"What *is* it?" Anna repeated. "I can't stand not knowing!"

"Hand me that shovel." Kenny gestured toward the farthest wall, where it lay against a support beam.

Anna seized it.

"What are you going to do?" she asked, handing him the shovel. "*Hit* the thing?"

"No! I'm just ..."

Kenny stuck the flashlight in his mouth, brought the shovel towards the tremulous, leathery thing, then ... poked it.

A series of wild screeches!

Things, dozens of them, fluttered into the air!

Anna leapt back with a scream.

Kenny fell onto his side, the shovel dropping with a dull clatter.

A flurry of large bats flew from the corner; ghastly creatures swooping and diving like mad. One landed in Anna's hair. She screamed, violently striking her own skull with her flashlight.

The bat emitted a high shriek, then fell to the floor.

It righted itself onto its belly, began to crawl, its black beady eyes fastened on Kenny. Only a bat—yet how vicious it was! Its tiny fangs gnashed at the air.

Kenny scuttled backwards like a crab. The bat followed on broken wings, its mouth open wide, shrieking.

"Oh, no, you *don't!*" Anna brought her foot down hard.

Tiny bones crunched underfoot.

Now, a long bloody strand stretched from the sole of her shoe to the black lump on the floor. With a groan of disgust, she scraped her shoe upon the ground, smearing the clinging viscera.

Aside from the occasional screech, the bats now huddled quietly in the rafters—as if fearful of sharing in their brethren bat's gruesome end.

"That's right," Anna shouted. "I'll squish all of you!"

"Shush." Kenny picked himself up, dusting off his professorial sweater. "They won't bother us now."

"The hell they won't." Anna trembled, catching her breath. She didn't mind breathing in the green fog anymore. Just so long as she didn't have a bat in her hair. She shuddered at the memory, all too fresh in her mind.

"Let's look in the corner; seems like they were huddled around something." Kenny trained his flashlight. Now that the bats weren't obscuring it, protecting it, they could see what it was:

A plump, pink organ of many intricate grooves and fissures—slick, wet, quivering in its gelatinous profusion.

Kenny kneeled beside it. He groaned. Not only did his back hurt, now his knees ached. *Such are the vicissitudes of old age,* he mused. He squinted, examining the brain's peculiar topography as if he were a neurosurgeon.

"Oh, God." Anna turned away, bent over, and vomited.

"You grossed out?" Kenny asked without removing his gaze from the specimen.

"Nope. Definitely not."

"Come on, Anna. Train your light on this."

Anna trained her light, though refused to look at it. She gazed into the basement's dark green spaces.

"It's connected to the floor," Kenny observed, prodding the fleshy brain with his index finger. The brain was warm, wet ... and vibrating.

"It's *what?*" Anna asked for confirmation.

"Strands of dendrites, or some other thin, fibrous tissues are connecting it to the floor. Kind of like roots."

"The house has grown a brain, Kenny? Is that what you're saying?"

"Precisely."

"This is crazy shit." She closed her eyes, breathing deep.

"No crazier than anything else we've seen tonight."

"The house is alive then," Anna reflected, still refusing to look where her light was trained. "And it's growing a brain."

"No," Kenny said. "It's *grown* a brain. Past tense."

"Great. Now, get out of my way."

"What?" Kenny looked up.

"Get out of my way," she urged. "And keep your flashlight on it."

"What are you planning?" Kenny frowned, nervously.

"Watch."

Anna gently pushed him aside. She stood over the moist slimy brain, still keeping her eyes focused on the cobwebbed ceiling. Yet had she looked down, she would have noticed the tiny red bubbles secreted between the gyrus folds—then, if she'd looked closer, she'd have observed the brain *pulsing*—as if laboring over secret cogitations, as if it were *thinking*.

'We came down here to find a way out," Anna said, raising her foot above the brain. "This, perhaps, is the beginning of one."

Kenny grimaced, covering his eyes.

Anna slammed down her foot.

The brain *squelched*. Black blood ejaculated, splattering her legs, the stone walls, the floor. She gagged, then stomped on it again.

Then again.

One time more.

Suddenly, from behind: the *thump-thump-thump-thump* of things dropping in rapid procession. Anna was reminded of October apples falling in a strong wind. They whirled around, flashlights pointed in the direction of the din.

The bats had fallen from the rafters. *Lifeless.*

They resembled lumps of coal on the ground.

Their collective brain had been obliterated.

Smashed underfoot.

Destroyed.

The basement remained silent. They heard their own breathing—rhythmic exhalations of green fog—as well as the footfalls of rambunctious children running around upstairs. Jumping on the living room couch. Chasing each other through the kitchen, the library, every room on the first and second floor. Chortling. Shouting. Giggling. The kids still thought this was all a joke.

Kenny stared down at the deceased night-fliers.

"What a perplexing phenomenon." Kenny adjusted his glasses. "Still, I doubt even a brainless house will let us leave. The doors will remain locked. The windows unbreakable."

"So what do we do now, Professor?"

"We search for where the house stores its emotions," he replied, ignoring Anna's teasing. "Metaphorically at least."

Anna blinked at his seemingly strange statement.

"I keep having to remind myself," she said, "that we're not in Kansas anymore."

"Exactly. We're in Morton Manor. The rules of reality are very different here. I say we inspect the attic next."

"Why the attic?"

"It's the second most obscure place in the house. I suspect that's where the Manor keeps its most important organ. Not a brain, no, but—"

"A heart," Anna finished for him.

"Yes," he smiled, pleased by her completing the puzzle. "The heart of the house."

They climbed the creaking stairs. What they didn't notice, didn't observe in all their fear and excitement, was the trail of blood along the stairwell wall—how it led out the basement door, dripped across the kitchen, then smeared up into the parlor's fireplace chimney.

One of the bats had not only lived but escaped.

Just enough neurons and dendrites, apparently, survived in the trampled brain for the sustainment of a single creature.

The bat flew out the chimney, high and away, and Charles Vallancy possessed its wings; one speck of consciousness flapping across the moonlit night, soaring over houses and buildings and streets crowded with concerned parents.

It flew to the Sweet Hollow Police Station.

Maurice Wainscot, receptionist, stepped outside for a cigarette. He'd been fielding emergency calls all night. All of them the same: *Where's my child? What's going on with the old dark houses? Why don't the police just break in and save them, for Christ's sake?*

Charles Vallancy swooped down, slipping through the station's door a second before it shut. He had someone he wanted to visit—a faithless fool, a buffoonish betrayer called Thorn—who lingered and festered in a jail cell.

Maurice groaned pleasurably, enjoying a well-deserved cigarette break. He hadn't an inkling of what was about to transpire, nor that the police station he was obligated to protect was surreptitiously under siege.

He smoked his cancer-stick down to the stub.

Then lit another one.

Chapter Fifteen

Four teenagers made out in Ted's parents' basement. It was well-furnished down there, with a shag rug, couch, hi-fi stereo, and a flatscreen television spanning the length of one wall—Ted's parents were loaded.

They'd all planned on staying up till dawn, watching horror movies and smoking pot. But once the bizarre lights shone outside the basement's narrow egress windows, plans changed.

Now, they would go to the mansion.

Forget the slimy green of Morton Manor, or the candy crimson of Bannatyne House. *Those* were for kids.

In preparation for this nocturnal outing, Ted rummaged up some alcohol.

"This wine's been down here since before I was born." Ted grinned, grabbing two bottles out of a large cabinet built into the far wall. "I say we get this party started!"

He dusted off an old corkscrew and popped the first bottle. The others laughed, joining him beside the liquor cabinet. A dusty agate bar stood in the corner.

"My parents quit drinking a long time ago," said Ted. "Which means more for us, right? Hey, Darren, take a whiff of this."

Darren took up the bottle, sniffed, nodded approvingly, then handed it to Clementine. She held the bottle under their nostrils, delighting in the fruity aroma.

Clementine handed the bottle to Sandy, Ted's girlfriend. Although far from a connoisseur, Sandy picked up on its more lavish notes; strawberry, oak, and orange blossom.

"They should bottle this smell," said Sandy. "Make it into a scented candle."

"Go on," Ted grinned. "You take the first nip, Sandy."

"You're not going to pour us glasses?"

"If I grab any from upstairs, it'll make my folks suspicious," Ted explained. "Just take a sip!"

Sandy obediently sipped, then passed it to Clementine.

Clementine brushed back her long, auburn hair. Far from being shy, she took a good long pull. Darren liked the look of her wet lips and Dionysian smile. Suddenly, he longed to kiss her all over again.

"Here, babe." Clementine handed it to Darren.

Darren took an even bigger pull before handing it back to Ted.

"That's the spirit, gang." Ted gulped until the bottle was half-empty, then sighed with satisfaction. "We'll drink this whole thing now, then take the second bottle with us."

"We better go soon." Darren checked the time on his phone. "I doubt we're the only idiots heading for those lights. It'd be awesome if we were the first ones there."

"Let's get drunk quick then." Ted passed the bottle.

The bottle exchanged hands until empty.

Then they loaded a backpack with flashlights, candles, lighters, a bag of marijuana, and the second Merlot. Darren offered to drive them all to the Vallancy, but Ted shot this down. "Better to hike through the Northwoods," he said. "I know the old trail pretty well. It'll be spookier that way."

Ted turned up the volume on the TV, letting *Shudder* play its curated selection of horror films. This way, his parents would be less suspicious, less inclined to sneak downstairs and see what they were up to.

Silence implied making out, perhaps even a quiet orgy. But the sounds of screaming, grumbling chainsaws, and butcher's knives slicing the air? Simply kids enjoying a relatively innocent—albeit gory—Halloween.

Not drinking alcohol.

Not having sex.

And *certainly* not sneaking out of the house.

The four of them, quiet as cats, lurched up the carpeted stairs.

Passed through the kitchen.

At the front door, they glanced into the darkened living room. Ted's parents lay on the couch—voraciously making out!

Sandy and Clementine palmed their mouths, stifling an uproar of giggling.

Darren's eyes went wide. He looked at Ted, and silently mouthed the word *Gross!*

Ted rolled his eyes, and motioned for them all to get out, get out, before anything more happened.

They all got out.

The door clicked shut.

A Cheshire moon gleamed in the sky and made twisted shadows of the trees. Stars glimmered above like distant snow crystals. Winter loomed ominously near; the wind whispered as much. An icy breath stirred the dead leaves at their feet. Twigs and branches snapped underfoot like bones.

"How much longer?" Clementine huddled against Darren as they walked.

"Almost there," Ted groaned, tired of her complaining. "Have some wine! It'll warm you."

"I don't *want* any more wine. I *want* out of these creepy woods."

"More for me, I guess." Ted tilted his head back, downing the delicious Merlot.

"Give it here, I could use it." Sandy stumbled around random shrubs, laughing. Ted caught her from falling twice, laughing with her.

"You sure you could use it?" Ted asked. "Seems like you've had enough."

"I'm cold!" she exclaimed.

"Then get warm." Ted gave her the bottle. "Get hot, even!"

Sandy chugged, then handed it back. Less than half the bottle remained. Somewhere, a wood owl hooted and made them all jump. They laughed—a noise much too loud for these nearly silent woods.

"All better now," Sandy grinned, then clamped both sides of Ted's face and began kissing him. Ted's eyes went wide, feeling her wine-slicked tongue roving inside his mouth.

"Eww!" Clementine grimaced.

Darren grinned.

Sandy broke from the kiss, then said, "How's *that* for hot, Ted?"

She led the way now, up to her ankles in frosted leaves, swaying drunkenly and dodging trees. Despite her prodigious inebriation, she moved steadily northward. A well-trodden trail led them through the moonlit woods. Sandy had steam behind her; all that wine and grass providing a novel euphoria. Her calves burned on the uphill terrain, but she relished it.

All followed her lead.

Lingering sweetness danced upon their tongues.

The moon rose higher; all prayed thanks to its cadaverous hue: they had never known a night as bright as this.

"I'll never think of red wine the same way again." Ted smiled, sharing the last of the vintage with Darren.

Darren tossed the empty bottle over his shoulder. It thunked against a tree.

All laughed and joked except for Clementine; she had come to her senses. She sulked, longing to return home and crawl into bed. She began thinking the Vallancy was a terrible idea—a sense of danger, perhaps evil, lingered in the night air.

"There it is!" Sandy shouted. "We made it!"

The trees thinned and they stepped onto a gravel road.

A tall iron gate hung wide open.

Beyond the bars, an astonishing sight!

Clementine's jaw dropped.

Darren blinked, wondering if it wasn't a wine-induced hallucination. He shook his head, as if to clear his vision. Nothing changed. He examined his friend's faces; they saw it too.

Ted shivered at the sight.

"Holy shit." Sandy's labored breath fogged the air. "It's *gorgeous!*"

The Vallancy Mansion was striking enough—an immense gothic domicile of ghostly, underwater lights—yet the glowing legion of jack-o'-lanterns were another matter entirely.

How many leering faces? Hundreds? Thousands?

They passed through the gates. No one spoke.

They walked solemnly, as if entering a sacred cathedral. Orange faces peered out from tall white grass; faces of the dead whose eyes and mouths and noses were lit by the flames of Hell.

The four teens ambled down the gravel path, taking in the numberless glowing countenances. Some were frightening; eyes of vermillion flame and teeth full of malice. Others appeared odd; buck-toothed mouths, circular noses, gaunt and withered cheeks, shocked and widened eyes uncannily human.

"It's as if the ground has absorbed a thousand dead," said Clementine, no longer conscious of how cold she was, "and given birth to them once more, their spirits resurrected in the flames of jack-o'-lanterns."

All nodded, quietly.

Clementine observed the ground—how torn up the soil was! As if these haunted faces had emerged from the earth fully formed ... but that couldn't be, she told herself. Such a notion was impossible.

The narrow path came to an end.

The porch steps began.

A fog eddied beyond the open doors—its sapphire swirls moved in crazed patterns, a maelstrom of jade and indigo, beckoning them forth! The fog resembled a gleaming crystal, whirling in an ethereal dance; ghosts waltzing in the graveyard blue.

Tentatively, all four stepped onto the porch.

"Maybe we ought to head back." Darren smiled falsely. "I don't like the look of it."

"We walked for miles...." Ted protested, yet secretly wanted to turn back as well.

Sandy heard the trepidation in their voices. "You guys, do you realize that if we don't explore this mansion, right *now,* we're going to regret it forever? We'll look back on this night and curse ourselves for being cowards."

"She's right." Clementine stepped to the threshold.

All turned, examining her with surprise.

She'd been so resistant, so lame before! Out in the woods, shivering against Darren's shoulder, refusing to drink wine! Now, as if provoked by some unseen spirit, she thirsted for adventure.

"It's the most beautiful thing I've ever seen." Her dilated brown eyes shimmered, roving the Mansion's gothic facade. "Whoever designed tonight's creepy shenanigans is a genius. I've got to see what they've set up inside...."

"Well, if you're going," Darren said, putting an arm around Clementine's shoulders, "then I guess I am too."

Ted stared into the doorway of blue fog. "If we're doing this," he sighed, wishing he had more wine, "then let's not take all night."

"Then it's decided." Sandy interjected, taking one last look behind her at all thousands of orange, giddy flames. "So long as we don't leave each other's side, we'll be all right."

Silently, reverently, drawn by sheer curiosity, they entered the Vallancy.

Ted half-expected the doors to creak shut behind them, just like in the movies.

There was no creaking report, nor outright slamming shut of a doors, for which Ted was grateful. The blue fog was so thickly luminous, however, one couldn't see the doors. Maybe they had closed—silently.

"Hey, Darren?" Ted strained to keep his voice level.

"What's up?"

"Go back a few feet and check the doors, will you? Make sure they're still open."

"Ha! Okay ..." He disappeared into the blue billows.

"Well?" Ted asked, staring nervously into the fog.

The fog furled and unfurled, like flexing tentacles.

All held their breath.

The mansion possessed all the solemnity and silence of a sepulcher.

Suddenly Darren emerged from the haze, laughing—and all exhaled in relief.

"The doors are fine," he grinned, nudging Ted's shoulder. "What's the matter? You afraid Charles Vallancy's ghost might lock us in?"

Ted laughed as if such a notion were ridiculous—as if it hadn't been *exactly* what he was thinking.

"Impossible to see anything in here," Darren muttered, now turning about. "But let's keep going. Maybe our eyes will adjust."

A stupid thing to say, Ted thought. *One's eyes adjust to darkness. Not fog!*

But as they explored the parlor, their eyes indeed adjusted.

Either that, or the fog thinned.

Almost as if it wants us to explore the house, just so the fog can thicken up and we lose our way.

Several ripped-up couches were strewn about the room. Warped and damaged bookshelves. Crusty old rugs. A magnanimous fireplace of blackened bricks and one lonely ash heap.

Ted's heart quickened. He fantasized about the doors creaking shut; being locked in; trapped like tonight's trick-or-treaters had been trapped. He'd seen all those parents on the street, attempting to break into the Bannatyne and Morton Manor—how sad and desperate!

A cold skeleton hand snatched Ted's arm.

He jumped, emitting a thick-throated wail.

Sandy laughed, kissing him on the cheek. "Hey, scaredy cat," She winked, pulling him close. "Wanna be my Halloween beau?"

Ted forced a smile. The powerful bravado he'd felt while marching through the forest and gulping wine had long faded. He was supposed to have an exciting life ahead of him—dying in the Vallancy a month shy of turning eighteen was not part of his plans.

"No splitting up, okay?" Clementine reminded everyone. "That's what happens in horror movies, and look what happens to *them*. Darren and I will lead from the front. You guys stay in back. Always remain within earshot. We'll call to each other once every minute, just to make sure we're all here."

Walking in twos, they stepped out of the parlor and into a long misty hallway.

Like a trickle of icy water, the group flowed from one room to the next; there was little to no deliberation.

"Group check!" Clementine called. "Everyone here?"

All four confirmed as much, even though Ted and Sandy could barely make out the back of Clementine and Darren's heads. The fog swirled around them in miniature cyclones, pushed by some sporadic, unfelt draft.

How is the fog shifting? Ted wondered, uneasily. *The fog I get, sure, that's easy. Vents installed in the walls and ceiling are pushing this stuff out. I can even buy the color—hidden LED lights, what else? But the constant shifting, swirling, rotating movement? The Vallancy's walls seem to have completely blocked off the outside breeze....*

The hair prickled on Ted's arms.

The fog curled about his body.

His sweaty palm glued to Sandy's hand. Occasionally, she leaned over and kissed him on the mouth. Her lips still tasted of fruity wine, and Ted swayed with the impulse to bow down and worship her—Sandy, the Goddess of Wine and Fertility.

This isn't so bad, I guess. So long as she keeps kissing me....

They discovered an enormous kitchen with rats in the sink; their pink tails swishing about clogged pools of black water. Then a billiards room with a vaulted ceiling. Next, a library crammed wall-to-wall with bookshelves lined with musty tomes. Finally, they entered a dining room with a long oak table. A dozen chairs bordered each side, plus one at the head and foot. Candelabras festooned with cobwebs; plates and silverware coated with dust.

A dinner for the dead. Ted shuddered, thankful to pass through.

Room after room; so many chambers! How many had they entered and exited? How many had they leisurely strolled through, not knowing the room's purpose? Some were empty. Others filled with furniture. Several with rats sniffing and scuttling about the corners—they stared with beady red eyes, as if conspiring to charge in one verminous mass....

Something furry scampered over Sandy's shoes.

She squealed. Ted held her, whispering words of reassurance—words he needed to hear just as much.

Every minute, the four of them called out.

Each time, everyone answered.

Then, near the far back of the mansion's first floor, they came to a tall black door with a chipped knob. Until now, every door had remained wide open.

This one was closed.

Just a narrow slab of wood, really. Ted thought. *But why is it closed, when all the others are open? What ugly secret might it harbor?*

Beyond the door—the trickling, running of water.

They clustered around the door. A wet slosh, like a tide of dirty dishwater, splashed over their ankles.

"Ugh!' cried Sandy. "My shoes are soaked!"

"Jesus!" Darren shouted. "We're standing in like two inches of water...."

It's blood, thought Ted. He kneeled and put his fingers into the frigid liquid. Bringing his wet hand near his face, he sighed with relief.

Water, after all.

Not red, nor slimy or coppery.

"You all hear that?" Clementine put her ear to the door, ignoring the icy water soaking her socks.

All leaned forward, ears against the door.

A steady trickling of water.

A rushing stream.

Like a waterfall inside a cave.

"Stand back," Darren said, and everyone obeyed.

He opened wide the door.

They peered through the blue fog, down into darkness. A pool of water glimmered about the top of the stairs, their reflections staring back at them.

"Holy shit," Ted muttered. "This basement's been turned into a goddamn swimming pool."

Ted saw his reflection—it grinned hideous sharp teeth.

He blinked hard, seeing it was just him and his friends, staring into the flooded basement. Still, did not their reflections seem odd? Perhaps a trick of the light. A trick of blue fog on black water to make their faces seem ghoulish.

"Who wants to take a dip?" Darren chuckled.

Everyone ignored his imbecilic joke.

Clementine gasped, then leapt backwards. A black snake slithered across the flooded stairs, slipping out the door, sliding over their feet.

Sandy's face blanched white. She opened her mouth to scream—nothing came out.

Ted squirmed where he stood; he *hated* snakes!

"Aww, you guys are a hoot!" Darren laughed, shutting the basement door. "Come on, let's get out of this water before our feet are soaked."

"Too late," Sandy grimaced.

Now chilled to the bone, they explored the remainder of the first floor; their tennis shoes soaked and squishing. Room after room; chamber after chamber; infinite antiquity and dust and shadows and mildewed walls and scampering rats.

"Let's return to the foyer," groaned Clementine. "I've seen enough."

"We haven't even been upstairs, babe." Darren sulked like a child.

"I'm with Clementine on this one," Sandy interjected. "This place is cool and all, but now my feet are wet and I'm goddamned *freezing!*"

They'd been wandering the mansion for what felt like hours. Enough rooms on the first floor to keep them occupied for days. They turned back the way they'd come, but each room proved unfamiliar, as if they hadn't passed through before.

"Where the hell are we?" Ted asked, having had enough of the ominous quiet.

Silence met his query. Evidently, nobody knew.

"Hey," shouted Ted, growing cranky. "Does anyone know if we're going in the right direction, or we just walking aimlessly?"

Again, silence.

Ted stood still. "Guys?"

He was alone.

Alone in a dark, silent, foggy room.

He stared into depthless blue haze.

At the top of his lungs, he shouted, "WHERE THE HELL ARE YOU GUYS? STOP FOOLING, GODDAMN—"

The scuttling of rats.

The creep-crawl of spiders.

The snap of a silk thread in midair.

The creak of a door, somewhere, in front or behind.

The dreadful, dreary din of Vallancy Mansion. The walls, floor, windows, and doors seemed to listen; delighting in Ted's increasing fright. His heart pitter-pattered in his chest. A hot rash spread across his back, then up the side of his neck—this happened whenever he was truly afraid, ever since he was a little kid afraid of monsters under his bed.

Ted now felt terribly abandoned.

As abandoned as Vallancy Mansion itself.

The room in which he stood was large and obscured; the blue fog thickened. Still, he discerned gilt-framed paintings upon the walls, a rotting rocking chair, yet another fireplace, and a window where the moonlight streamed through—

There!

Three silhouettes stood before the window.

Ted fervently hoped it was his friends—for to whom else could those shadows belong?

But what if that's not Sandy, Clementine, Darren? Could be another group of kids come here to explore. Or some bad people I don't want to meet … people who call this ugly old mansion home.…

Then Ted heard a sound which invoked simultaneous pity and relief—Sandy was crying. Unmistakably, the sound of her sobbing! It broke Ted's heart whenever she cried; a wail of fear and grief that could belong to no other.

Ted crossed the room. He stood beside them, facing the window.

"Sandy, what's wrong?" he asked. "For Christ's sake, why didn't you guys answer me when—"

Now, he saw.

They all saw.

Gathered around the window, they stared at each other's reflected faces—their old, wrinkled, bruised faces; corpse-white beneath the moon.

"M-must be this fog," Darren shuddered. "It's poisonous. Toxic chemicals in it or something. I mean, it's made us so, so … *old!*"

Sandy wept openly.

Clementine stared in disbelief at her hands—her pruned, shriveled hands like wadded up gloves.

Ted felt for his own face now, and knew he was no longer seventeen. On the outside, on the superficial skin-surface, he was sixty, maybe seventy years old.

An old, old man.

A group of teenagers had entered Vallancy Mansion on Halloween night. A group of old men and women would leave—if the house permitted as much. If those terrible front doors hadn't creaked shut, as Ted feared, locking them in forever.

"Let's get out of this fucking place," Darren shouted, then kicked at the window with his shoes. When this didn't work, he wrapped his fist in his shirt's long sleeve and punched the window. He reeled backward with an aching hand. Then they all pounded and slammed and kicked— the window glass refused to so much as crack.

"Ah, forget it!" Darren gasped, waving dismissively at the window. "Everyone keep together, remember?"

They walked side by side, holding hands in a chain of four. They toured room to room, chamber to chamber, the cold foggy mustiness all the while leaching into their crumpled flesh.

Endless!

Infinite!

Tears dripped down their rugged faces. None could discern whether they were getting closer or farther away from the entrance. Numerous windows were attempted—none unlocked, and none gave, despite their battering fists. They turned left, right, then right again, then left—the rooms shifted, rearranged, morphed. Inexplicable shadows shrunk and stretched in the fog. Chittering, clawing, groaning noises resounded in darkened corners—the source of these disturbing utterances yet to be established. All sense of direction vanished entirely. The effects of the wine had long faded, too, and now only hopelessness formed the draught of the souls; for they were drunk on misery.

A ship adrift at sea, lost in a swirling blue fog.

CHAPTER SIXTEEN

They mistook Harry Thanatos for a ghoulish Halloween prop. The kids poked and prodded his wrinkled corpse, marveling at the 'realistic' texture.

Deputy Johansen observed the crowded parlor with horror and wonder. She could hardly believe her eyes. "What the *hell* is going on?" she asked the children. None heard, and thus none answered. They continued jostling Harry's corpse, where it lay slumped on the divan.

Are these truly children? she thought.

They rather resembled four-foot-tall adults. Some in their fifties, others approaching seventy. Age descended with its ragged claws and branded their faces. No longer were they pretty, young, or charming. Time disfigured their youthful flesh; a permanent and existential tattoo.

A fairy wearing a silver tiara suddenly screamed. She'd glimpsed her reflection in a mirror—a cracked reflecting glass hanging askew in the parlor. Now, she buried her face in her hands; hands like large pale prunes.

Each child took a turn.

A devil stared into the mirror. The red grease paint flaked and twisted on his sagging skin. The boy tore off his horns and sobbed. His dyed red tears slipped between his fingers like liquid rubies.

Next, a witch studied her reflection. Her costume, it seemed, had become a reality. Despite being only seven, she accepted her morbid and magical misfortune. She did not weep.

"I'm a *real* witch now," she said, turning away from the mirror. "And what are *you* going to become, Missus Officer?"

The twenty-nine-year-old deputy braced herself.

She stood before the mirror.

Her eyes stung with sudden swollenness. She had been young before tonight. Beautiful, even. Now, deep lines around her mouth formed a perpetual frown. Her neck hung in a waddle; her earlobes drooped; her forehead forever furrowed like a well-tilled field.

The Harvest of Time had reaped her body.

As for *where* the crops of her youth had been stolen to, she hadn't a clue.

Her heart pounded; regular and steady, a reliable organ with a resting rate of forty-five beats per minute. Her heart had served her well in this life, and continued to do so, for she now remembered the old man's dying words:

The attic. That's where the heart is. Kill it, and maybe that door will ...

Johansen's face resembled a Halloween mask—that of the *old hag.* Her appearance deeply frightened her, yet she regarded the mirror as nothing more than a funhouse joke. An illusion. A trick. Besides, if a little girl could be stoic, surely a mature woman (an officer of the law, no less) might achieve similar equanimity.

The children took off their masks. Beneath all that plastic, rubber, and silicone—yet another guise; time's mask of weathered flesh, something they were far too young to wear.

Though I wear a grotesque mask with the rest of these poor children, my heart is untouched. I can count upon it. I know I can, and I must.

Johansen's heart guided her up the stairs (which did not creak, but were of smooth polished boards), then down the hall where the floral wallpaper was fixed and taught, no longer peeling away in brittle slices.

She reached the end of the hallway, and, gazing up through sanguinary nebulae, grabbed the dangling pull-string.

Down with the accordion steps.

Up with Deputy Johansen.

The attic was dark. The fog thinned to a blood-mist.

She listened to her quickening heart: *buhthump, buhthump, buhthump* ...

She'd never felt her heart race so fast! Her internal organs seemed to be catching up to the age of her feeble face, her harried hands, her sadly sagging breasts.

Did this rapid beating belong to *her* heart? Truly?

Harry's dying whisper: *the heart is in the attic* ...

Moonlight sifted through the attic's window cupola, drenching everything pallid white. She rummaged around cardboard boxes, crates, old trunks, clawed past sickening scrabbling spiders and their sticky strands of web....

Once upon a time, Cambria Balustrade was eight years older than her brother. Now, she was *eighty* years older.

Caleb, never inclined to tug his forelock, told her as much.

"This green stuff," he said. "It's gotten into your skin! You look like one of those evil old witches, straight out of the movies."

"Shut up," she cried. "You don't look so hot either, creep!"

Caleb shut up. He hadn't meant to make his sister cry. Not precisely. He'd only wanted to point out how ugly she was.

Besides, she was not alone.

He too had become ugly.

He'd caught his reflection in the scummy kitchen sink; the clogged pool served as a black mirror, and as he'd gazed down, noticed his white makeup had worn away, revealing an old, cadaverous face.

His skeleton costume was glow-in-the-dark green.

He blended in with his surroundings—a skeletal chameleon.

Soon, he feared, his flesh would wetly prune, sag, then fall off his bones like hot dripping wax. All that would be left was bone, then *not even* bone, only fog ... doomed to become a verdant haze drifting about the house, smothering the walls and floors for eternity.

Caleb grew frightened, disoriented. Now *he* wanted to cry!

Although he loved his sister (even if he'd never admit it), he found her quite useless. She'd huddled into the kitchen corner, rocking back

A Pirate, an Astronaut, and Cinderella turned from the wall.

and forth, ever since the changes began. The change in their faces; the gradual donning of ancient masks. Who, then, was to protect *him?*

"This is my fault." Cambria buried her face in her hands.

"You're silly," said Caleb.

"This is punishment. For something *I've* done!"

"What have you done?" He scooted close beside her.

"I damaged Mrs. Thanatos' car! Slashed her tires, scratched horrible words into her hood."

"That was *you?*"

"Yes. All me. And now, God is punishing us all for it."

"That's stupid, Cambria. God would never punish anyone for that. In fact, you've probably gotten on his good side. Nobody likes Mrs. Thanatos. She's mean."

"That doesn't make what I did right," she sighed, wiping her runny nose. "But I know you're trying to cheer me up."

"Well, what can I say? I try."

Cambria looked up. Her brother's voice carried a sense of normality, something she desperately needed. Anything to distract her from the sheer nightmare of their situation—the swirling green fog, their rapid aging, the eerie rehabilitation of the Manor.

She kissed Caleb on the forehead, where new lines grew fast as jungle vines.

"Yuck!"

"You're welcome," Cambria playfully punched his arm. "Now, let's say you and I explore upstairs? Maybe we can find an unlocked window to escape through."

"I guess." Caleb yawned, stretching his green bones. "Anything is better than you crying."

"What are you kids *doing?*" Anna froze in the hallway.

A Pirate, an Astronaut, and Cinderella turned from the wall.

Weary, furrowed faces stared up at her, the bags beneath their eyes violet, lumpen, disturbed. Grim scowls creased their mouths.

Their fingers ceased scratching at the wallpaper.

"Picking scabs," replied the Pirate.

"Seeing what's beneath," said the Astronaut.

"It isn't pretty," Cinderella added.

"Leave this hallway," Anna demanded, disturbed by the children's ghoulish countenances. "Back downstairs, with everybody else! This hallway is off limits."

"Says who?" the Pirate grimaced, an old, weathered man of the sea; the spray in his bloodshot eyes, the turbulent waves in the scars of his face, the stubble of black beard on his tiny chin.

"Says *me,*" Anna snarled her teeth, and as she did, two yellow molars slipped over her lips, clicking upon the floor like fallen pearls.

The children's eyes bulged from their sockets. Skirting the wall, they backed away, then rushed downstairs.

Downstairs—a gymnasium of children packed into each room, sobbing, screaming, laughing madly, the lucky ones sleeping. Fear was exhausting to endure, and a few had passed into unconsciousness.

"You're losing teeth." Kenny stood beside her now, his face scrunched with concern.

"Let's not talk about it," she replied, absentmindedly tonguing the new spaces. "Look at this." She stepped toward the wall. A portion of wallpaper had been torn away. Her index finger prodded a fleshy hole where a deep wound had been exposed.

Wet red mucus.

She pushed her finger in—the wall reflexed backward, inching away from her finger.

"A pain response," Anna grimaced.

"A biological development," Kenny removed his glasses, and thoughtfully nibbled at the triangular tips. "We've destroyed its brain, but it still has blood under the flesh of its walls."

"And veins, too. See?" Anna peeled off a wide strip of wallpaper. Beneath, pulsing wetly, making a sucking sound—a vacuum with its intake hose partially covered—a great red expanse with purple veins thick as tree roots.

The veins were slick, slippery, sluicy....

The house groaned at her touch.

"Pain," said Kenny. "The house is witless, thoughtless, yet it still feels *pain.*"

"It *feels*," said Anna. "That's the key word. We've got to get to the center-core of the house's feeling."

"A house is not a house without a heart," said Kenny.

From behind: "*Pssst!*"

They spun around.

Cambria Balustrade stood in the hallway, holding hands with a green, glow-in-the-dark skeleton.

"We know you guys are looking for a way out," Cambria offered a smile. "Do you mind if my brother and I join you?"

Kenny and Anna exchanged glances.

Old eyes met old eyes.

"You both seem sensible enough," Kenny shrugged. "If you find anything that resembles a human heart, let us know."

"A heart?" Caleb crossed his skeletal arms. "That some kinda joke?"

"Far from it," Anna replied. "We're not stuck in just any average house, if you hadn't gathered. This house is *alive*. A living creature. It's greedy, famished, consuming all of us minute by minute. Taking away our youth. Soon we won't even be *old* anymore."

"We'll be dead," Kenny nodded, causally putting his glasses back on. "We've found its brain already. In the basement. Squashed it good, too. Now, we're after its heart."

"You sound like a couple of lunatics," Cambria pursed her rumpled lips. "Then again, what hasn't been lunatic about tonight? Count us in."

Their footsteps echoed in the sweating hallway; the floorboards swaying subtly beneath their feet. *Everything was breathing.*

The green fog pulsed; a moving, sentient vapor.

They discovered a small flight of stairs. It led up to an attic door.

Armed with flashlights; their faces set in grim determination; they did not dawdle.

Anna pushed in the door.

They knew the treasure they must find.

A beating, palpitating heart.

A heart that must be stopped; stomped; squeezed until every drop of life is vanquished.

This, they fervently hoped, would cease their minute-by-minute deaths, unlock the windows, and open wide the front door....

Johansen's hands trembled over the music box.

At least, that's what she thought it was—one of those trinkets where you opened the lid and a ballerina popped up on a spring, slowly pirouetting to the tinkling of silver notes. A waltz. A melody to comfort; to make you smile; to drift asleep to.

She'd had one as a little girl. Her mother had gifted it to her.

It was lost in the fire. Johansen had lost everything in the fire, including her mother and father.

She'd been adopted when she was ten, by a police officer named Dale. Far from being a resentful adoptee, Johansen greatly admired her foster father. Never would she have entered the academy had she not followed faithfully in his footsteps. She was an exceptional deputy, and was often told as much, yet she longed for something greater. Someday, she hoped to become Sheriff of Sweet Hollow.

That is, if I ever get out of this damned house....

Her hands quivered—an old woman's hands. She knew not if this was due to sheer terror, or from the raw nerves that jangled in her palms, the backs of her hands, her knuckles, the joints in her fingers....

Over the space of several hours, she'd grown into an elderly woman.

In the broken mirror downstairs, her mother had stared back.

Now, as she bent over the ochre box, listening to the intense thump of her heart, and of the thing *inside* the box, she thought of fire, of high red flames, and of the red mist enveloping her until she crumbled into ash.

She was crying; tears rained onto her liver-spotted hands.

She heard the music of two hearts beating too rapidly, too fast!

Slowly, her eyes stinging with tears (*smoke*), the redness all around her (fire, burning), unable to look away—she opened the box.

No music came out of it. No ballerina swung up on a spring to dance. There was only the steady *whump* of that dreaded, palpitating organ.

The heart is in the attic. Kill the heart, and maybe ...

A groan in her throat.

She abhorred to touch it yet reached into the box all the same—

146

like witchy hands lowering into a cradle to strangle the baby.

"Hush," she whispered, growing dizzy. "Don't beat a word."

It throbbed in her hands. She squeezed. It slipped from her palm like a bar of soap. She picked it up, both hands constricting.

She felt like an Aztec, clutching the still-beating heart in her hand.

The Heart of Bannatyne House.

Buhthump-buhthump-buthump!

Her fingers laced over the jutting aortas. In a gasp, in a stomach-churning shudder, her palms squished what felt like a giant pulsing maggot. She squeezed tighter, and tighter....

The floor sweated beneath her; she slid around in the slick dew.

The walls silently screamed.

The fog scurried—turned ragged, rippled, running tendrils of red mist.

The air itself bled.

Her fingers dipped into the heart, forming fleshy indentations.

The heart is a hard organ to crack, she thought absurdly, mind reeling, spinning, not sure if she was really doing this, if this was reality or nightmare.

Sweat stung her bulging eyes.

Her own heart beat ravenously, a machine gun within her chest.

Her fingers caved in the red walls, and she felt the pit of the heart, and slowly, with a sickly wet tearing, she tore it in two.

The beating ceased—immediately.

Johansen collapsed onto the damp floor, breathless, chest heaving, with a broken heart in her hands.

She dropped the two chunks—*splat*—onto the floor.

The box remained open, empty, lifeless—no music.

And like a sudden gale on a calm day, she rippled with laughter. Not the laughter of madness or delirium, but of sheer relief.

"Thank you, Harry," she whispered, shakily. "I did as you told me. Your dying wish. And now ... *what?*"

She fantasized about the front door, opening wide—the thought of those children stepping into fresh night air. She thought of her mother's elderly visage fading, and her own face, her young, pretty features returning in full bloom.

In a sudden surge of hope, she scrambled toward the opening in the floor, down the accordion steps, brushed past the frantic children downstairs and ran for the front door.

She gripped the doorknob with blood-stained hands.

She yanked, pulled, gritted her teeth, groaned.

Senseless! Futile! Wretched!

"*But I've crushed your heart,*" she screamed. "*Your hateful, horrid heart!*"

The red fog smothered her, painful on her sensitive skin, burning her spirit with its insufferable flames. She cried against the door's fresh cedar, cursing her fate.

Somehow, she knew.

Bannatyne House did not *feel* anymore, but still it *thought*.

CHAPTER SEVENTEEN

The Manor's attic smelled like an Egyptian tomb: dusty, dry, and desiccated. Afraid the door would lock of its own volition, they propped it open using one of the loft's random chairs. For obvious reasons, the house could not be trusted.

Now, the four youths gazed in awe at the attic's bizarre tenants.

Rats the size of newborn babies scuttled the floors; impossibly corpulent, furry creatures with sharp ruby eyes. Their long tails dragged, forming patterns in the dust. Their large yellow teeth chattered.

Cambria put her hand on her mouth, staggering backwards.

The rats had quadrupled their natural size. For it was not merely the wood and plaster of the Manor which spontaneously renovated—the creatures lurking within the house's walls had likewise transformed. The rats, of course, were integral to the Manor; a legion of white blood cells performing their work within the house's greater anatomy.

"Good lord," Anna whispered, her flashlight roving the horrors on the walls, floors, and ceiling. Spiders crawled about on television-antenna legs; their bodies bulked as basketballs.

"Merely daddy longlegs," Kenny joked, but no one laughed.

Caleb's voice piped up: "Is it true what they say? Daddy longlegs are the most poisonous spider in the world, if only they had teeth big enough to bite you? 'Cause if that's true …"

"No, it isn't." Cambria shook her head. "That's a myth."

She sounded uncertain. Her bulging eyes surveyed the things scrabbling everywhere; the walls encumbered by grotesque creatures with six legs and eight eyes. Cobwebs hung thickly in the rafters where black-winged pomegranates buzzed, stuck in the webs.

Scuttling of rat claws.

Trickling of spider legs; the sound of pattering rain.

The staticky buzz of enormous flies; trapped in a tapestry of silk.

Hideous bats hung from the rafters, too—the size of owls. Their vermillion eyes glared in the verdant mist. They were much larger than the bats Anna and Kenny had fought off in the basement. Much larger, and much more ... observant.

The bats *watched,* their unnatural stares demarcated by raw, alien intelligence; a studious presence observing all.

"Everyone?" Kenny whispered. "No sudden movements, please."

"This was a terrible idea," Anna's voice shook. "Let's get the hell out of here."

"We knew this might be dangerous, Anna."

"Yeah, but this isn't just dangerous. This is fucking crazy."

Cambria impulsively snagged her little brother's arm and pulled him into a hug. Caleb grimaced. His arm hurt where she'd grabbed it— the calcium in his green bones apparently diminished.

"We need to move forward," said Kenny.

"We need to leave," Anna quipped.

"We're going to take it slow, okay? Let's not draw attention to ourselves, if possible."

Silently, they moved as a group. A rat the size of a small dog waddled across their path—all paused, as if waiting for a green light. Once the thing had crossed the room, intent on nibbling at a musty cardboard box, everyone moved forward again.

One.

Step.

At.

A time.

Occasionally, Kenny sidestepped a rat. They paid him little mind, seemingly too lethargic to care about anything at all. One of the spiders

150

creep-crawled past, its eight onyx eyes shimmering curiously. How thick and intricate their webs in every corner! Within those gray, sticky lattices, spiders the size of melons—all mating, fighting, sleeping, spinning silk!

"The heart," Anna pointed to an antique trunk, upon which the attic's largest spider reposed, "is inside that trunk. It must be."

The spider's hematite sclera glimmered, observing their every movement.

"How convenient." Kenny rubbed his tired eyes, hoping the spider would disappear when he looked again—it didn't.

The spider was king; the trunk its mighty throne. Eight legs straddled the wood: three on the left side, three on the right, with two dangling over the latch. Its octad eyes shone from across the loft; obsidian mirrors reflecting Kenny, Anna, Cambria, and Caleb where they stood. They stared at their reflections—all felt, intensely, what it might be to see themselves through the eyes of a predator.

"Hold the goddamn phone," Cambria blurted. "You guys mean you're going to disturb that thing, just to see inside an old trunk? I mean, what if the heart isn't even in there?"

"She's got a point," Kenny admitted. "We might risk our lives for nothing."

"You're both wrong," Anna replied. "Can't you hear it?"

"All I hear is this freakish jungle we're standing in," Cambria said.

Caleb nudged his sister in the ribs, signaling for her to shut up.

Cambria shut up.

They all did.

They listened.

Beyond the ubiquitous scuttling of the hideous, overgrown creatures—that unmistakable, steady thump of a beating heart.

The heart was a tell-tale.

And the tale was this: *I am in the trunk, beneath the throne of the Spider-King whose legs shall not courteously unwrap for you, only to skitter away to some far-flung corner. Try if you dare, but beware those fangs poised to bite, the ever-watchful eyes, and the whiskered legs long enough to penetrate your ear and scramble your brains....*

Try it.

Try me.

"Anybody have a weapon?" Anna inquired.

"Your merciless stomping feet?" suggested Kenny.

"Funny. Anything else?"

"Nope."

"Right, then ..."

Caleb, still trapped within his sister's embrace, spoke up: "I've got an idea."

"No, you don't." Cambria hissed, squeezing him tighter. She didn't want to let him go. Didn't want him to risk his life. "Now isn't the time to do something stupid."

"On the contrary," Kenny interjected. "Now's the perfect time to do something stupid. We haven't many options, exactly."

Caleb pushed away from his sister. She let out a small squeal as one of the melon-sized spiders skittered over her feet. Cambria kicked it hard, like a soccer ball. It struck the far wall—*splat!*—then slid down the wood planks in one wet, massive goop.

"Jeez, Sis." Caleb blinked, astonished. "You should try out for the team."

"Oh." Cambria covered her mouth. "I think I'm going to be sick."

"What's your idea, Mr. Glow-Bones?" Anna asked, facing the boy.

Caleb shared his idea. It was simple. And, indeed, arguably stupid.

"What the hell?" Kenny shrugged. "Personally, I can't conjure up anything better."

"You've got to be kidding," Cambria shook her head. "Please, *please* don't do this. Guys, this is suicide!"

The prospect of their survival was gloomy at best. Still, it was better to act brave, hoping in the process to *become* brave. Truly and stoically brave. Like this: Kenny and Anna pocketed their flashlights for they no longer required them. A cold crystal moon spilled through the gable windows. They could see the spider. The old trunk. Their trembling hands.

Anna approached from the left.

Kenny from the right.

Slow, steady, and silent as lions on a midnight Serengeti.

The spider's eyes quivered within its fleshy bulk.

It quickly grew suspicious, and rightfully so. It did not budge from its throne; it was King, after all, and a King budged for no one.

152

Except for its usurper, Anna thought, the inside of her mouth parched with fear. *History is full of such moments. One king slain, then another takes its place. A cruel and brutal tradition ... but we're doing it for the heart. Everything for the heart ...*

Caleb approached the spider straight on; slow, shivering, sickened to his stomach.

Cambria remained behind them, relegated to the lowly position of cheerleader. Her hands clasped nervously. A millipede the size of a garden snake trickled past her ankle. She barely suppressed a squeal.

"Caleb," she whisper-cried. "Be *careful!*"

"I will," the boy replied, staring ahead. "Believe me, I will...."

Thus the strategy:

Three humans to one gargantuan spider.

A triangulated attack.

The creature's legs tapped against the trunk. It was nervous. Its legs drummed the wood like fingers on a stair banister; rhythmic, impatient....

The fangs flexed. Two daggers, dripping ... *what?*

Poison. Anna shuddered. *What else?*

The onyx eyes reflected only Caleb now, until its body began to rotate left, then right, processing glimpses of Anna, then Kenny, then Anna again, now Caleb....

All approached closer.

The legs excitedly fluttered against the trunk, like skeletal fingers drumming the underside of a coffin lid.

All three stood close.

Too close.

The spider would leap upon any of them in a second. Sink in its fangs. Weave hot silk around their bodies. Cocoon them into tightly knit, suffocating sleeping bags....

Caleb shouted: "NOW!"

Anna shot in from the left, grasping four knobby, prickly legs in a bunch. Kenny snatched the other four, bundling them in an iron grasp.

Like an aimless ball in the middle of an ocean, the spider's bulk twisted, quivered, spasmed with rage! Its mouth hissed, fangs dripping black bile. Its glabrous eyes shone with outraged panic.

The legs felt like brittle bamboo stalks within Anna's grasp. They shifted, jerked, trembled! She must not let go. "Lift it up, Kenny!" she screamed, locking her hands tighter. "Let's put it on the floor!"

Caleb prepared himself. His part was soon to come.

Kenny grunted, heaving his half of the spider off the trunk. He hated the sensation of those long, hairy legs in his hands. Loathed the feel of its stiff hairs pricking deep into his palms. He wanted to scream, to let go, to run away. Yet to do such a thing would prove himself a coward—likely one that would be chased down and bitten.

The spider hissed, twisted, nearly ripping free.

"*No!*" Anna shrieked. "Hold it!"

Suddenly they had the spider on the floor. Its sweaty bulk writhed in a display of agitation.

"Caleb," screamed Kenny, "get on with it!"

"No!" Cambria ran to him, seizing his hand. "Get *away!*"

Caleb ripped from her grasp, then ran forward, leaping into the air. He came down hard and fast, his feet pummeling straight down upon the spider's back.

The spider's mouth opened—a train-whistle *shriek.*

Writhing! Throbbing! Thrashing!

The boy stomped, as if destroying a rotten jack-o'-lantern. A thick, black ooze collected beneath his feet. Ebony gore splattered his shoes and legs. He jumped and bellowed wildly, until the spider's infernal screeching ceased, and Kenny snagged the back of his costume and yanked him away.

"Enough, kid," he scolded, out of breath. "There's nothing more to smash."

The boy glanced down at his work, observing the grotesque remains.

King Spider hadn't simply been usurped—he'd become a gooey lump of broken leg-stalks, hair, and steaming oily innards.

Caleb panted, wiping sweat from his withered brow. "I don't wanna look at it anymore...." He joined Cambria near the attic door.

The other spiders in the room nestled into the far corners, afraid *they* might be stomped to death next.

Cambria's eyes roved the room; the spiders were at rest, though the bats still glared from the rafters with hatred, and the rats scampered about freely, along with a variety of bugs much too big for comfort. She'd always hated bugs, no matter their size. Her stomach churned, on the cusp of vomiting. She couldn't even look at Caleb. All that gore on his costume! *Disgusting!*

"Well," Anna almost cried with relief, "now that we've got *that* out of the way."

"Let's hope to God it's inside." Kenny bent over the trunk. He flipped up the unlocked clasp, then lifted the screeching lid.

"Home," Anna murmured, gazing into the trunk with fascination, "is where the heart is."

"The weirdest thing I've ever seen." Kenny spoke softly. "Stranger than the brain, even. Look at it, Anna. It's ... *pulsing!* As if still pumping blood ..."

"That's because it *is*."

"Impossible," he replied. "It's in a trunk, isolated, unconnected to anything. There's nothing for its aortal valves to *attach* to."

"Nothing is impossible in an old dark house," Anna smiled ironically. "Look around, Kenny. You ought to know by now."

Kenny admitted she was right. The isolated heart didn't make sense, but then again, nor had the brain in the basement, nor a single thing that'd transpired within the last twenty-four hours.

They were living in a different world.

A different planet.

The planet of the Old Dark House.

Kenny stooped down, reaching into the trunk. His hands grasped the bleeding, pulsing organ. It throbbed between his palms, warm and wet, pumping every ounce of blood within the Manor's walls.

"Now what?" he grimaced, holding it up in the moonlight.

"Now," Anna nodded curtly, "we break its heart."

Chapter Eighteen

Maurice Wainscot disposed of his cigarette into the plastic receptacle near the front door. It'd been a good smoke. One he'd needed. Even the blood-curdling scream resounding inside the station did not totally unsettle his newfound calm.

The hobo, he thought, with a sigh. *He's gone absolutely mad. Well, of course he has. What better time to lose your sanity than Halloween night?*

Maurice's shoulders slumped with exhaustion. Endless phone calls flooded the station lines, each stating the identical emergency. Calmly, politely, over, and over, he informed parents that the entire Sweet Hollow police force was working on a solution.

Nearly midnight. He was ready for bed. Beyond ready. For the foreseeable future, however, he was stuck at the station.

And now the crazy homeless guy is wailing like it's the apocalypse. Like he's watching the death-comet plummet from on high. Good lord, what a racket!

Maurice unlocked the door that led from the waiting room into the offices, then entered. The desks were empty, save for piles of paperwork, heaps of paperclips, rubber bands, and scattered pens. He rubbed his eyes, cheeks, and chin. Yawned. Picked a crumb from his mustache. The phone rang. He answered it. Delivered the same speech. Hung up.

Normally at this time of night, there'd be a few people with feet up on their desks, drinking coffee, awaiting calls for backup. Now, the station was vacant.

Maybe that's why his screams are so damn loud. No bodies moving around to dampen or block the sound.

The keys on Maurice's belt jingled as he walked down the carpeted hallway. The phone rang behind him; he ran back, answered, delivered, the speech, then hung up. Passing the sheriff's office, the staff lounge, the evidence storage room, the booking room, locker rooms, the report and complaint offices, employee bathrooms, and a janitor's closet, he at last arrived at the steel door which led into the men's detention cells.

He clanged the door shut behind him. His feet echoed on concrete.

Thorn shrieked like a crow that'd just been doused with boiling water. He threw his body against the bars of his cell—Maurice heard, though did not yet see him. With all his years on the force, he was familiar with the din of madmen slamming their bodies against iron.

"Calm down!" he shouted, rounding the corridor. He arrived at the last cell in the row. Then his mouth dropped open.

Blood.

Never had he seen so much.

Dark crimson splattered the brick walls, iron bars, and concrete floor. Thorn had his back turned, trembling from head to toe. The madman staggered. For a moment Maurice thought he'd topple onto the concrete, but suddenly Thorn swiveled around. His blue eyes were shot wide with terror; the overhead fluorescents dancing in his wild gaze. He clutched his throat, blood gushing over his fingers, down his ragged clothes, splashing onto the floor.

"*H-helllp!*" Thorn gurgled.

Maurice observed the creature gnawing at the man's throat. It was black, leathery, and emitting tiny, erratic shrieks.

Ebony wings stretched out and flapped, brushing against Thorn's unshaven face.

"Jesus H. Christ!" Maurice struggled with the keys on his belt. They jangled as he pulled on the wind-up elastic cord. His fat fingers fumbled the keys.

"*P-please . . .*" Thorn croaked, swaying on his feet.

At last, Maurice shoved the correct key into the lock. The cell door creaked in its iron track as he slid it back.

Thorn collapsed onto his side.

The bat feasted upon his gashed throat, growing fat with blood.

Thorn's eyes emptied, became vacant and glazed. He stared as if into a distant space; and a distant space stared into him.

Seemingly satiated, the obscene creature waddled across Thorn's chest. Its wings fluttered once, twice. Then its head pivoted on its black furry body and looked up.

Maurice shuddered, frozen in the cell's open doorway.

Every hair on his body stood straight, his nipples hardened, and a terrible coldness nestled inside his heart. *It doesn't behave like a bat,* he thought, vaguely. *It acts like a human, trapped inside of a bat.*

An absurd notion.

It was all Maurice could think of.

He stood petrified, blanched, and shivering.

The bat's beady black eyes fastened upon him—a cruel, hungry gaze. Its blood-slicked snout wriggled at the air, sensing Maurice's raw fear.

As a child, he'd lay awake nights feeling the terrifying presence of ghosts in his closet and monsters under his bed, but it all paled compared to this moment. This instant. Now.

But it's so small. Such a tiny creature. I could run forward, right now, and smash it under my heel! He glanced at the corpse with its jugular veins torn to ribbons and thought better. This is no ordinary animal.

Slowly, he backed away.

He shuddered with repulsion.

The bat toddled forward, its wings streaking blood across the concrete. Its gray gnarled face writhed like a lunatic with a spreading grin. Tiny, blood-stained teeth gnashed the air.

A scream caught in Maurice's throat and came out as a trembling groan. A warm stream trickled down his pant leg. He tripped over his own feet. Landed hard on his tailbone. A shot of agony radiated up his spine. He grimaced, eyes clenching shut.

When he opened them, he glimpsed a blur of blackness—as if the night had settled its sable velvet curtain over his vision.

A sharp serrating pain pierced his pale throat.

He screamed. His panicked hands clawed at the creature fluttering at his neck. He racked fingernails into its furry body, tore at its head, then grasped the wings, attempting to rip them apart. Sharp teeth sank deeper into his throat, as if the bat intended to devour his Adam's apple—a delectable Halloween treat.

Maurice writhed on the floor, blood gurgling in his throat. His hands imprecisely jabbed and tore at the animal. His thoughts turned in on themselves; he couldn't believe what was happening to him, couldn't comprehend anything except raw unbearable pain.

Layers of flesh peeled away, the thyroid cartilage torn, then the jugular sliced.

Maurice flung onto his side, staring straight into Thorn's vacant death-gaze.

An identical expression dawned upon Maurice's face; slackened mouth, glazed eyes, his throat gushing a geyser of gore.

The man within the bat—a three-hundred-year-old ghost named Charles Vallancy— screeched wickedly, flapped his wings, then flitted out between the bars in the cell's high, moonlit window.

CHAPTER NINETEEN

Parents and grandparents, teachers and shopkeepers, cops and firefighters, neighbors, and tourists—all stood in the street, beholding the slow-burn evolution with enraptured gaze.

Before everyone's eyes, the Bannatyne House *transformed*.

New shingles, sparkling black in the night. Crisp white clapboards with nary a scratch upon them. Windows gleaming crystal and brilliant over the red fog. The front porch rebuilt with refurbished oak and gingerbread trim in the high corners.

Every minute, a scratch, a dent, a nick vanished. A fresh coat of paint applied. A window-crack mended. The warped boards unbent and became smooth and perpendicular. All accomplished by unseen hands!

Ghostly hands, it was rumored; spirits of the past restoring what was once theirs.

"Remember the old dance hall?" asked Howard Philip, owner of the town grocery store. "They knocked it down last year. Some said you could see dead people screaming in the windows when they launched the wrecking ball into it."

"Superstitious mumbo-jumbo, dear," his old wife retorted. "You know that."

"How the hell else can you explain this, lady?" Officer Dalton's hands were on his hips. His blonde hair, usually combed prim and proper, hung disheveled over his forehead. There'd been a lot of theorizing tonight. Some chalked everything up to ghosts; others to God or Devil or witchcraft. Dalton, eventually, had sided with the spiritualists. He'd seen a ghost once as a child, and he'd been raised by a family of believers—who was to say that tonight, prior to demolishment of the houses, *they* had not returned to claim what was rightfully theirs?

Sheriff Bradley, meanwhile, was having none of this nonsense.

"I'll kindly ask you to stay off the property," he shouted, waving people off the Bannatyne's front yard. "This is an official crime scene, folks."

A flustered mother retorted, "You cops aren't doing a damn bit of good! Let me have a try at those windows—bet it can't keep *me* out!"

"I know you want your children," Bradley held out his hands, addressing the crowd. "I promise, we'll get them back to you. Tonight. But pounding on the doors and windows has already been tried. We're going to need to think our way inside these houses, you see? So *think* a little more, please, and back off."

The crowd groaned amidst the curses, shouts, and threats.

Bradley ignored them, pacing the front porch. *What the hell to do? If stainless-steel battering rams can't break into these houses, what can?*

The sheriff jammed two sticks of cinnamon gum into his mouth. It helped him think. He paced.

Christ! I sure could use a glass of whiskey.

He halted. Stared at the house across the street. The two ivy leaguers, Peter Petrie, and David Chambers, sat in rocking chairs upon the front porch. Debating, philosophizing, and getting very drunk.

"Uh-huh." Bradley shook his head, then approached Officer Landis. He stood gazing up at the Bannatyne's attic window, attempting to discern movement behind the crimson glass. "Hold down the fort here, Landis," he ordered. "I'm going to have a talk with the two fellas across the street."

"Sure thing, Sheriff." Landis nodded, grateful to have been assigned a task. He stood before the Bannatyne's newly remodeled façade, frowned at the jeering crowd, and crossed his arms like a bouncer.

Bradley crossed the street, then climbed onto Peter Petrie's front porch.

"Marvelous night, isn't it, Sheriff?" Peter raised his glass.

"Aye," David chimed, his eyes glossy as buttons on a tweed suit. "Such a spectacle ought never to be taken for granted."

"We've been studying your every movement, Sheriff," added Peter. "You're doing all you can, you know. There would seem, regarding this highly phantasmic situation, to be very few *logical* moves one can make."

"Tonight has been quite unlike a game of chess," David observed.

"Listen, old-timers," Bradley spoke curtly. "If you know something I don't, you'd better tell me ... right ... *now*."

Peter and David cocked their heads. Their eyes sharpened, now studying the sheriff as if he were a curious insect beneath a microscope.

"We are only spectators amongst the teeming crowd, Sheriff Bradley," said Peter, with a wily grin. "We're here for the show. The hoax. The fantastic fabrication of fairy tales. These houses are a chimera, you see? A magic trick! And a stunning one at that, one which my friend and I can appreciate, though not completely understand."

"A magic trick all the same," added David. "Any enlightened creature must agree."

"Yes, I know all that." Sheriff Bradley muttered. He gazed over his shoulder, over at the house that was, moment by moment, renovating itself. *Do I know that?* He second-guessed. *Do I know it's all just a hoax, a stunt, a trick? Or is it something ... more?*

Sheriff Bradley frowned deeply. He was beginning to believe in ghosts. A magic trick? All of this? The foggy lights, the mending of the houses, the hundreds of kidnapped children, not to mention the disappearance of his best deputy? A magic trick of this magnitude seemed almost as improbable as the existence of ghosts.

He turned back to Peter and David, about to tell them as much.

They stared up at him, blinking curiously.

They're watching me. I'm a spectacle just as much as the houses are. The lights. The disappearing children. Well, I guess they're entertained, the ruthless, unfeeling bastards....

"Say, boys." Bradley licked his dry lips. "You mind fixing me a drink? I don't do gin. Whiskey would be good."

"It'd be an honor, Sheriff!" Peter went into the house, and when he came back, handed Bradley a highball glass of amber liquid. "Drink up, Sheriff. It will enliven your consciousness."

"An eye-opener, we used to call it." David lifted his glass high. "May those restless spirits of Morton, Bannatyne, and Vallancy be with you!"

They drank.

Bradley downed half his glass in one gulp. Once more, he looked over his shoulder. A few in the crowd were watching him, shaking their heads (*drinking on duty, what a shame!*).

It'd been a long damn night.

What an unsettling feeling, to be sheriff of a small town, a person everyone counted on, and yet unable to do a goddamn thing to improve their situations. He thought of Johansen, trapped inside the Bannatyne's red foggy labyrinth. Tears rushed to his eyes, though he forced them away.

He felt useless. A trapped pawn.

Tonight had come to a stalemate.

"The Vallancy," Bradley reflected aloud, his eyes catching on the lapis-lazuli hues gleaming above the hills in the northern sky. "It's a big place, that old mansion. Could be something there, a clue to what's going on."

"Perhaps so," grinned Peter Petrie.

"Perhaps, indeed," grinned David Chambers.

Bradley frowned, handing Peter his empty glass.

"Well, I'll leave you two incorrigible bastards to your vicarious entertainment. How's *that* for vocabulary?"

Feeling lighter after his drink, Sheriff Bradley crossed the street. The two old men remained upon the porch, where'd they been all night, watching, studying, cracking jokes, pouring "eye-openers."

"Well?" Officer Landis raised his black bushy eyebrows. "Any news?"

"No news," replied Bradley, "But I'm considering the Vallancy Mansion. Seems to me we ought to check it out. See if the doors and windows are just as unbreakable as here and the Manor. At this point, it's the one thing we haven't tried."

"Right." Landis nodded. "Who should I enlist for backup?"

"Grab Dalton, tell him we'll stop by the station to gather supplies.

Then we'll head for the Vallancy."

After climbing into his cruiser, Bradley radioed back to the station, letting Maurice know they'd be back soon, and would he mind brewing a fresh pot of coffee?

"Maurice? Pick up and confirm, please."

Silence.

Very unlike Maurice Wainscot not to answer the phone. Not to be at his desk. Not to be doing his job. Very unlike Maurice, indeed.

Just fucking splendid, thought Sheriff Bradley. *Now what?*

"Don't cry, Missus Officer," the Witch cooed. "Everything will be all right."

Deputy Johansen sat in the entry hall, her back against the front door. Tears blurred her vision, making everything resemble one great smear of blood. The floorboards gleamed in their refurbishment. The walls stood whole and new. Not even the swirling red fog could obscure the pristine quality of Bannatyne House—nor could it hide the four-foot-tall witch standing before her.

Johansen remembered how the girl looked just two hours ago—how young, unblemished, her little cheeks pinching whenever she smiled. Now, she resembled a ghoul, or a medical curiosity out of the Guinness Book. The gnarled oak tree of her face suggested advanced age, though little to no wisdom.

In the Witch's hand, a shiny red apple.

"Here, Missus Officer. Eat this. You'll feel better."

"Where did you get that, little girl?" Johansen dried her eyes.

The well-worn, haggish face gazed up at the coat tree in the corner. A lone jacket hung there, ominous as a noose in a tree.

"From that jacket," nodded the Witch. "I believe it belonged to the old man, before he got so old he died. It's not his anymore, so now you can have it. Here!"

The Witch handed her the apple.

"Thank you." Johansen polished the apple on her uniform shirt. "That's awfully sweet of you."

"Do you think we'll ever get out of here?"

"I don't know, kiddo. I hope so."

"Well, if we *are* stuck in here forever, do you mind sharing that?" the Witch asked. "I already ate all my Halloween candy. I'm gonna get hungry, Missus Officer."

"Of course I'll share, so long as you call me Johansen." She smiled, handing the apple back. "You take the first bite, how's that?"

"Gee thanks, Missus Officer." She grinned, bringing the apple to her mouth. "Er, I mean, Johansen."

The Witch opened her mouth.

And took one large bite.

CHAPTER TWENTY

The children in Morton Manor no longer ran amok. They'd long ceased having fun, their youthful exuberance traded in for madness and fatigue. No more did they leap on the divan, bang fists against windows, or play games in the barren rooms.

The elderly creatures had long given up.

Spines brittle and twisted like dying trees. Backs badly bowed. Faces sallow and sagged.

Exhausted. Hungry. Sleeping.

On the edge of death: a razor's edge.

Their slumped forms lay scattered about the house. Even speaking required prodigious effort—their young voices now croaking, ragged, rusting with age.

The candy in their bags and buckets was gone. There was nothing sweet about life anymore. Nothing young, free, or vital. The costumed creatures now retired; devils and demons snoozing restlessly in the verdant forest of the house. The green fog swirled and contorted. Verdant tendrils drifted up into nostrils to poison their brains, sometimes floating into their sleeping mouths for to slumber sickly within hearts and lungs.

Unexpectedly the green fog flickered—as if experiencing some electrical defect.

One by one, the lumps upon the floor sat bolt upright.

The children who were not children blinked, rubbed groggy eyes, and, at last, summoned the energy to stand.

Something was happening.

They could feel it—how a mummy must feel upon awakening in his sarcophagus after millennia of sleep! The dust of time sifted from their forms. The grains in their eyes were wiped away.

"My spine," said a little Devil. "It don't hurt anymore!"

"My eyes," said a Princess. "I can see again! Even through this fog, I can see!"

"My joints," said a Skeleton. "In my fingers, toes, knees. They don't ache at all!"

Everyone in every room of the house, upstairs and downstairs, stood up, some even *leapt* up, and rejoiced with their neighbor on the curious recession of their ailments and maladies. How sweet it was to stand, to talk, to *breathe!* A sense of the miraculous enlivened them.

"My memory is back," exclaimed a Zombie. "I remember my parents' names! I remember who I am! My name is Sam Dolphy. My parent's names are—"

"I can dance!" shouted a Ballerina. "I can dance again, watch me, watch me!"

Thus Morton Manor rejoiced with painless Devils, perceptive Princesses, perfectly-jointed Skeletons, and performing Ballerinas.

"What's with the fog?" observed an Astronaut. "This planet's atmosphere has gone even stranger! Has anyone ever seen a fog *flicker?*"

The lines, crevices, and pockmarks upon their bodies began to fade.

The fog flickered once, twice, then blinked *off.*

Morton Manor grew dark. Several screamed.

Then, *shadows* in the moonlight.

Four shadows, moving, weaving, writhing in serpentine fashion—out of the attic, down the stairs, then through the parlor to the front door.

The door opened to the night, letting wan streetlight in.

The shadows flitted out.

Kenny, Anna, Cambria and Caleb stepped onto the front porch. Their faces were young and unblemished; the pain in their backs, joints, and memories wondrously alleviated. The moon bathed their skin and the cold wind had never felt so blessed.

The crowd in the street widened their eyes, opened their mouths, pointed!

Cambria and Caleb raced across the lawn, tightly embracing their parents in the street. Meanwhile, Anna and Kenny stood safely beside the hedgerows while a deluge of parents flooded into the front lawn, shouting their children's names.

"Stand back!" A policeman shouted.

No parent obeyed. They wanted their children. Right *now.*

The kids ran screaming out the front door and into their parents' arms. Devils, skeletons, pirates, and warlocks all found home within warm embraces, held close to swaying chests, accompanied by grateful whispers: "Oh, thank God! You're *alive!* I was terrified...."

Words of gratitude drifted on the air, mingling with the prayers of one family, then conjoining with affirmations of love from another— like ghosts of good-will, flowing hither and thither about the space of yard and street and sky.

Anna and Kenny held hands, smiling at the sight of so many young faces, including their own. Their hands were sticky with blood; the blood of Morton Manor itself. For they had destroyed its heart, and now the house was dead—truly dead.

They watched as an inky blackness leached into the Manor's yellow door. The clapboards weathered. The pain peeled into curlicue strips. With a screech, the rain gutter bent. Shingles stripped and rained off the roof. The foundation sunk four inches into the ground—once again the house sat at its customary cock-eyed angle.

"Everything has been set right again." Kenny fumbled with his glasses, a dead giveaway that everything had *not* been set right.

"You're troubled." Anna observed. "So, what is it?"

"Undoubtedly there's kids still trapped in the Bannatyne," Kenny frowned. "Maybe even Vallancy Manse. Who knows how long they'll survive? Considering these houses' ability to radically age its occupants, time is of the essence."

"We need to tell everyone about the hearts and brains." Anna added, the wind making Medusa's snakes of her hair. "Where to find them, and to kill them."

"Bannatyne House is the closest," said Kenny. "But perhaps we should make the hike up to the Vallancy. That's where all this began … isn't it?"

They turned now, gazing apprehensively at the streaks of blue light swimming about the northern stars.

Yes. Of course.

The Vallancy. The oldest house in all Sweet Hollow. A mansion once owned and curated by a greedy, narcissistic, vengeful man who'd stopped at nothing to preserve his legacy. They'd learned all about Charles Vallancy in history class. Kenny had even interviewed Patty Keepwell for one of his school essays.

A chill ran down Kenny's spine—from now on, they wouldn't merely be dealing with houses coming alive, but with a man who refused to give up his own ghost.

Charles Vallancy. The name whispered on the stars, on the moon, and in the wind that wound its way through the Manor's rusted, leaf-choked gutters.

"Let's not waste time." Anna grabbed his hand. "Besides, our parents have probably gone up there, thinking they'd find us. The truth is, *we* need to find *them. They* need *us.*"

They fetched their bicycles. Then, riding up Bloch Street together, they weaved around families heading home after the longest night of their lives. Leaves swirled in yards; tornados of gold and vermillion; and the corpse-pale moon made desolate and ghostly shadows of the town.

Anna and Kenny's legs pumped fast, working the pedals, striving northward.

"Here you go, Miss J." The witch smiled. "Your turn. It's delicious!"

Johansen politely accepted the apple with three bites taken out of it.

Such a sweet, charming little girl—it only took seeing through that hideous mask! The mask the house had gifted her.

Gifted them all, in fact.

Johansen selected a shiny red portion of the apple. She relished the crisp sweetness as her teeth sank into the fruit.

She hadn't eaten since yesterday's breakfast. Her stomach gurgled, demanding she take another bite. She brought the apple halfway to her mouth, then paused.

"Here you go, honey," she smiled, handing her the apple. "You should have the rest."

The witch accepted it greedily. Turned it in her pruned hand; a little red world in a big red fog, orbiting, turning in her fingers, until she found the spot that looked tastiest.

A glossy red portion, with a small blemish in it, a tiny slit in the crisp flesh of the apple—such a minor defect only lent the apple further appeal.

The Witch giggled, as six-year-olds do.

The Witch bit into the apple—then shrieked.

The Witch's mouth hung open, her tongue now a dangling waterfall of blood.

Chapter Twenty-One

"We've one murderous son-of-a-bitch on the loose." Sheriff Bradley scowled down at Maurice's bloody corpse. "Notify everyone on the force. Let them know what we're dealing with. Any out-of-towner on the street tonight ought to be stopped and questioned."

"I'm on it, Sheriff." Dalton proceeded to radio back to the cruisers stationed outside the houses.

Within minutes, he learned that over a hundred children had escaped Morton Manor. Meanwhile, Bannatyne House remained impenetrable as ever, with still no word from Johansen.

Bradley crouched beside the body, which lay sprawled in the main isle between cells.

"Christ, Maurice," he muttered, wiping his teary eyes, "Who did this to you?"

Truthfully, he wasn't sure he wanted to know. What he *wanted* was to return home and lie in bed. Sleep. Drink. Forget the world. But as sheriff of a small town, that wasn't possible. People counted on him. His colleagues. His friends and family. Hell, every man, woman, and child in Sweet Hollow.

He closed his eyes, weary of staring at his friend's gory remains.

The veins in the receptionist's throat had been ripped out. Blood pooled beneath him, darkly shimmering beneath the fluorescent lights.

Dozens of small, razor-sharp indentations (*teeth marks?*) surrounded the wound like scattered buckshot.

"You there, Landis?" Bradley called over his shoulder.

"Yes, sir?" He stood in the doorway, arching his thick eyebrows.

"Call the state police. Notify them of our situation. This is bigger than we can handle."

"Roger that."

"When you're done, collect some shotguns from the armory. They might come in handy when we investigate the Vallancy."

"Sure thing, Sheriff."

Landis' footsteps echoed down the hall.

Bradley stood, turning away from the grisly corpses—Maurice in the alley between holding cells, Thorn splayed on his side with his ashen face awash in moonlight creeping down from the barred window. Bradley ambled out of the jail, into the station's main hallway, then entered his office.

He didn't bother shutting the door.

He opened his bottom desk drawer. Took out the bottle of Wild Turkey. Poured himself a paper cup. Emptied it in two gulps.

He fished around his pants pocket for cinnamon gum. He plucked out the package, stared at its fire-red logo, then tossed it into the wastebasket.

He took up the bottle. Poured another cup. He did not want to go exploring the Vallancy. Did not want to see what sort of hell awaited him there.

"Doesn't matter what you *want*, buddy," he spoke aloud, fidgeting with a callus on his right thumb. "It's a matter of what must be *done*."

He downed the cup, crumpled it, dropped it into the garbage. Then he walked fast into the station's reception room. Dalton and Landis waited beside the front door.

"I've loaded our cruiser with shotguns," Landis stroked his beard, soberly. "The state police are on their way."

"We should move now, Sheriff." Dalton brushed the blonde hair from his sweaty brow. "If we don't act quick, more lives may be lost."

"You don't have to tell me twice." Bradley nodded. "Let's go."

Elise Thanatos parked outside the wrought iron gates. Slowly, she opened her car door and stepped out. A field of jack-o'-lanterns, radiant with sherbet flames, burned warmly in the field beyond.

Jason Hardy's pickup truck squatted adjacent in the dark. It lay empty.

So then, they've gone into the Mansion. What are they up to? Are they the people behind this ghastly field? Those eerie lights all over town? Or are they merely trying to find out what the hell is going on, like myself?

Elise wanted to blame tonight's anarchy on Patty Keepwell and her accomplices. Still, she reminded herself, she could be wrong.

She'd been wrong about a lot of things.

She'd been wrong to treat her husband so terribly—always accusing, scolding, reprimanding him for his honest nature. He'd done his best to make her happy over the years, but she was rarely happy. That wasn't any fault of Harry's.

"Are you in there, Harry?" she whispered, gazing up at the mansion. "Are you afraid and alone?"

She didn't know.

She'd find out.

Tonight.

She was exhausted of all this raucous. Weary of not knowing why Harry hadn't come home, why the houses mended themselves whole, and why the children were inexplicably locked away.

She braced herself against a gust of iceberg wind. Dead leaves swirled in wet tornados. Her hair stirred wildly. The moon shone its cadaverous light down upon the Vallancy's renovated slate roofs, gingerbread vergeboards, and high polygonal chimney pots. The Manse was a gothic Gargantua, darkly looming, and newly awakened from eons of demonic slumber.

Beyond the field of fiery winking eyes and glimmering dagger-teeth, the indigo luminescence beaming from the windows flickered—*only once.*

Elise smiled softly. This confirmed a defect in the lights; a fault attributable to their designer. This singular deficiency, it seemed to her,

175

suggested a chance to set things right. Maybe tonight's perpetrator didn't have everything under their control, after all.

She pushed through the creaking gates, strode confidently up the path between a thousand Satanic faces, up the newly minted front porch, then pushed in the (*unlocked!*) mahogany doors.

She stood at the threshold.

The blue fog cloaked her shoulders, as if reaching out to embrace.

Thick unease curdled in her stomach. She placed a hand under her blouse, feeling the slightly raised scar. The trauma from that dreadful night fleeted through her mind, and she winced as if stuck with a knife.

For this was the house the man had taken her into.

Now, she prepared herself to enter it for the first time in decades.

She closed her eyes, breathed deeply, thinking other things:

I'm going to singlehandedly get down to the bottom of everything that's happened tonight. Then the town will celebrate in my honor. A wonderful dinner party with fancy foods, fine wines, even a marble statue constructed in my likeness and set in the middle of Sweet Hollow Park. I will not think of the past. No, no, no, the past does not exist. There is only now, this moment, my first step over the threshold and into the house....

The old dark houses were a thing of the past—but as Elise Thanatos stepped into the Vallancy's foyer of marvelous blue light and swirling fog, it seemed obvious her future lay ahead.

A future of respect, honor, and love It was all she'd ever wanted.

She tip-toe-danced to the sound of silent cheers, venturing deeper into the mansion, eyes squinting against the fog, searching the spacious foyer for tonight's troublemakers.

The doors behind her, quickly, though silently—shut.

The Witch lay on the floor. Blood flowed steadily from her mouth. Her black pointy hat lay crumpled under her head, serving as a cushion.

Johansen's eyes swelled with tears, watching the little girl sleep. The pain had been too unbearable for her to remain conscious. Lord, how she had shrieked, her sliced tongue dripping crimson, her hands fluttering the air in exasperated agony, panicking, not knowing what to do....

Blood seeped out of the girl's mouth, pooling thickly onto the floor only to shrink and vanish—the floorboards drank thirstily.

"Damn this house," Johansen cursed; her voice a whistle passing over the lip of an old glass bottle. She lay beside the girl, stroking her long white hair. She'd managed to pull the razor blade out of the roof of her mouth—it'd not been imbedded deeply.

Johansen thanked God the razor hadn't been swallowed.

"Poor, poor sweetie," she whispered. "How could anyone do such a thing?"

She gazed over at Harry's corpse on the divan—a shriveled mummy with a tobacco pipe on its lap.

How could you?

The apple had been inside his jacket, Johansen had discovered. She'd rifled through the pockets, finding pipe-cleaners, matchboxes, and his wallet. Just whom had he intended to give the apple to? Or, yet another possibility—had someone gifted it to him?

Her forehead scrunched. A thousand furrows formed their field.

She'd never known Harry Thanatos to have a bad bone in his body. His wife from city council, on the other hand ...

She observed a rivulet of blood escape the corner of the girl's mouth, drip down her chin, splash the floor, then sink into the wood.

Bannatyne House seemed eternally parched—a vampire never to be satiated.

Where does all that blood go? The basement, I suppose.

And if there was a heart in the attic ... what the hell is in the basement?

A pair of lungs? A stomach full of intestines, livers, gallbladders, all growing out of the walls?

... how about a brain?

Her eyes shot wide.

An awareness dawned within her weary mind—an awareness that could only be described as the discovery of some great truth. She stood up, slowly—the only speed she was capable, these days. She limped through the red fog of the rooms, stepping around the fatigued, sleeping children now hundreds of years old. Her legs ached fiercely. Her hips, too. *Come to think of it,* Johansen thought, *everything aches.*

Just past the kitchen, she came to a door within a pantry nook.

There were no shelves along the nook's walls, no distinguishing features whatsoever—only the door.

The door was tall and black with a crystal knob.

The red fog thickened, obscuring her vision—a definite sign she was close upon something the House didn't want her to find. She opened the door. Blackness opened up below. The smell of wet earth clung to her nostrils, bringing to mind a legion of dead rotting things.

Fumbling with her utility belt, she retrieved a small flashlight.

Flicked it on.

Steep steps led down into pitch darkness. She peered over her shoulder once more, curious as to whether or not this was a good idea. Would she return from this basement alive? Would her next choice prove fatal?

"It's only a matter of time before we all get old and die," she mumbled, ignoring a fresh wave of shudders. "I have to get down to the bottom of all this...."

The damp mustiness clinging to her flesh, she stole her breath, then got down to the bottom.

The paved streets of Sweet Hollow eventually gave way to dirt roads on the town's outskirts. Forests thick with gnarled, leafless branches clotted the hills. Owls hooted from swaying eaves.

The moon—a dead man's eye.

The hills—a flowing opal sea.

Sheriff Bradley clenched the wheel, eyes fixed on the road. One had to be careful out here. The deer population was terribly high. One never knew when a deer might jump out in the middle of the road, offering itself up as an idiot sacrifice. Still, he stepped on the gas.

He was doing sixty miles per hour, well above the speed limit, but his guts told him to arrive at the Vallancy as soon as possible. Briefly, his eyes flicked to the rearview mirror, making sure Dalton and Landis were following close behind. Thankfully, they were.

Something waited at the Manse, he knew.

Something darkly hideous, perhaps stranger than anything he'd ever known.

As Sheriff of Sweet Hollow, Bradley had seen *a lot* of strange things. The town, though quiet most of the year, had a reputation of making up for all those quiet days with wild, unhinged nights such as this—as if the pits of hell suddenly opened beneath their scorched feet, and one had only a precarious rope-bridge to cross the chasm.

He wondered who, or what, might be discovered in the Vallancy.

Would he meet the person responsible for tonight? The impenetrable fortresses of the houses? The numerous disappearances? Maurice and Thorn's death? Was a *person* responsible for all this?

Several persons, more likely, Bradley guessed. *Who could pull off a stunt like this without multiple hands working behind the scenes?*

He remembered theater shows he'd seen as a kid, all the stagehands scrambling in the darkness. And when the lights came on—how everyone gasped, amazed by some fantastic new set design far too complex, too dreamy to have been constructed in a matter of seconds.

Yet even as a child, he'd known it was all an illusion. A magic trick. A *chimera,* as those old ivy league coots had termed it.

"Almost there," Bradley gritted, strangling the wheel. "Almost."

He braked hard, then rounded a corner—behind him, Landis and Dalton's cruiser followed the turn in a spray of gravel.

His headlights revealed two vehicles parked outside the Vallancy. A blue Chevy truck, which he immediately recognized as Jason Hardy's—a local artist who hauled canvases, paint cans, and easels everywhere. The second vehicle was unmistakably Elise Thanatos's Buick. It might've sported brand new tires with full tread, but the hood still featured its crude vandalism: *I AM A WICKED OLD HAG.*

What was Elise doing here?

What, indeed? Bradley's eyes squinted in suspicion. He pulled onto the opposite side of the road. Stepped out of the vehicle. Went around to the trunk. Opened it.

Landis and Dalton pulled up behind him, cutting off their lights. Emerging from their cruisers, their faces were hard and grim—the night's events had rendered them fatigued, irascible, and nervous. Witnessing the dead body of their colleague, Maurice Wainscot, hadn't done them any favors either.

"Here," Bradley said. "Arm yourselves."

He handed them each a twelve-gauge Smith & Wesson shotgun.

"We might require firepower," Bradley explained, "though I hope to God we won't need it. If anything, the very sight of these arms should elicit a bit more intimidation than our service pistols."

"Who exactly do you think we're up against, Sheriff?" Officer Dalton shifted uneasily, pointing at the vehicles. "Looks like some town regulars parked out here."

"My concern isn't with townspeople, Dalton," Bradley spoke levelly, feigning stoicism. "We're bringing the shotguns in case we run into strangers. People capable of murdering Maurice, Thorn, and God forbid, any children. Now, let's keep our cool, search this mansion with utmost diligence, and see what we can find."

The three officers passed through the open gates. *CLANK!*

The gates closed behind them—pushed by the wind, or so they reasoned. The sound of iron slamming shut made Bradley shiver—like he'd stepped into his own jail cell. One he might never escape.

A narrow path split a field of jack-o'-lanterns. The orange, lustrous faces gawked at them; grinning sharp teeth! Glaring ember-eyes! And did they not *turn, pivot, swerve* just the slightest quarter-inch as they marched past?

Officer Dalton, at least, thought they did—their gazes following him all the way to the Vallancy's porch steps.

A spidery creep-crawl traced the back of his neck.

Officer Landis nudged him. "Keep alive, Dalton."

"Trying my best, partner," Dalton whispered. "Believe me."

Sheriff Bradley half-expected the double-doors to be locked. Instead, he saw an eerie light spilling through the one-inch gap. He smiled. He got the idea the Vallancy *wanted* them to enter—or, more precisely, tonight's criminals did. Bradley steeled himself, then pushed the doors wide open.

Vigilantly, they entered. The blue fog swallowed them.

PART III:

THE HEART AND BRAIN OF CHARLES VALLANCY

Chapter Twenty-Two

Charles Vallancy glided through the rooms, a gray shadow in the fog. Upstairs, downstairs, attic, basement—the walls and ceilings were no obstacle, for his flesh was the flesh of space and time.

Sixteen souls wandered his mansion. Sixteen little flies scurrying about, buzzing madly against the windowpanes, seeking escape; a freedom they would never attain, for Charles obstinately concluded they should stay forever.

The old ghost floated in the attic now—a cavernous room where grotesque creatures crawled, scampered and groaned in the hideous dark.

Charles' heart lay beating in the wine case, upon a barrel beneath the moonlit window. With severest vigilance, he would protect it.

The hearts of the other houses had been destroyed. At least Bannatyne House still possessed its brain, although that terribly industrious Johansen would locate it soon....

It was inevitable—the children of Bannatyne House would be freed, just like those within Morton Manor. This, however, would not lessen Charles' vitality. The youth now embedded within his mansion's renovated walls made him impervious.

Sixteen souls! He'd committed their names and faces to memory; the teenagers; the parents; the police officers; Mrs. Thanatos; and the ghosts of Harry Thanatos, Thorn, and Maurice.

Charles' dead eyes gazed out the attic window. The jack-o'-lanterns winked below; each ghastly face a memento of some spirit he'd trampled on in life. He was cheerily reminded of Vlad the Impaler, whose own courtyard was often strewn with victims.

This was the natural order of things: to obtain what one desired, to leave behind an enduring legacy, one was required to destroy the lives of lesser beings.

Charles was better—always, and in *all ways.*

As a man of prodigious intelligence, capability, and vision, how could this not be so? After all, no common plebeian could rightly claim to be a thinker, a dreamer, and writer. For he'd composed tomes on the history and lore of that great green land of Ireland—the land where Halloween was born. Indeed, nothing outshone his utmost passion for that beautiful country. He would've lived out the remainder of his years in Ireland, if it wasn't for the villagers of Killarney chasing him out with torches, pitchforks, and all other tools which fools, serfs, and slaves are wont to use.

A frown creased his mouth, remembering the fateful night he forsook his quaint Irish abode.

All the fault of one woman.

A natural damsel of the village. Dazzling blue eyes! Fire-red hair! Her body classically lithe and pale; Michelangelo might've eagerly sought her for an intimate portrait. Charles enjoyed her for a time. His mistake had been to marry her—thereafter her tones of affection grew into intonations of nagging, griping, lecturing. Always demanding he stay home, all cooped up in that old dark house! Always insisting he love her, and *only* her.

The madame hadn't understood him; and so his nights in the town pub grew long and plentiful. In the dead of night, he journeyed home with any woman he fancied, married or not, and ravished them before his wife's teary eyes.

One evening, when his wife's voice had come wrenching into his mind, twisting his sanity out of shape, he clutched her lily-white neck with his bare hands and did not let go until she was dead.

Charles smiled, scratching the bald scalp beneath his wig.

How right it had felt! His hands around her neck—her soft, white, vein-gorged neck! How her blue eyes had *bulged,* and her crimson hair, red as blood, had fallen disheveled onto her pallid face!

The moon shone upon his spectral form, and it reminded him of her. The moment she'd fallen dead to the floor, her vacuous eyes gazing from a face as worn, pale, and pocked as the moon.

After that cruel midnight hour, it'd been only a matter of time before the woman's father, a well-respected man about Killarney, discovered what Charles had done. Subsequently, the village mob burnt his house to the ground, chasing him with torches, knives, and muskets. Charles, however, was discreet as a black cat on Samhain night—two fortnights after the murder, he'd boarded a ship for America.

After three months on the ocean, the ship docked at Narragansett Bay. He thereafter began his search for the land upon which to build his mansion. He'd maintained the majority of moneys from his book royalties, had saved all cash from his university lectures, and no one knew of his dishonorable exodus from Ireland—for in all the years he'd resided in that green land, he'd never once told a soul of his profession, nor even his real name. He'd married that Killarney woman under a false identity. Exceedingly shrewd! Charles was many things, but a fool was not one.

Now, he sensed the souls of Thorn, Harry Thanatos, and Maurice Wainscot stir about the rooms below, lingering in the oil paintings, wallpaper, floorboards, and flooded basement.

He felt, too, the four teenagers buzzing about the ground floor.

Three police officers with shotguns.

Two lovers, a boy and girl, searching for their parents—likewise, their parents searching for *them.*

Elise Thanatos roved the foggy chambers; her fingers grazing the scar on her belly; fighting tears; searching for her husband; and hoping, in the process, to discover what on earth was happening tonight.

Charles despised her completely, for she possessed the nerve to destroy his mansion. Destroy *him.* In a way, she was no different from that woman in Killarney!

Ahh, yes. Charles would deal with Elise accordingly—and soon.

Lastly, there was Patty Keepwell—the benevolent woman with a fascination for history and a fondness for old dark houses. Indeed, she possessed the only item Charles considered a threat—the blueprint to his mansion. For Charles could alter the fog, induce it to swirl and mix in disorienting ways, but he could *not* physically rearrange the rooms—thus, aided with the blueprint, they would locate his brain, his heart, and thus, himself.

Charles whistled an Irish ballad to the jack-o'-lanterns below. The macabre gourds pivoted in the dirt and gazed *up* with fiery grimaces. How Charles adored his possessions, his souls! For they made him strong, secure, indomitable.

His transparent form sank into the attic floor and hovered down through the ceiling of a spacious bedroom. There, he hid himself in a darkened corner.

With a vile leer on his face, he waited.

Waited ... *for her.*

Elise Thanatos stretched out her arms, advancing half-blind through the fog. She wanted to fall to her knees and weep. How many rooms had she stumbled into? How many stairs ascended? It was all so impossible to navigate!

She stopped to catch her breath. The blue fog obscured everything. She swayed on her feet, sweating profusely.

Climbing the stairs onto the second (or was it third?) floor had been a mistake. The rooms went on endlessly. The hallways twisted and turned. Her every attempt to relocate the main staircase proved a failure—she was irrevocably lost!

Taking several deep breaths, she straightened.

This is a test of strength. A test, that's all. It's been a terribly long night, and your nerves are fraught, but you will get through this, you will....

Impossible to see through this swirling, oceanic fog!

Even her tennis shoes were obscured; there could be anything down there. For all she knew, rats and cockroaches scrabbled about her feet.

She tried not to think of it.

She shambled forward, hands outstretched like a blind woman in an unknown town.

She'd learned if she didn't walk with her hands out, she'd bump into something. Reaching up, now, she rubbed the lump rising on her forehead. Downstairs, she'd rammed her face into a doorframe. The pain had been exquisite, enough to sting her eyes with tears. That was *after* she'd heard voices—Patty Keepwell's voice, she imagined.

She'd ran toward Patty's voice, intent on grabbing hold of her jacket collar, shaking her, and screaming, *Just what the hell do you think you're doing here!? What have you done with my Harry?*

But her quick movements had been rewarded with pain—the smack of wood against her skull. Blood trickled down the bridge of her nose. She'd wiped it away with the fringe of her angora sweater. Tears stung her eyes, but she refused to let them fall.

Blood might fall, but never tears.

Elise was determined to remain strong. She would not cry like the others, like the low-lifes one saw in the movies or read about in melodramatic books. Damsel in distress, she certainly was not! Although she *was* exhausted. Undeniably so.

"How tired I am," she groaned, stumbling in the foggy dark. "How very, very tired ..."

Her knees banged into a piece of furniture. She fell forward, her hands catching onto something soft and padded.

She squinted, waved the fog away, and glimpsed old quilts laid out smoothly with nary a wrinkle. Two pillows, soft and plump. An ochre post, one at each of the four corners.

A lovely, impeccably soft bed.

She gazed about the crazy blue world—foolish to lie down. Foolish to do anything but search for her husband, or Patty Keepwell, or at least a way *out* of this dreadful place.

How was it, she wondered, that she could feel so tired? As if the fog had taken everything out of her, leaching her soul of energy; a blue, swirling vampire that did not bite her neck so much as cloak her body with lethargy. The fog soaked into her skin, her pores absorbing its parasitic atoms.

Elise climbed into the bed.

She wriggled under the sheets. She sneezed thrice, pulling the dusty covers to her chin.

"Must rest a little," she muttered. "Five minutes."

Her eyes fluttered shut.

Almost immediately, she knew.

Someone was in the room with her.

Someone impossibly cold; a moving ice sculpture, or a ghostly galleon adrift on the Arctic—moving toward her in one frigid wind!

Her eyes shot open.

A white silhouette stood at the foot of the bed.

He was tall, a strange shade of pale, leaning toward her with a ghastly grin....

Elise's heart thundered in her chest.

The fog parted like a curtain.

He wore a curly wig. His black eyes shone like lifeless buttons. A pale grin stretched to his ears, and his hands, his wicked hands touched her, *touched!*

Elise released a blood-curdling scream; the serrating shriek of a banshee; she writhed in the bed; his wintry hands grasped her throat!

Choking. Her mouth opened, closed like a fish. She battered at the man with her fists—to no avail, for her fists seemed to move *through* him.

The world dimmed into a thin blue line, and Elise thought of the man who'd taken her inside this mansion all those years ago. The young handsome stranger with promises of adventure, who'd ruined her on the dark, musty second floor of the house, who took out a knife and branded his first initial—'V'—into the soft flesh of her stomach.

There was no knife now, but there were hands.

Hands tight around her throat.

No air, no air, no air!

She hadn't enough breath to scream.

Elise's eyes rolled back into her skull; two bloodshot moons full and bright.

Chapter Twenty-Three

A wild shriek disturbed the mansion's otherwise silent air.

"The hell was that?" Anna's eyes darted around the billiard room, an expansive chamber featuring a wall-length whiskey bar, pool table, a stand of pool cues, and a blackjack table with moldy playing cards fanned across the green felt surface.

"I don't know." Kenny shook his graying head. "But it didn't sound pleasant, did it? Let's keep walking."

They walked.

Then froze where they stood.

A tall dark figure stood in the doorway to the next room.

"Who is that?" Anna whispered, her face delicately wrinkled. The Manse had aged them both at an astonishingly rapid rate; faster in its effects, even, than Morton Manor had been.

Kenny's tongue clicked in his mouth, unable to speak. The shadow crept closer. Tall, dark, gliding toward them …

The fog parted around its face.

Long, pale, gaunt features with blue eyes staring wide. Dirt and grime coated the man's cheeks. A bloody bundle of jugular veins dangled from his throat like a grisly Christmas ornament.

Kenny wanted badly to grasp Anna's hand and run away—he stood petrified. His heart pounded in his chest. Worse still, the eerie sensation that he'd seen this man before, pushing a shopping cart of trash about town ...

Kenny took a sudden step forward.

Just one step, but it was firm.

"What do you want?" Kenny gritted his teeth, anticipating the man to reach out with gravestone hands, grab him tight, then pull him away into the fog. Anna would be left alone then, screaming his name, but he would be taken forever.

The grimy man tilted his head; his portrait one of supreme sorrow.

He spoke, and the blood gurgled in his throat. "*Beware the creatures ... in the attic! For if you don't ... you'll be Charles Vallancy's slave ... forever....*"

Thorn's eyes shot wide, the pupils darting fearfully about the room as if he'd heard his master beckon his name. His lips quivered. He glided backward into the fog, reduced to a silhouette, then nothing at all. The fog flowed and swirled like a crazy river.

"I think we just saw a ghost." Anna blinked. "One kind enough to warn us ... or so it seemed. Beware the creatures, he said. *What* creatures?"

"I'd rather not speculate." Kenny shuddered in the chill air cloaking his pruned flesh. "Let's just find our parents, okay? I have the feel that if we don't keep moving, something terrible will happen."

At the south end of the billiard room, they arrived at yet another door.

"Look." Anna pointed to the number carved into the door's top mahogany panel:

21.

"Someone's numbered the doors," she noted, running her fingers over the light groove of its numerals.

"Smart," nodded Kenny. "Like leaving a trail of stones in the forest to find one's way back home."

They passed through the door, feeling one hundred times their age. Kenny gripped Anna's hand, a great comfort to him. He tried not to think of the grotesque ghost that'd appeared before them, but only of their mission to locate their parents—he hoped they'd find them, and soon.

Their breath labored, their backs ached, and time was short—*such is life.*

Sheriff Bradley gazed up the red-carpeted stairs that led up into nowhere.

Into fog-land.

Into the Twilight Zone.

"That scream," he muttered. "It came from upstairs...."

Red stairs.

Blue fog.

He squinted, unable to make out the landing.

He shouted, "Ma'am? Are you all right?"

He shut his eyes. He felt like an idiot. What good could come from hollering into the dark? Still, there was someone in trouble up there. His obligation was to serve and protect. He turned, gesturing for Dalton and Landis to provide cover.

Slowly, the three officers crept upstairs with shotguns.

No more screams.

Only eerie silence.

"Who's up there?" Bradley called again. "This is the Sweet Hollow Police...."

Bradley froze on the sixteenth stair—a silhouette stood at the top landing.

"M'am?" he asked softly, raising his shotgun.

The silhouette was short, stout, rotund in the belly. A vaguely familiar shape. It began descending the steps.

"Hands up!" Bradley ordered, his finger locating the trigger guard. "Stop right where you are. This is the police."

The short, squat figure halted.

A moment. A beat.

Then, resumed its gradual descent.

"Freeze!" Officer Landis shouted, peering down the barrel of his weapon.

Dalton shook where he stood, terrified, fumbling his shotgun into position.

Only a few steps above them, the figure froze again.

They observed its thick body, the black pants and untucked blue shirt, the pale hairy arms by its side—still its head remained obscured in the fog.

Its upper torso jerked forward then, and the face was revealed.

Sheriff Bradley clamped his eyes shut, opened them, then shut them again.

Had he gone insane? Was he *seeing* this?

"Oh, dear God," Officer Landis whispered, lowering his weapon.

Dalton let out a low, agonized moan. He gripped the banister, nearly stumbling down the stairs.

Sheriff Bradley opened his eyes again. "Maurice?" he stared wildly. "For God's sake, is that you?"

Maurice Wainscot smiled hideously. His teeth were red with blood. Leaning forward, he tugged at the veins in his open throat as if straightening a tie.

"*Best of luck, boys,*" he croaked vilely. "*Charles Vallancy is a wicked man. You've got your work ... cut out for you.*"

Maurice laughed; the sound of a crow in a dark wood.

The blue curtain pulled shut between them; Maurice faded into the fog.

Bradley turned to his men. He opened his mouth to speak, then didn't.

There was nothing to say.

Now, he knew for certain: this was no magic trick. No ruse, stunt, or chimera.

This was *real*.

Dalton covered his mouth with one tremulous hand. He'd suspected all this, somehow. He'd known, in the deep cold shiver of his bones, something supernatural was afoot in these old dark houses.

"Listen, Sheriff," Landis growled now. "I'm an officer of the law, not a ghostbuster. I'm getting the fuck out of here."

"Don't be a coward." Bradley gripped the officer's shoulder. "What would your old man think, Landis? You know better than anyone how proudly he served on this force for twenty-eight years."

Landis, having turned to leave, stood still. He grimaced with equal parts fear and rage, scratched his beard with agitation, then released an exasperated sigh. He still had his pride, after all.

"Christ on his throne." Landis grated.

"Believe me, men," said Bradly, gazing about the foggy stairwell. "I don't want to go upstairs either. To be honest, I'm scared shitless. Have been all night. But if people need our help, then let's find them and help them."

They passed the spot where Maurice Wainscot's ghost had stood moments prior, ascended the stair landing, then stalked down the twisting maze of shadowy hallways on the second floor.

Chapter Twenty-Four

P atty dusted oak splinters from her hands, then pocketed the Swiss army knife. Number 27 was now prominently carved into the door. She studied the blueprint, nodding satisfactorily. This was indeed the twenty-seventh room on the ground floor—the ballroom.

In a trepidatious waltz, they advanced onto the dance floor. A great saloon stretched along one wall. Dusty bottles glimmered beneath cobwebs. A wall-length mirror reflected the room where Patty, Jason, and Alice huddled together in a sky of blue cirrus clouds.

The dance floor reverberated with notes of silence.

"Let's keep moving," Patty said, consulting her blueprint. "Room 28 should be the main dining room."

"Yes, let's do." Alice replied in a show of confidence, though the hope of locating her son seemed remote. Two hundred and fifteen rooms! All this bizarre fog! They were destined to become ghosts, forever haunting the chambers, hallways, and stairwells in search of their lost children....

Jason touched her left shoulder.

"Take heart," he said, gently. "We'll find them."

Lying. As much to himself as to her.

If he'd been telling the truth, he would've said, *We're on a wild-goose chase, Alice. We'll find nothing in this fog. Nothing! We'll only get older and older, our skin sagging until it falls off our bones, then we'll wander through the afterlife as desperate skeletons. God, I'd feel better if only I didn't have this sensation that something ... anything ... might find us. There are things around here ... can't you sense them, hear them? ... up on the second floor, or in the attic ... scampering, crawling, groaning ... things I never expected to find in this place ... but, then again, life itself is often unexpected....*

He expressed none of these frightful ruminations. A maxim his mother taught him as a boy floated through his mind: *if you haven't anything nice to say ...*

The blue fog shed a brilliant incandescence. Jason carried flashlights in his backpack, though they didn't require them just now. One was a waterproof headlamp, the kind you cinched around your forehead—very useful for deep-sea diving or spelunking. That's what it felt like they were doing now; delving into a dark, watery cave. One with half-shadowed creatures scrabbling around the place, obscene, hidden, lurking.

Jason paused to listen.

From beneath their feet ...

What sounded like a running river. An ocean swell. A lake lapping at the shore. Jason heard it whenever cocking an ear toward the floorboards: the whoosh of wave, the trickle-drip of a creek, the sluice of water or slime.

Patty led the way with sagacious discretion. Her familiarity with the blueprint saved them from getting lost at every turn. Before entering each door, she carved a number into the wood.

Now, Patty cut deep splintery grooves into the dining room door: 28.

Warily, they entered. In the middle of the room stood a long oak table, prepared with tarnished silverware, plates, and a candelabra. A dozen chairs lined each side, with one at the head and another at the foot. Thick cobwebs festooned from the chairs. No one had dined here in at least a century. Only spiders dined here, wrapping bugs in white wads of web, then, for a ritual dessert, biting off the heads of their mates.

"In the early nineteenth century," Patty began, her eyes absorbing the room's faded grandeur, "Charles Vallancy hosted dinner parties nearly every night. Even in his twilight years, he was regarded as Sweet Hollow's greatest celebrity. Everybody came to his parties. Young and old, rich and poor. Charles wasn't finicky regarding who came to worship his wealth, elegance, and fine tastes. Anyone at all would do. An elitist to his core, though an egalitarian when it came to admirers! Now, here we are, two centuries after his death ... his latest guests."

"I don't like the sound of that," Alice said, an ache worming its way into her stomach.

"Neither do I." Jason agreed.

High above them, the attic suddenly creaked, groaned, shuddered. Dust sifted down.

"What the hell is *that?*" Alice's head darted toward the vaulted ceiling. Everyone stared up into impenetrable fog. Then, before anyone could speculate as to the din in the attic, there arose an altogether different sound:

Voices.

Perhaps two, or three. A conversation.

Drifting somewhere beyond the dining room doors.

"Hello?" Patty shouted. "Anyone there?"

Silence. Not a pin drop—even the ravenous movements above ceased, as did the river sounds beneath the floorboards.

Then Alice's eyes grew wide, livid, shimmering with hope. Her son's voice floated beyond the room: "Ms. Keepwell? That *you?*"

"Oh, thank God," Alice exploded with a sob and ran for the door.

"Wait!" Jason snagged her arm. "You'll get lost, running from room to room. Let him come to us."

"He's right, hon." Patty cupped hands around her mouth. "Follow the numbers carved into the doors, Kenny! We're in Room 28!"

"We're in 26!" Anna shouted back. "Almost there!"

Jason Hardy grinned. His daughter's voice sounded like wind chimes of diamond and tinsel; of brilliant sun pouring off the shimmering notes, forming melodies of honey to drowse the otherwise ghastly air; and that melody was called *Anna.*

He'd never felt so relieved.

"Follow our voices!" Jason bellowed. "You're almost there, honey!"

Two silhouettes entered the dining room. Alice and Jason ran for them now, wrapping them into tight hugs. Their children had grown elderly; wrinkles clustered their mouths and eyes, and furrows etched their faces into unreal masks. Jason and Alice hardly cared. They kissed their children, so happy to hold them once again. Anna and Kenny, likewise, saw past the ravaged, wrinkled faces of their parents, and embraced them.

"I was so frightened," Alice whispered, holding Kenny in her arms. "I thought we'd be searching for you forever."

"Mom, please," Kenny grimaced. "You're strangling me."

She apologized, sniffed, and loosened her embrace.

"We're all together again," Patty nodded with approval. "That's well and good, but let's not waste time. We'll need to locate the front doors."

"The entrance is useless," Anna stated, matter-of-factly. "It's just like Morton Manor. Every door to the outside is locked. Every window unbreakable."

"I repeatedly threw a chair at one of the foyer windows," Kenny added. "Not even so much as a crack. As for the front doors, they open for nothing, save their own free will."

"Thankfully," Anna said, "we discovered how to escape the Manor. We believe the same trick will work for Vallancy."

Patty tilted her head. How greatly these children had learned in so short a time—an entire life lived, examined, ruminated upon in the course of a single night. Wisdom creased their formerly young faces, and it was honest, well-earned wisdom; the kind that arises through trial-and-error, through sorrow and struggle, through pain and endurance.

"Consider my curiosity piqued," Patty smiled. "Tell us, how the hell *do* we get out of here?"

Anna opened her mouth, thought a moment, then laughed.

"It sounds crazy." She shook her head.

"We're open to crazy," said Jason Hardy. "We've been seeing it all night, sweetie. Go on."

Anna told them.

The heart in the attic.

The brain in the basement.

The veins, blood, and sinew behind every wall.

The living soul who animated the houses; the man named Vallancy.

"Then it is as I suspected?" Patty Keepwell's tone grew hushed and reverent: "It is truly *his soul* animating the houses, in quest of power?"

198

"Charles Vallancy lies behind everything tonight," Anna replied, confidently. "He's the man behind murders, the houses, the aging—"

"*A man? Well, not quite . . .*" A voice sounded from across the room; a voice both old and young; aged and fresh; pruned and full-bloomed.

They whirled around.

"*To call me a man is dubious. A phantom, however? Most certainly.*"

Instinctively, Jason and Alice clutched onto their children—yet they tore from their parent's grip, eagerly leaning forward, peering at the astonishing visage before them.

Patty Keepwell took slow, cautious steps toward the floating presence.

"Sir," she greeted, recognition glimmering in her eyes. "It is, admittedly, an odd pleasure to meet you."

Charles Vallancy stood not twenty feet away; an historical figure Patty had read (and written) multiple biographies of, and had studied ceaselessly for years. Now, his opaque, semi-translucent form wavered before them; like a ripple of water.

The fog around him dispersed, revealing his extraordinarily tall height. His gaunt moon-white features glowed like a distant star. A malicious grin spread across his youthful face—for he'd died old, but the souls in his Manse had seemingly gifted back the smooth complexion of his youth.

"*Welcome, my guests,*" he replied, bowing slightly, "*to my humble Mansion. A delight to have you all here. A sheer delight, indeed. How sublime your frightened countenances! How delectable your earthbound forms! You may stay as long as you like. Stay forever, in fact.*"

The phantom laughed, and it was the laugh of a thousand devils.

His form faded into a pale outline.

The fog took his place.

CHAPTER TWENTY-FIVE

The teenagers wandered for what felt like years through the foggy labyrinth of rooms.

Ted and Sandy.

Darren and Clementine.

Were these their names? They'd begun to forget....

Blue fog obscured every corner. It felt as if they'd awoken on an alien planet—one which may be home to hostile creatures. Whenever gazing upon each other's faces, they shuddered and cried.

How old they'd become, how ancient!

They ambled through the chambers like the walking dead, like wandering mummies, like hideous ghouls.

The Vallancy had done this to them. The Fog. The endless maze of rooms and hallways.

Their feet were sore from miles of walking. Their backs ached. Their lungs ached. Their hearts ached. Everything *ached;* a painful, marrow-deep cancer ruminating in their skeletons. Solemn creaks lifted from the floorboards, and the creaks echoed in their bones. They might fall apart, just as this mansion had once fallen apart.

Forever, they walked.

Voices drifted in and out—human voices, a group, but from what room, what floor? Impossible to tell.

God, when will this end? Ted wondered, holding Sandy's pruney and sweaty hand. *I just want to wake up and find this has all been a dream....*

"Look," Darren rasped, wiping long white hair out of his eyes. "We're in the dining room again. We've come full circle!"

They all groaned—indeed, it was true.

The dining table stretched before them. Each place prepared for a guest—guests long dead, and who'd never arrived.

Ted yearned to sit down in one of the chairs. Just sit down and lay his head upon a dusty plate and sleep, sleep, sleep until he never woke up. That is what would happen, he knew, if he sat down. He'd grow older and older until his heart withered into a clot, his lungs shriveled into dried apricots, and his brain liquified into a moldy lump, unable to think, reflect, or remember who he was and what they were all doing here, here in this cursed oblivion....

Ted grabbed the chair, scooted it back, content to plop down—

He froze.

Voices. Close, this time—in the next room!

The four teenagers gazed at each other's creviced, paper-white faces. For a moment, they hardly believed it. They'd been lost in this mansion for what felt like an eternity, and now, the heaven's opened a crack, and voices spilled through—were they to be saved?

A woman's voice.

Followed by a man's.

Sandy began to weep; she wished they'd all spent the night drinking in the woods. She couldn't think clearly, her brain as foggy as the chamber they presently stood in.

Clementine cupped a hand behind her left ear yet heard nothing, as her eardrums had decayed to semi-deafness. Darren began shouting wildly, and then they all began to shout:

"In here, we're in here!"

"We're lost. Help us, *please!*"

"We're in the dining room, we need HELP!"

Voices of rust, flaking pipes, corroded batteries.

Voices of sarcophagus dust and porous rocks.

They screamed.

Ted began to think the voices had been an auditory hallucination—

an illusion of the mind and ears—but when the voices *replied,* there was no mistaking it.

They were not alone.

A woman in the next room called out: "Follow our voices into the billiard room! I've got our flashlight trained on the doorway. Can you see it?"

Dimly, about twenty feet away, they glimpsed it.

Like a softly radiating star, the rectangular doorway glowed.

With haste, they entered the room where five people awaited.

All possessed kind faces, although lined and aged just as their own.

"How long you kids been lost?" asked Jason Hardy, astounded by their crinkled tissue-paper faces.

"Ages." Sandy wiped away tears. "Years!"

"What did he say?" Clementine shouted. No one replied, for she wouldn't hear their answers.

Ted stepped forward and introduced everyone.

"I'm Ted. This is my buddy, Darren. And this is Darren's girlfriend, Clementine."

"What?" shouted Clementine.

"And this is my girlfriend, Sandy," Ted explained. "It was a mistake, obviously, our coming here. We thought exploring the Vallancy on Halloween would be, well, *fun....*"

Ted winced as the words escaped his mouth; he felt doltish, absurd, a fool.

"You poor kids." Patty Keepwell shook her head. "Caught in here for hours, you say? Years? Ages? Well, I believe it. The Vallancy is a strange place tonight. Stranger than can be known."

"Does anyone know what the hell is going on?" Ted asked, exasperated. "I don't understand what's happening to us. Why the doors or windows won't open. I don't understand *anything.*"

"The houses," Kenny piped up. "They're alive. Anna and I were caught like flies in Morton Manor for quite some time. Obviously, we escaped."

"Escape?" Ted's brow furrowed into a thousand creases. "How did you guys manage it?"

"The same way we'll get out of the Vallancy," Anna interjected.

"There's a heart, brain, and soul to these old dark houses. If we kill the heart and brain, the soul will take care of itself."

"Only then will the doors open," added Kenny, "and the windows break."

"Crazy talk." Ted swallowed, his throat like a dry riverbed. "But somehow, I believe it."

"Me too," said Darren.

"*What?*" Clementine hollered, more confused than ever.

"So then," Sandy interjected. "How the hell do we kill this heart and brain then? Where do we even find them? Let's get it done."

Everyone now laid expectant gazes upon Anna and Kenny—they knew the secret to escape, or so they claimed. Now, it was time to prove it.

The hallways twisted like gnarled branches. Bending, winding, coiling—a tangle of rooms and halls with unsuspecting corners. Everything met at odd turns; an impractical, if not outright fanciful, geometry.

Sheriff Bradley led his men down the halls with his shotgun drawn.

They were in the right place, he knew—despite how wrong it felt being here. The walls seemed to seep something sinful and sinister, and the floor reeked with malodorous age; and the fog resembled the blood of a ghost—remnants, perhaps, of the infamous, if not legendary, Charles Vallancy.

The Manse is undoubtedly where tonight's trouble originates, Bradley reflected. *It is the eye of the storm. The center of a black hole. I can feel it.*

Indeed, his was the intuitive knowledge one always feels deep down, as opposed to knowing it intellectually. Bradley had never been an intellectual man, anyway. Nor did he have any interest in resembling men like Peter Petrie and David Chambers, two Harvard graduates whose pride exceeded reason—this, despite the fact that they considered themselves the kingly exponents of reason.

No reason here in the Vallancy.

No logic or rationality.

No mathematical formula to explain why Maurice Wainscot, found dead at the station one hour ago, now shuffled about the mansion with his bloody throat torn open.

No consistent philosophy to understand the mysterious, foreboding thumps and scratches resounding directly above their heads, in the attic—Bradley shuddered at each noise. *What the hell is crawling around up there?*

"Dalton? Landis?" asked Bradley, staring straight ahead.

"*What?*" they chorused behind him.

"Nothing. Just wanted to make sure you're both still with me."

"On your heels, Sheriff," Dalton replied.

"Better keep it that way." The sheriff halted in his tracks—so abruptly his fellow officers ran into his back.

He held up a hand for a silence.

He turned toward the open doorway to his left.

Up until this point, every door on the second floor hallway had been closed, as if tenants slept soundly with *Do Not Disturb* signs hanging from the handles.

This door, however, stood wide open.

Bradley faced his comrades.

"We're going in this room," he spoke quietly. "I have a feeling we're going to find something. Something we won't want to see. But if we should run into some, well … ah, Christ! I'll just say it. Listen: if we run into a monster, or some ghoul or vampire, then *cover* me. All right? Just don't get stupid and shoot some innocent kid. There's bound to be plenty of kids roaming the Vallancy tonight. That's partly the reason why we're here. To find them, bring them out, get them home. Got it?"

Dalton and Landis nodded slowly.

Reluctantly. Regrettably.

They wanted to head downstairs, find the front doors, then drive home.

Home to their wives, heated up leftovers, and a soft warm bed.

Now, despite better instincts, they followed Sheriff Bradley into the room.

CHAPTER TWENTY-SIX

Patty Keepwell dreamily recalled that morning's rainstorm, before the sun had risen over Sweet Hollow. How cozy she'd been, sipping cinnamon tea and gazing through the sliding glass partition into her backyard; observing dead leaves swirl in tiny maelstroms, the bending branches of apple trees, the rain pattered glass.

Difficult to believe that'd been less than twenty-four hours ago.

She gazed down into the Vallancy's flooded basement, thinking of the storm. Water sloshed at her feet, pooling over the door's breach—as if all the rain had fallen only to collect here, in the Vallancy's basement, patiently awaiting her submergence.

The group stood behind her. Quiet. Reflective. Growing older by the minute.

All gazed down at the stairs.

Was it true? Had the Manse grown a literal brain, and did it hide beneath that murky surface? The stairs led down into a dark, cold abyss. Simply to stare at it was to shiver. Large rats swam about the surface—desperately scrabbling for dry land.

"Are you kids positively certain?" Patty turned around. "The brain is ... down there?"

"This *is* the basement, isn't it?" Anna asked.

Patty unrolled her blueprint, pretending to check.

"Yes." She sighed. "It is."

"Then it *must* be down there. Perhaps in a trunk, or in an obscure corner. It's likely hidden."

Without further word, Patty stuffed the blueprint into the inner pocket of her wool coat, then shrugged out of the coat and handed it to Anna. "Keep this safe, dear. My mother gifted it to me before she passed."

"Wait a minute," Jason Hardy scoffed, then stepped forward. "You're not going down there, are you?"

Patty bent over and untied her boots. "I take it you have objections, Mr. Hardy?"

"Damn right he has objections." Alice Vandermeer crossed her arms. "I do too. Patty, you'll freeze in that water! You'll drown."

"Well, I appreciate the vote of confidence." Patty removed her fashionable, calf-high boots, stuffed her socks inside, then handed them to Kenny. "Please keep these dry, if you can manage it."

"Patty." Jason frowned. "I appreciate your bravery. But don't you think—"

"The brain of Vallancy Mansion is in that basement," Patty spoke evenly. "Quite simply, I intend to find it and destroy it."

"Listen why not let me go instead?"

Alice flinched. Truly, she didn't want anyone going down into those frigid, scummy waters. One was bound to die of hypothermia, or become prey to whatever hideous thing might be lurking down there....

"I appreciate the offer, Mr. Hardy," said Patty. "But how good of a swimmer are you?"

"I'm a fair swimmer."

"And did you win seven medals for fastest relay on your college swim team?"

Jason blinked. It was an odd rhetorical question, and he considered whether or not it warranted a reply.

Patty awaited his answer.

He replied, with a small laugh, "No."

"Well, have you ever participated in the annual 'polar plunge,' where one dives into the icy January waters?"

"I have not."

"Well, Mr. Hardy, I have. You may be a fair swimmer, but I'm an *excellent* swimmer. I'm also accustomed to cold waters, being the sort of person who enjoys ice baths with some frequency. Now, Anna? Hold my coat. Kenny? Keep my shoes. I'm going in."

Patty stepped upon the first stair, submerging to her ankle. She took a deep breath, then exhaled. She did not shudder. She took another step, the icy water numbing her calves.

Jason tapped her shoulder.

"Here, at least put this on," he said. "It's waterproof."

"Much obliged." Patty donned the headlamp. Tightened the straps. Flicked on the switch, and a beam shone out of her forehead like a third eye.

"Wish me luck." She slowly descended the stairs, submerged to her waist, then breasts, then shoulders. Goosebumps formed on her arms and legs. She took a final deep breath, then only her hair floated atop the dark waters.

She dipped out of sight.

Bubbles spit at the surface.

Kenny Vandermeer shone his flashlight over the stairs.

The bubbles ceased. The waters grew eerily still—even the rats, it seemed, had drowned.

Everyone watched.

Waiting for Patty to breach the surface for a breath of air.

Waiting for her not to.

A lime-green carpet cushioned their footfalls. Officers Landis and Dalton bracketed the sheriff on his left and right. All advanced into what could only be the Manse's master bedroom. The fog congealed into a thick blue cloud.

They wandered the room blindly; discovering the room's characteristics like a photograph gradually revealed, portion-by-portion.

An armoire stood sentry beside the door. There was a writing desk, as well, elegantly carved with inlaid floral design. A divan of gold-and-red brocade squatted in the corner. On the opposite wall hung a large mirror one couldn't see until standing less than two feet away.

Officer Dalton caught his reflection in the mirror.

He screamed.

Landis rushed to his aide, shotgun drawn, only to find himself pointing the barrel at his own face—his face in the mirror blanched, then sagged.

"Get your head together, Dalton," said Landis. "It's just a mirror."

"What's happening to us?" Dalton shivered. "We look different. Older."

Landis gazed into the reflective glass, then shook his head. "A trick mirror, that's all."

Sheriff Bradley hissed, "*Focus!*"

The officers resumed their positions, covering the sheriff as he moved deeper into the room. A large four-poster bed emerged from the fog. The wood was of fine, sturdy oak, and an emerald-hued cloth formed the canopy.

In the bed, a woman.

"You there," Bradley growled. "Are you all right, ma'am? Say something if you can hear me."

Stiff as a corpse.

Still as a starless cosmos.

Silent as a windless sea.

The woman lay with eyes closed, mouth slackened.

Bradley bent over her grotesque form.

"Good lord," he whispered, his eyes huge in his skull. "It's Elise Thanatos...."

Dalton and Landis peered over his shoulder, fumbling for an explanation. They knew not what to think, save that an autopsy would be required.

Bradley examined the purple bruises around the woman's neck. The marks of someone's fingers. Undoubtedly, they belonged to a man with large, thick hands.

He placed two fingers beneath Elise's jaw.

No pulse.

He expected as much.

Bradley closed his eyes. He sighed, lamenting yet another death.

When he opened his eyes, the woman was staring at him. Two blue beams—like miniature spotlights—glowed out of her skull.

Bradley leapt back with a shout, stumbling into Dalton's arms.

Silence sealed their lips. They retreated with every hair on their arms standing straight, shivers snaking up their spines. They scrambled toward the door, the door, the door—somewhere back there in the fog!

The woman jerked up in bed.

Her eyes—two severe blue lasers jutting outward!

Bradley shielded himself; half out of sheer terror, half out of fear of being blinded.

Elise's mouth opened impossibly wide. A sharp, vivid beam shot out. It was as if she hadn't a brain inside her skull, as if her cranium were a mere home for the ethereal light teeming out of her sockets and flooding over her purple lips.

She lit up like a human jack-o'-lantern.

Her body trembled; twitched spasmodically; on the cusp of explosion.

The light beaming from her face flickered like a strobe; then the mouth stretched wider, wider, until her lips cracked and curled in on themselves. Her mouth turned inside out and swallowed her entire skull. Suddenly Elise no longer possessed a head—only a great, indistinct blur of sapphire hovered above the neck. The light grew white-hot, like a solar flare, creating spots to float about the officers' unbelieving eyes.

Bradley spun around, the shotgun dangling in the crook of his arm. He fumbled along the wall, hands outstretched, searching, and, at last, found it—

"The door!" he shouted.

In a scramble of legs, Dalton and Landis followed him out.

They slammed the door shut.

They breathed heavily, hands on their knees, eyes trained on the closed door. Would the knob turn? Would the door open, revealing an undead Elise Thanatos, her skull a veritable beacon of supernatural flame?

"I'm not going back in there." Landis breathed heavily. "Sure as shit I'm never going in that room again!"

"Let's get the hell out of here, Sheriff." Dalton gagged, about to vomit onto the hallway carpet. "This whole thing is bigger than we imagined. We're not equipped. Too many rooms. Too many ... *impossibilities!*"

... only a great, indistinct blur of sapphire hovered above the neck.

Dalton tossed up his hands in exasperation. Sweat slicked his blanched face. His hair had gone snow white.

The men caught their breath. Straightened. Looked at each other.

"Sheriff?" The lines around Dalton's mouth pinched. "Something's happening to your face … your stubble has gone white. There are … wrinkles around your eyes."

"It's happening to all of us," Landis remarked, his eyes suddenly foggy with glaucoma. "The mirror in that room … well, you were right, Dalton. It's sure as hell no funhouse trick!"

"Listen, men," Sheriff Bradley spoke up. "Let's forget about our pretty faces and keep moving, okay? We need to find the culprit behind all this. And if not that, we need to locate whoever else might be lost in this dump."

"Seems like Mrs. Thanatos could've used our help quite a while ago," Landis grumbled. "Lot of good we did her!"

"Sheriff," Dalton pleaded. "If we stay in this mansion, we're going to die."

"He's right," Landis nodded. "We need to save ourselves if we're going to save anyone else."

"You think *I* want to stay here?" Bradley scowled. "No, but I'm doing my job anyway. Serve and protect, remember? You two cowards head on home, if you like … good luck finding your way out."

The sheriff walked away.

Landis and Dalton exchanged glances through the fog.

The fog, the fog, the roiling, swirling, blinding fog.

"Ah, fuck it," Landis groaned, catching up the sheriff. "We'll stick with you, boss. And whatever happens, happens."

Dalton squared his shoulders, preparing for a long night ahead.

"That's more like it, fellas." Bradley half-smiled. "Let's keep along this hallway. See what we find."

They advanced down the hallway.

A lime-green carpet lay beneath their feet, green as an Irish spring. Paintings of random country scenes lined the walls—rolling emerald hills, cows in the pasture, yellow turnips in fields of clover.

"Sheriff," Dalton blurted out, unable to keep silent on the matter, "What the hell do you think happened to Mrs. Thanatos? That blue

213

light! It beamed out of her face like, I don't know … like something out of a goddamn *horror movie.*"

"How the hell should I know?" Bradley replied, stiffly. "I know about as much as you do. Besides, I'd prefer to keep my mind on those who might still be alive—and human. Look steadfast, Dalton. Don't dwell."

Don't dwell? Dalton rolled his eyes. *After what we witnessed back there?*

In his mind, Dalton replayed the image of Elise's hollowed-out face; a grotesque lighthouse, gleaming its eerie blue light to attract the wandering undead.

Landis, meanwhile, feigned a hearty stoicism. He set his jaw with determination, stared fixedly into the fog, and attempted to block out the ghastly images crowding his mind—in particular, that of Maurice Wainscot floating atop the stairs with his throat ripped out.

We've seen some terrible shit, Landis reflected, grimly. *But I've a feeling we'll be seeing a hell of a lot worse before the night is through.…*

Chapter Twenty-Seven

"**I**s she all right?" Clementine frowned, peering at the stairs. "She's been submerged a long time…."

"It's been forty-two seconds," Jason replied, checking his wristwatch. "Just seems longer."

"What?" asked Clementine.

Jason held up his watch, showed her the digital numerals adding up, and mouthed the words *Only fifty seconds.*

Anna and Kenny stood nearest the door, staring down into black tepid waters.

"If she's under for two minutes," broke in Alice Vandermeer, "I'll be forced to jump in after her. I'm a decent swimmer too."

"Mom." Kenny looked at her skeptically. "You were on a college swim team twenty *years* ago."

All remained silent, observing the frigid waters with a shudder.

Anna wondered what it was like down there—other than dark and freezing—in that legendary basement. Would Patty find the brain? Or would there be too many things cluttering up the place? It seemed entirely possible the endeavor to locate Vallancy's brain might take hours … and if such was the case, would they even be alive by the time Patty found it? Would *she*?

"One minute, twenty-five seconds," Jason announced. "And if she's

215

... then swam into the middle of the immense basement.

under for two, *I'll* be the one going in to fetch her out."

The waters lapped calmly at the top stair.

They all waited. Watched. Worried.

Patty Keepwell was enveloped in a dark watery world.

Her headlamp was impressively bright, illuminating the drab surroundings. She reached the bottom stair, then swam into the middle of the immense basement. Iciness cloaked her skin like a frozen blanket. Particles of dust floated everywhere, illuminated by the headlamp. Old crates bobbed around the basement. She grabbed one and easily removed the top.

Inside, dead rat carcasses.

They floated up out of the crate and swirled around her head. Patty pushed them away, and they drifted into the dark corners—like rejected comets into a starless universe. She was more careful opening the next crate.

Patty pulled off the top with a swift yank, then the lid drifted away. Old clothes floated out: a red scarf, white tunic, brown trousers, green waistcoat, a silver pocket watch on a chain— still ticking; black leather shoes with golden buckles, and a gross yellowed wig.

She wondered if these items hadn't belonged to Vallancy himself, perhaps in his formative years.

She pushed away the crate. It drifted until hitting the far stone wall. She wondered, vaguely, why the basement should remain flooded. Surely the two-hundred-year-old mortar between stones would be porous, and not solid enough to hold so many gallons of rainwater?

Perhaps it is not mortar anymore.

Beyond the stones could be blood, sinew, flesh.

And flesh is quite solid ... how well it contains one's blood, veins, organs, everything a living creature requires....

She swam toward the stairs, compelled by the need for oxygen. She'd pushed her lungs to the limit. Now, they might explode. She hauled herself up by the railing. Her knees scraped the stairs, collecting splinters.

At last, she broke the surface.

She sucked in the air.

"One minute, fifty-eight seconds." Jason grinningly held up his wristwatch. "You're a champ, Patty!"

"Are you okay, hon?" Alice gritted her teeth, freezing at the mere sight of Patty's drenched form. "You know you don't have to do this, if you don't want to."

"I'm … I'm fine! Water is w-warm." Patty smiled.

"Take as long as you need." Jason restarted his stopwatch at zero.

Patty practiced her diaphragmatic breathing technique—a training she'd gleamed from her competition days—then dipped down out of sight.

She returned to the top of the stairs multiple times, sucking in enough oxygen for another descent into the basement. The duration of her trips decreased; her lungs grew tired, the muscles in her arms and legs ached, and it felt as if her bones had turned to brittle ice.

She'd opened every crate, box, and trunk in the basement.

And yet, no brain.

The empty boxes and their archaic contents floated about her like lonely planets in space. The sun fell upon them on from time to time— the light of her headlamp. Now, her hands fumbled along the stone walls. She traced much of the basement's perimeter, moving as quickly as she could.

She couldn't stay down here much longer. No breath! No warmth! The chill waters soaked into her bones, replaced her blood, merged with her skin.

She traced the basement walls.

She came to a long bench built into the southward wall—what must've been a work bench. Then, she spotted it.

Located at the end of the bench—a large, hand-crafted toolbox.

A morose thing of dark, rotting wood; perhaps as old as the manse itself.

Many drawers were half open. Inside were nails, washers, screws, bolts. All of them little piles of orange rust.

She fumbled with the shelves, tugging them open.

The drawers resounded with a dull wooden *clunk;* the water muted everything. It was eerily silent down here, so otherworldly calm that one's own movements couldn't help but startle.

Patty's heart raced.

Her lungs burned.

She had to find the brain—*now!*

She yanked one drawer clean out of its box. Rusted bolts floated downward like dead minnows. Finally, she opened the bottom drawer, the deepest of them.

Patty grinned, despite her frigidity. The water chilled her teeth and made them ache.

She reached inside the drawer and pulled it out.

It weighed approximately three pounds. Soft, wet, slippery.

She couldn't believe it—what she held in her hands.

She was careful not to drop it.

Like a football, she clutched the slimy thing against her breast. Swimming one-handed back to the stairs, she gripped the railing, then climbed.

At the surface, she took in several tremulous gasps.

She spit water. Choked. Vomited.

A hand reached down, pulling her up the last few stairs.

Anna Hardy's hand.

Now, Patty stood shivering in the billiard room; her clothes sopping wet, dripping onto the ancient carpet, pooling water at her feet. In her arms, she held it.

And *it* was alive.

Thumping, pulsing, quivering!

"Good Lord." Jason Hardy blinked hard, as if to change the picture before him.

Everyone echoed his sentiment.

Ted held a hand over his mouth.

Darren and Clementine looked away.

"*Disgusting!*" Sandy grimaced. "Get rid of it, for God's sake. Isn't that what we came here to do?"

"Agreed," Anna replied. "Destroying it is the first step to escape. The sooner the better."

"Give it to me," said Jason Hardy, hardly believing the words forming on his lips. "I'll do it."

"Be my guest," Patty trembled as she handed him the slick pink mound. It made a *squish* sound when Jason grabbed it, then squished again when he set it upon a pool table. A red, slimy puddle spread around the organ.

"Everyone? Feel free to avert your eyes." Jason grabbed a pool stick from the nearby rack, dusting off cobwebs. "This won't be pretty."

Sandy looked away. Everyone else watched, eyes riveted on the fleshy brain upon the pool table's felt green surface.

It rhythmically pulsed, as if *breathing*.

The plump organ quivered now, as if with anger—its internal thoughts surely of the most violent and vile variety.

Jason stood over the brain, raised the pool stick as if he were Ahab before the great whale, then launched it downward. The stick easily impaled the brain—everyone grimaced at the woody knock as the cue stuck through to the table.

The brain spasmed at the end of the stick.

Kenny suspected that if the brain had a mouth, it would've screamed.

Jason withdrew the stick, rose it above his head, then jammed it down repeatedly. Raw, gaping holes formed within the vulnerable organ—which began resembling what could only be described as a large moldy block of Swiss brain-cheese.

The brain writhed like a suffering creature; a squid impaled on a hook.

Then, suddenly, it lay still—lifeless.

Now, it was no more than a bundle of disconnected ganglia. Its distended neurons gushed outward, and its watery, synaptic gunk pooled freely into the pool table's four pockets.

"Well?" Jason breathed heavily, tossing aside the stick with a clatter. "Now what?"

The blue light flickered around them—an unsteady energy buzzing through the fog. Everyone felt it. A change in the air; a decrease in static. The fog thinned, becoming no more than a diluted blue mist. The corners of the billiard room became visible.

"Now," said Anna, her elderly face set into a deep frown. "We go after the heart."

Patty returned from the corner, where she'd stripped out of her soppy sweatshirt and donned her dry wool coat. She'd put on dry socks and boots as well. Her jeans, however, remained pasted to her frozen legs.

She retrieved the blueprint from her coat pocket, unrolled it, studied it for some moments, then pointed to the topmost structure on the map. "The attic is here. And we're down *here*. We need to locate the main stairwell, then find the attic door, which, obviously, will be on the second floor."

Patty rolled up the map. "Let's get going." Her voice remained even, despite her shivering from head to toe.

Anna and Kenny exchanged impressed glances—for Patty had only just emerged from the icy basement waters, had in all probability contracted hypothermia, and yet here she was pushing *them* all forward. When she went to consult the number carved into the door of the billiard room, she half-smiled at the sight of smooth, unblemished wood.

The number she'd carved had faded away.

The door had healed itself.

"No worry," she told the others. "The numbers were extra protection. So long as we have the blueprint, and study it carefully, we should be all right. I *hope ...*"

Patty led them from chamber to chamber, toward the foyer with its elegant staircase. It was significantly easier to navigate the rooms now that the fog had diluted. At last, they arrived at the foyer's main staircase. They all paused, staring up at the red-carpeted steps with terror brimming in their hearts.

Despite apprehensions regarding what might be discovered on the second floor, or in the attic, Patty led them upward, and onward.

All followed—a battalion on a life-or-death mission.

221

Chapter Twenty-Eight

Charles Vallancy paced the attic; his transparent form hovering and gliding a foot above the floor. Grotesque creatures scurried around him—those who had grown fat and plump with life. Just like himself, they had fed upon youthful souls, imbibing freely in their blood and flesh and spirit.

His heart thumped inside the wine box; the finest vintage of all.

And yet ...

Everything for which he'd labored was now threatened. His life's work teetered on the edge of oblivion. His legacy. His mansion. His *memory*.

To exhale breath and not to take in another is not to die—not truly.

To grow corpse-pale within a coffin is neither to die.

To die, then, is to not be remembered.

To die is when one's heart and brain are lost to time and amnesia, to bulldozers and wrecking balls, to new life built upon the graves of old.

Charles felt this in his bones and in his heart, though no longer in his brain.

He did not *think* anymore.

Only felt.

Felt what needed to be done next.

For even a ghost may stay alive—if they are remembered.

Charles stood before the wine box, where it lay upon a hefty old barrel beneath the window. The moon sank eye-level with the windowpane. Its silver beam filtered through the dusky glass, and Charles let this dead planet bathe his immaterial form with the purest light.

Still, he himself was not purified.

He shrunk himself down into the box, and once inside the dark enclosed space, curled up inside the heart and waited.

Waited for those damned fools to enter the attic.

Little did they know a terrible surprise awaited them.

My, how his attic creatures scrabbled, scurried, scraped!

Long teeth, sharp claws, immense breadth of wings!

His wine box would never be opened.

They would never discover him, curled up within his own heart.

Death would come tonight—yes.

But to Charles Vallancy? Not tonight. Not ever.

The old ghost closed his eyes.

Within the cold beatings of his own heart, he slept soundly.

At the end of the great twisting hall, a narrow stairwell led up to a modest oak door. A door so modest, in fact, it seemed its very design was intended to be inconspicuous. A little door to nowhere—so why bother?

Bradley, Dalton, and Landis huddled beside the door, their ears flat against the wood. Their shoulders rubbed against each other, due to the stairwell's extreme enclosure. Unearthly din resounded from the topmost room—a cacophony of scratching, scuttling, shrieks, and screeches.

"Why do I have the feeling," asked Landis, wiping sweat from his brow, "something unbelievably fucked up is going on in there?"

All three stood back from the door.

Sheriff Bradley inhaled a sharp breath and, feeling ridiculous, went ahead and did it anyway—he lifted his fist and rapped against the door.

"This is the police! Open up!"

Groans. Mewls. Snarls.

Indeed, no pause came from the hellish sounds beyond the door.

"Sounds like a goddamned jungle in there," said Dalton, embarrassed by his own tremulous voice.

Everything about tonight had left him permanently terrified: the impenetrable houses; the field of sentient jack-o'-lanterns; the eerie sight of Maurice Wainscot's ghost, the macabre luminescence of Elise Thanatos; and now, having hiked up this claustrophobic flight of stairs, they faced a door shut against what could only be a forest of wild beasts.

Perhaps this door is intended to stay shut, Dalton thought. *Perhaps we shouldn't go trampling around forbidden places....*

But they weren't in a forbidden place—not truly. They were in the old Mansion, a derelict structure familiar to Sweet Hollow residents for over two centuries. Everyone knew about this place since the time they could talk. Charles Vallancy, indeed, was a name forever whispered on the air, discussed in history class, and bandied around boyhood campfires.

"Okay," Bradley sighed. "On the count of three, I'm going to open this door."

"No!" Dalton blurted.

His colleagues frowned.

With his remaining pride, Dalton adjusted his tone. "All due respect, Sheriff, but that's an *awful* idea."

"Don't you get it, Dalton?" Bradley snapped. "Merely running away when things get scary isn't part of our job description."

"Steel yourself, Dalton," Landis added. "We're going to open the door, that's all. Doesn't mean we have to step inside, right? At least, not yet ..."

Bradley reached for the doorknob.

His hand rested on cold brass.

"One," he whispered.

Dalton and Landis stood behind him, shotguns in hand.

"Two ..."

He turned the knob.

"Three!"

Sheriff Bradley flung the door inward.

225

A musky, sulfurous odor blasted in their faces—the fetor of ashes and burnt leaves and damp, ancient woods. The maddening shriek and chitter of creatures resounded in their ears.

Bradley stepped inside the attic.

In a few moments, his eyes adjusted to the darkness. He glimpsed a cupola window on the northward wall, looking out on the courtyard. Beside it, a barrel with a slim, narrow box upon it. A wine box, it looked like.

This was not all.

Far from it.

Covering every inch of wall, trim, and floorboard, a veritable ecosystem of creatures spawned and sluiced, crawled and clambered, slithered and flew. Things roamed this attic—now an alien world with green and yellow lichen spread across the walls. Cobwebs cloaked the ceiling in a sticky white canopy.

Bradley's heart thudded hard in his chest; his breath caught in his throat; he stared with incredulity.

Immense, bear-like beasts thudded on all-fours across the floor.

Bradley squinted his eyes.

It took him a moment to realize what they were, but when it finally clicked, he let out an audible gasp. *Overgrown rats.*

Their beady eyes glowed ruby red, and their tails were thick enough to snake around one's throat and suffocate.

Then, the termites—the size of small dogs, long and slimy, with a million tickling legs. Their mouths opened, grinning teeth full of slime. Next, spiders a foot in height, with legs thick as broomsticks. They scrabbled across the ceiling, weaved impossibly thick webs in the rafters. Within the webs, melon-sized flies buzzed with distress.

A garden snake, the size of a mature anaconda, slithered toward Bradley's feet. Its silvery tongue darted out, tasting the air. Its beady eyes fastened upon the human standing before it. The sheriff released a prolonged moan, stumbled backward, then slammed the door shut against the terrible attic jungle. The serpent scraped its side against the door, then slithered away.

Bradley tumbled down the stairs. His partners caught him in their arms. Together, they jostled down the stairwell, then stood in the hall.

The noises above sounded a little more distant, though this provided no sense of safety. Dalton gazed up at the door, fearful it would fly open. He imagined all the creatures plunging down the steps. Rats, snakes, spiders, millipedes, every one of them capable of eating him alive.

The men stood in the hall; staring at each other; eyes wide with terror.

Landis kneeled, vomiting in the corner.

Bradley and Dalton looked at each other with old pale faces, their hair snow white, their eyes like weary husks in the blue mist. They hardly believed what they'd seen, yet were certain they hadn't seen *everything*— there'd been other creatures roaming the attic; they'd just hadn't enough time to know what they were yet.

A voice in the hallway: "See something upsetting up there, boys?"

Bradley and Dalton swiveled around, nearly tripping over their own feet.

A figure emerged from the mist.

"Ms. Keepwell?" Dalton squinted.

"Officers," Patty nodded, pulling her wool coat tight around her neck. Her pale lips trembled. She longed to draw a steaming hot bath and lie in it until some semblance of warmth returned to her bones. Never had she felt so frozen. Her head ached like someone who'd eaten an ice-cream sundae much too fast—no amount of pressing her tongue to the roof of her mouth was likely to cure her agony. Only warmth could do that. Warm blankets, central heating, and dry clothes.

Silhouettes emerged behind her, coming into focus.

Alice Vandermeer and Jason Hardy, two well respected working-class parents about town. Their respective teenage children, Anna, and Kenny, whom Sheriff Bradley had known since they were tykes. Then, four high schoolers whose names he couldn't recall. Or, at least, he thought they were high schoolers, but with the extreme age of their faces, how could he tell?

"What the hell are you people *doing* here?" Bradley asked, both grateful and anxious to learn he and his partners were not alone.

"We're here for the heart, Sheriff." Patty shrugged, as if the notion should've been utterly obvious. "The heart of Charles Vallancy."

Quite naturally, Sheriff Bradley hadn't the foggiest inkling what she meant.

Each member of the group stepped forward to provide a piece of the story. Everyone had a small monologue, a scene to share, and a role to play in tonight's Theater of the Bizarre.

Piece by piece, Bradley stitched together a semblance of the night's events. Most importantly, he grasped the importance of the brain, heart, and soul of Charles Vallancy. It all sounded like a fantasy, and it was, and yet he realized it must be true.

On this Halloween night, fiction had become as fact, and fact as fiction.

It dawned upon him that all of this could only have happened on October thirty-first—the eve of demolition for the old dark houses, as well as the most magical night of the year; a time of myth and marauding monsters; when skeletons and moonlit-clowns were accepted into society with open candy bags and a mirth of laughter. For this night possessed a sense of horror and mystery stretching back thousands of years, even to the ancient Celts of Ireland. The pagans had celebrated Samhain, when offerings were procured for the deceased, turnips had been hollowed out and carved with eerie faces, and people believed in such things as malevolent spirits and fairies, and would dress up to resemble them, and march in a grand procession out of the village and up into the green hills, for to lead the spirits up and away from camp.

Sheriff Bradley had read of such things in a history book as a child, and had been ravenously interested. Now, for the first time in well over two decades, these fascinations returned in all their macabre glory, and he had to physically shake himself back into reality.

"Look, we can't go into that attic." Bradley sighed, all the while knowing they must. "You guys don't know what's up there."

"We've got a pretty good idea, actually." Kenny removed his glasses and nervously toyed with them. "Giant insects, perhaps? Sure. I can tell by the look on your face, Sheriff."

"Truth," Anna confirmed, shuddering at the memory of the Spider King in the Morton's attic. "We've got a whole crew here. And *you* guys have shotguns. Kenny and I managed to kill a monstrous spider with our bare hands. And we're just kids … right?"

Sheriff Bradley gazed over at his partners—pale, sweating men sick with fear.

"All right," Bradley replied soberly. "But before we all risk our lives, let's drum up a plan."

Chapter Twenty-Nine

Sheriff Bradley decided all prior procedure and police protocol should, under the bizarre and phantasmal circumstances, be abandoned.

"Since my fellow officers and I have shotguns," he said, "you three, for a time, will protect yourselves with our service pistols. I ask that you keep your fingers off the trigger unless you intend to fire. Be extraordinarily careful where you aim. Understood?"

Jason Hardy frowned at the pistol that was handed him. Not being fond of weapons, he found the solid weight of cold steel in his palm to be genuinely sickening. Still, he did not refuse the gun.

Alice Vandermeer, meanwhile, palmed her Glock 19 with familiar affection—she was well acquainted with the local shooting range. "As a single mom," she explained to Bradley, "I've taken the protection of my home and child somewhat seriously."

Officer Dalton, baring a reluctant grimace, bequeathed his own pistol to Ted. The boy was only seventeen years old. "I shoot guns with my old man every other weekend," he claimed, and thus his amateur practice elected him among the most trustworthy to handle a firearm.

"You say you found a brain in the basement," said Bradley, turning toward Patty Keepwell, "and that it was destroyed, and that's why this fog has thinned. Now, you claim there's a living heart in the attic. I want you to locate it, Patty. Me and my partners will cover you, should anything attempt to ... well. Should anything *get in your way*, let's put it like that. Now, as for you kids," he gestured toward Anna, Kenny, and the others. "All of you stay here, save for Ted. No wandering off. And under no circumstances are you to enter the attic. Got it?"

"Um, Sheriff?" Anna rubbed her crooked, aching fingers. "All due respect, but *I'm* the one who discovered the brain and heart of Morton Manor. Shouldn't I be—"

"No." Bradley shook his head. "You've braved enough terrors for tonight. But thank you, Anna. You're a courageous young woman."

Kenny gripped Anna's hand. He didn't want her to risk her life. Didn't want to her to die up there in that jungle of beasts.

"Stay with me," he whispered. "They've got this."

"Bull*shit*," Anna rolled her eyes, yet effectively stayed put. She'd come all this way, had survived so much. She didn't want to be left out.

"Okay." Bradley spoke calmly. "I need everyone to remain focused. Do not let fear cloud your minds. For everyone's sake, *keep alive*."

He gazed at the weary, worried, wrinkled faces.

Faces he vaguely recognized; masks of entropy; veneers of old age.

He reached into his pocket, retrieved a stray stick of cinnamon gum, then voraciously stuffed it into his mouth.

He bounded up the narrow stairs.

Placed his hand on the doorknob. Turned it clockwise.

"Count of three," he said, and the others gathered behind him. Bradley chewed his gum. Wiped the sweat trickling down his forehead before it stung his eyes. He thought of the serpent, hoping not to find it waiting for him, coiled, oily black, prepared to spring, constricting around him....

"One ...

"Two ...

Breathing hard, he turned the knob.

"*Three!*"

They burst into the attic.

All around them, the malodorous musk of primeval woodland. Damp, rotting floorboards nibbled by centuries of termites. Mildewed rafters cloaked with spiderwebs. Leather-dried rat carcasses strewn in the corners. Knee-high mounds of guano piled like ashy dunes upon the floor.

The attic was a deep dark jungle for creatures to roam—creatures spoiled on the blood of life.

Rats the size of bears.

Termites big as terriers.

Humongous bats hung upside down, their vile claws pinching the rafters.

Infant-sized spiders, scrabbling on eight enormous legs ...

Slowly, and grotesquely, all eyes roved until fixing upon Patty Keepwell and her group of intruders.

Eyes of onyx and vermillion.

Eyes of quick death and slow decay.

They've not sunk fangs into us yet, Patty thought, still shivering in her soaked blouse and jeans, *but they're draining our blood just the same. Our every wrinkle, line, and white hair is due to the life leached from our flesh and given unto these ... things. And if we die tonight, this attic will be born anew; no mildew, no rot, no cobweb, not one speck of dust. This manse has rebuilt itself from the ground up, and this loft is the final room required to mend. If all goes to Charles' plan, his manse will become as dazzlingly elegant as when it was first built in 1812.*

Patty stepped further into the attic's vastness, fighting off the shivers racing across her body—shivers of cold fear.

Sheriff Bradley grabbed an antique straight-back chair and placed it beneath the doorknob. He suspected Anna Hardy, at least, would attempt breaking in to help them—this he would not allow. Keeping the teens out of danger was among his priorities. God knew he felt guilty enough having Ted come along.

Everyone spread out into a fan-like formation, guns raised. Patty stepped forward, taking the lead.

Sheriff Bradley joined his fellow officers, where they stood to one side. They stared down the barrel of their shotguns, eager to protect Ms. Keepwell.

It was dark inside the attic, despite the moon spilling through the cupola window. Multi-faceted eyes spied within the cobwebbed darkness—bundles of eight onyx lenses shimmering like moonlight on a dark river.

Jason Hardy saw something slither out of the dark.

He raised his pistol. It was black, oily, partially coiled, just to the left—the creature had been waiting. It slithered fast toward Patty's ankles. Raising its arrow-shaped head, it opened its jaw, exposing two dripping fangs.

Jason aimed the Glock, then pulled the trigger.

The snake's face exploded in a burst of black blood.

Patty leapt aside with a shriek.

The snake lay limp at her feet—like a fat, thoroughly drowned worm.

Oily blood dribbled down Patty's jeans.

"It's warm," she whispered, staring down in shock. "The blood, I mean. It's warm."

Jason stared widely, unsure what to say. The Glock trembled in his hands. He couldn't believe he'd hit the snake, and killed it, on his first shot. He'd never fired a gun before. He didn't know if he was naturally gifted, or if it was just sheer luck, though he leaned toward the latter.

Patty breathed in deeply, as if she were about to dive into water. She cautioned toward the moonlit window. There, a wine box lay upon an old oaken barrel. She sensed a new danger with every step. The wine box seemed miles away, and strange eyes stared at her from the dark.

Black eyes. Red eyes.

Some blinked.

Her heart thumped within her temples. She still had a migraine; worsened by a gunshot that'd made her ears ring.

A creeping suspicion dawned upon her—behind all those hundreds of alien eyes, one vast intelligence lurked ... mean, morose, and menacing, like a skeletal ghoul at the bottom of a black pond, reaching up for a swimmer's legs....

This intelligence, Patty intuited, was none other than Charles Vallancy. For the man's heart lay beating within that box up ahead; and all those eyes would never cease watching until she was destroyed.

Patty halted where she stood—a platter-sized spider scrabbled out of the darkness.

The arachnid halted midway across the attic, and for a moment its empty black eyes met her own—an instant of recognition. The creature scrunched down on its fat legs, and, like a springboard, leapt high into the air—it flew across the loft, its legs outstretched to wrap around her face—

BLAM!

A blur passed before Patty's eyes—a mixture of shattered sclera, broken legs, and a hairy, dislocated midsection.

With an audible *splat!* the spider collapsed upon the floor.

Sheriff Bradley pumped his shotgun, prepared for whatever came scrabbling out of the dark next.

Patty winced, stepping over the mound of gushing green guts, twitching legs, and leaky eyes. She was closer to the wine box.

Closer, yet still so very far away. The distance between Earth and Mars. She felt like an astronaut stranded on a hostile planet, a fatal leak in her helmet....

She took another step.

Then another.

Behind her, everyone kept pace, forming a semi-circle around her. If anything moved toward her, from in front or behind, they would fire—so long as they kept alert, aware, alive!

Eyes wide open. Guns drawn.

Hearts hammering. Stomachs clenched.

A vile *clicking* emerged ahead—the sharp lapping of a tongue. What followed could only be described as an unholy *screech;* a deafening, high-pitched noise.

Somewhere in the attic depths, the creature spread its enormous, ebony wings.

Its red eyes enlarged as it approached, like twin flames engorged.

Patty ducked with her hands over her head. A swoosh of air passed over, whistling across her knuckles.

A scream from behind.

Patty reeled around, then gasped in horror.

Officer Landis struggled beneath the beast. The giant bat flapped its wings, obscuring his screaming face. He'd accidentally dropped his shotgun and his hands were free to rip and tear at the leathery wings—

two prodigious fliers which embraced Landis' upper torso. Cobwebs stirred above due to the bat's violent gesticulations.

It clicked and screeched—its throat performing as amplifier for its monstrous vocalizations. Landis screamed; the blood gushing down his face, dying his white beard crimson.

Alice Vandermeer raised her pistol, aiming at the hideous creature.

"No!" Sheriff Bradley rushed to her side. "Don't shoot! You'll kill him!"

Alice spared a glance over her shoulder; her face cinched with panic. Dalton and Bradley laid their shotguns on the ground, then suddenly leapt upon the great bat. They tore at its great wings, intending to rip them clean off the creature's hairy, shuddering body.

Landis' agonized screams cut away—he slumped to the floor. The bat buried its gray, gnarled face into his throat—just as it had done to Thorn and Maurice Wainscot.

The officer's face was gone; only the blood, tendons, and skull remained.

He lay on his back, eyeballs darting wildly from his naked skull.

Blood pooled thickly upon the floor.

The boards drank the blood, until it was gone.

Gone—just like Landis.

Bradley and Officer Dalton now screamed—how the creature shuddered in their hands! After a series of spasmodic yanks, they managed to rip the bat away from Landis's corpse. Quickly, as the creature writhed within their grasp, they rammed it hard against the westward wall.

"Duck low!" Alice Vandermeer shouted. "Duck your heads!"

Dalton and Bradley instinctively obeyed the command. They tucked their heads into their chests, and Bradley leaned far to the left, and Dalton to the right. They held the jittering creature against the wall.

Alice aimed the pistol squarely between the officers—and fired.

The bat screeched its final hideous note, then silenced.

Its wings ceased fluttering.

Bradley and Dalton let the creature drop—*THUMP.*

Slowly, they turned around and stared at Landis' body—now a faceless corpse, the teeth shockingly white in the dark, the skull blood-slicked, the eyeballs bare and staring into nothing.

"I'm sorry," Alice cried, aiming her pistol at the things quivering in the dark, "but there's nothing you can do for your friend now. Please, if we're going to get out of here alive …"

"She's right, Dalton," Bradley muttered, picking up his shotgun. "Claim your weapon, man. Focus on Patty!"

Almost mechanically, Dalton picked up his shotgun. He focused on Patty's every advance toward the wine box. The shotgun no longer trembled in his hands, and his sweaty, blanched face resembled a blank note. Pure shock paralyzed his emotions; he moved as if pulled by hidden strings.

Patty inhaled the attic's earthy decay.

Her ears rang; her headache raged; her body shivered.

I can do this. Yes, I must … all my life I've wanted to do something great. Now, here's my chance.

Every step brought her closer to the window, the table, the box, his heart.

Along the wall, a blind thing crawled across the window, obscuring the moonlight. The attic went pitch-dark.

Blackness.

The moon eclipsed by an unknown shadow.

What remained: the ominous noise of chittering, clicking, growling.…

Then, like a blessed ray of heaven, moonlight flooded the window. Everyone observed the creature where it lay upon the large barrel. It possessed a trunk of many red segments, long furry antennae, and a million red legs repeatedly coiling and uncoiling, like a bodybuilder flexing his muscles.

The wine box disappeared beneath its slimy bulk.

Two dark red pincers quivered around its mouth.

The mouth opened, revealing a bundle of spikes for teeth. *Put a hand in there,* Patty thought, *and all you'll get back is a spurting stub.*

The millipede lingered, its antennae tickling the air.

Once more, Patty froze.

A low, blood-curdling growl—where from? It was close. Horribly, uncomfortably close, for she could smell its fetid breath!

Somewhere ahead, burning rubies winked.

She took a step back. Two steps. Three.

The millipede had suddenly become the least of her worries. She thought of the bats—there must be a dozen of those things, all mere seconds from screeching out of the dark and driving fangs into her vulnerable flesh. Slowly, like a bleak and ominous dawn, she knew—

"Oh, my God...," groaned Ted Gable, his hands quivering around the pistol.

Everyone muttered curses, followed by a simultaneous gasp of disbelief—

Six gigantic rats lumbered out of the thin blue mist.

A few stood up on two feet, their wriggling pink ears scraping the ceiling. Two sharp, yellowed teeth stuck out of their mouths; teeth designed to render flesh from bones. A chittering shriek resounded from their throats. Hungry.

Their red eyes, beaming like devil's eyes, locked upon Patty's retreating form.

Closer they came. Some walked stiltedly on two hind legs, others hunched down on all fours.

Closer, then closer still ...

Sheriff Bradley stepped in front of Patty, his shotgun raised.

Instinctively, Officer Dalton did the same.

Alice and Jason stepped forward.

Then the shivering, panicking, not-yet-eighteen-year-old Ted Gable.

They formed a solid row in front of Patty Keepwell—like a defensive line protecting the team quarterback. The largest rat of them all, standing nearly eight feet in height, shambled forward on its hind feet. Its sharp claws dragged across the floor.

Bradley fired.

A gush of blood burst from the rat's chest.

It hunkered down on all fours, quivering in pain. Then, incredibly, it elevated back onto its hind legs. It growled deeply, advancing turgidly with blood dripping down its pink-white belly.

The other rat-beasts launched into a rapid scamper forward, their claws clicking the floor in a charge—a wave of vile and vicious vermin! They would not approach one at a time, no—they attacked *en masse*.

A series of shots rang out.

Patty ducked onto her haunches, grimacing, covering her ears. The blast of guns bombarded the air, followed by the meaty *thump!* of four-hundred-pound bodies slamming onto the floor. The floorboards trembled.

Patty pivoted to one side, spying something in her peripheral vision.

Ted Gable successfully shot down one of the gargantuan rats. He did not, however, observe the creature behind him—crawling out of a darkened corner with glistening eyes.

Now, it was too late. Ted released a blood-curdling shriek—a veritable Wilhelm scream. A fat hairy spider with a basketball-sized midsection leapt upon his head. Its plump legs slid into his mouth, nostrils, and ears.

Patty's eyes swelled. She covered her mouth, stifling a horrified sob.

Officer Dalton turned from the massacred rats, alerted by the commotion behind him. He ran for the screaming boy. He aimed his shotgun, searching for a decent shot without Ted in his line of fire.

As Dalton charged forward, another spider leapt out of the darkness. Eight legs wrapped around Dalton's waist, and he collapsed under its weighty bulk. The shotgun flung out of Dalton's hands.

It skidded across the floor—serendipitously landing at Patty's feet.

Patty snatched it up. Pumped it. Took aim. She stared down the barrel, brought the spider nearly within dead-sight, yet could not get a clean shot.

Dalton didn't have the chance to scream.

The spider's toxic fangs sunk into the officer's skull. Blood gushed down Dalton's face, running into his trembling, gasping mouth. His scalp dissolved, the yellow venom instantly eroding the hard bone of his cranium. Dalton collapsed face down; his brains peeled away, melting onto his shoulders, tossing up thick smoke.

Bradley rushed forward, gripped two of the spider's legs, then flung it across the loft. It struck the floor, tumbled, dizzily righted itself on all of its legs, then leapt forward again—Jason Hardy took aim this time, and shot it dead.

Ted—still horribly alive—shrieked and thrashed upon his back while the spider's legs slid, inch-by-inch, deep into his eye sockets, his broken ears, and down his bulging throat. The boy still gripped the service pistol and fired blindly into the air. Dust and cobwebs drifted down from the rafters.

With a sudden crack—as of a tree splitting beneath a lightning bolt—the spider's legs broke through the roof of Ted's mouth and stirred his brains.

Sheriff Bradley, tears streaming down his face, shot both the boy and spider dead.

Ted twitched once, twice, then lay motionless.

Bradley plucked new bullets from his gun belt, fastidiously reloading despite his tremulous hands. His heart pounded in his chest; he could hardly comprehend everything that'd just happened—his fellow officers were dead, as was, quite obviously, the much-too-young Ted Gable.

Only Alice, Jason, Patty, and himself remained.

He wiped his tears; straightened his hunched shoulders.

Six dead rat-beasts lay upon the ground—fresh carcasses for the spiders and bats to feed, and feed they did.

From out of the dark, the creatures gathered around their fallen brethren, and, without mercy, drank and lip-smacked and slurped and grunted in a great, gory, gluttonous feast. *Good,* Bradley thought, feeling as if he might go insane. *A distraction for them. Temporarily, at least . . .*

He elbowed Alice and Jason to the side, then firmly pushed Patty back in front of them.

"Keep moving, Patty," he demanded, once again wiping his eyes.

"We've got you covered, I promise. Close the space between you and that box. Do it *now.*"

Yes. Patty nodded, shakily. *Because if not now ...*

She faced the moonlit window, and the winebox upon the barrel, and the colossal millipede coiled there—a paradox of monstrosity. Her heart pounded like marching drum. If she didn't get to that goddamned winebox, the death of her friends will have been for nothing.

She looked around her. At the feasting creatures. At the blood. The bodies.

Move! she commanded herself.

She strode forward, closing the distance. Fear and glory stirred her spirits, courage steeled her nerves, and destiny compelled her forward.

The millipede awaited.

Its red maw opened, flashing jaundiced needle-teeth.

CHAPTER THIRTY

Arching over the wine box, the millipede's body bent into the shape of a question mark. Its antennae twitched at the air—tentative and teasing. The mandibles quivered, and the legs all rubbed against each other in vile stridulations....

Merely looking at it churned Patty's stomach, as if she were seasick. Still, she did not turn away, did not even blink. She glimpsed a familiarity in the creature's face—true, the insect's countenance struck her as unbelievably alien, and yet ...

Charles Vallancy's presence lingered in its cruel, gleaming gaze.

The uncanny realization made Patty's skin crawl.

A gun shot rang out—a spider silently scrabbling toward her exploded like a heavy garbage bag full of wet viscera. She did not bother to turn around and see who shot it. Her ears rang terribly; she continued forward.

From out of the dark, the flapping of giant bats—Jason Hardy and Alice Vandermeer raised their pistols and shot them down. Then one of the few remaining rat-beasts lumbered into the moonlight. It was bigger than a grizzly, and its long pink tail aggressively thwacked the floor. Jason fired at it—and missed, striking the wall behind it. Wood splinters scattered everywhere. Sheriff Bradley stepped forward now, and shot the creature. The vermin collapsed with only half its skull attached.

Alice gritted her teeth, shooting the creatures as they emerged. When, finally, her Glock emptied, she shielded herself behind Jason Hardy.

He continued firing—occasionally missing his targets and cursing himself. He thought only of Anna, his beloved daughter—he must survive this night, must return to her safely.

Patty Keepwell stood only a few feet from the millipede. It arched cobra-like upon the table, its mandibles excitedly twitching. Jason intended to shoot the vile thing, but his chance was denied—still more creatures scurried out of the dark. At these, he was forced to take aim.

Sheriff Bradley set aside his emptied Mossberg and scooped a Glock 19 off the floor—the one Ted Gable had dropped prior to his violent departure. He fired relentlessly—at bats, rats, spiders, all freakishly huge and hideous and springing upon them all at once. His bloodshot eyes glared into the dark chittering jungle … yet did *not* see the gargantuan termite scrabbling above, emerging from the rafters.

Patty screamed as the beast's weight slammed down onto her chest. She pinwheeled backward, then slipped. The base of her skull thumped the floor. Everything blurred.

Tiny white specks whirled about her vision.

Her head throbbed, yet the pain was obscured by the sight of the grotesque thing buzzing on top of her.

In one horrible second, she thought: *termite!*

Its sightless eyes blinked on either side of its square brown head, and its jaundiced yellow body shuddered orgasmically, and the labrum above its mouth dripped mucus, and the antennae twitched, and the dark brown mandibles scraped Patty's cheeks, drawing blood, pulling her screaming face closer to its gnashing mouth.

The huge mandibles were sharp as blades

Should they close like a pair of scissors, they could easily cut off Patty Keepwell's head.

The gray compartment of its mouth slid open like a pneumatic door—beyond that, a bundle of razors; teeth capable of chomping through doors, galleon ships, draw bridges, and log cabins.

Two furry antennae slid behind her head, lifting her face closer, *closer!* Its teeth gnashed, and its thorax slid and warbled rhythmically atop her breasts. A hideous buzz resounded, and its cold breath blasted in her face and smelled of old, rain-dampened wood.

Patty's hands reached up and yanked frantically on the antennae, as if to snap them like twigs.

In that moment, molested by its six fumbling legs, submerged in her own horrified screams and the brown mandibles that pricked her cheeks and her hands grappling the hairy antennae, twisting, and tearing at them, the mouth of the insect looming closer, closer—

She saw it before she heard it—like lightning preceding a powerful clap of thunder.

A blotch of blood splashed onto her face.

The gunshot blasted out; deafening.

Patty screamed still more, recoiling at the black insect guts splattered all over her face. She tasted them in her mouth; a nasty sour porridge. She turned aside, spit out the lingering guts, then at last opened her eyes. Sheriff Bradley stood beside her.

He plucked up the dead termite, tossing aside its cumbersome bulk. Then he reached down, grabbed her hands, and yanked her to her feet.

Patty wiped the slime and mucus out of her eyes.

I'm alive, she reflected, utterly shocked by the fact. *That thing on top of me, driving me insane with its horrible gnashing teeth ... I'm alive? Truly?*

"Move, Patty." Bradley spoke firmly, yet with compassion.

"I'm fine," Patty nodded. She was pretty damned far from fine, but it was all she could say. She tried to thank him for saving her life; yet her tongue would not cooperate, and the words escaped her. Now, it was all a matter of one step in front of the other....

Patty stopped short of the millipede hunched over the wine box.

Instinctively, she knew what must come next.

She covered her ears and winced.

Jason Hardy and Sheriff Bradley opened fire. They each shot it once, twice, three times before both their triggers went—*click.*

The millipede spread its mandibles wide and screeched an unearthly, alien din.

Its legions of legs lay languid.

Its antennae wilted like dead flowers.

... she crushed the heart with her bare hands.

It slipped off the table, coiling onto the floor in a slick, slippery slump.

Patty stood before the barrel beneath the moonlit window—the wine box waited.

Her hands, numb and trembling, splattered with blood that was not her own, deftly slid open the box's compartment.

"A curious vintage, indeed," she whispered, reaching inside.

Now, Charles Vallancy's heart thumped between her palms. It was not the dry, dull, shriveled organ she'd expected. The heart was plump and slicked with fresh blood—the blood of Dalton and Landis, of Elise Thanatos, Thorn, Maurice Williams, Ted Gable, and others.

Like an ancient Aztec, Patty held the heart high above her head.

Felt its frantic beating between her fingers.

Moonlight gleamed off its crimson features.

The aortic valves pulsed, fluttered, hissed.

And the hiss formed words, as if Vallancy himself whispered in her ears: "*Return my heart to its box, you vile strumpet! Return me at once! I beg of you!*"

"Farewell," Patty Keepwell shouted at the top of her lungs, "and goodnight—you miserable, vain, murderous bastard!"

With all her furious strength, she crushed the heart with her bare hands.

Blood rained down—like warm water wrenched from a sponge.

Blood smeared her scarred cheeks like war paint.

The blue mist flickered, then faded entirely.

Patty gritted her teeth, sinking her fingers deep into the meaty organ. Then, with one tremendous pull, she ripped it into two bloody pieces.

Thus it may be said: Charles Vallancy, at long last, died of a broken heart.

Chapter Thirty-One

Darkness reigned supreme within the Vallancy, save for the moonlit windows. Jason Hardy retrieved a flashlight from his backpack, switched it on, and surveyed the attic with distaste.

Bats *thunked* from the rafters onto the floor; now lifeless piles of decaying meat. Every millipede, termite, and spider shrank down to average size, then rotted away into tendrils of steam. The rat-beasts withered into small dead rodents—common tenants of any old attic.

It all almost appeared ordinary.

As if the madness, terror, and fantastic horrors of the place had never existed.

Everything had grown silent. No longer did the loft resound with perpetual growls, racking claws, and grotesque burbles. Only one sound remained—that of fists pounding on the attic door.

Sheriff Bradley gave a wide berth to the grisly corpses of Landis, Dalton, and Ted Gable, sparing them not a glance. His jaw clenched and his eyes narrowed, yet beneath this veneer of callous authority, he was merely trying to keep himself together. He crossed the room, removing the chair from beneath the brass knob.

The door burst open.

Bradley lifted his hands to hold back the kids, but Anna and Kenny nimbly brushed past; their faces harried, their breath ragged, anxious to see their parents, to be sure they were still alive. All the screaming, shouts, and gunfire had induced them to panic.

Now, they stared at the chaos; blinking unbelieving eyes.

Clementine, Darren, and Sandy ducked past Bradley's outstretched hands, and entered the attic. Immediately, their faces paled.

Sandy screamed at the sight of Ted's corpse.

She fell to her knees at his side, sobbing uncontrollably.

"I'm truly sorry, Sandy." The sheriff placed a hand on her shoulder, his eyes red with tears. "You shouldn't be seeing this. Let's go home."

She nodded slowly. Her hands covered her face, tears slipping between her fingers. She'd not heard a single word Bradley had told her, yet seemed to understand just the same.

Bradley helped her up from the floor.

Grief possesses its own gravity, and Sandy felt as if she might crumple on the spot. She stumbled sideways. Clementine reached out, wrapping her arms around her. Without a word, the girls walked out of the attic.

"For God's sake," whispered Patty, shivering in her blood-drenched coat. "Let's get the hell out of here. I believe we've all had enough of Vallancy Manse."

None objected to this suggestion; indeed, everyone seemed on the verge of mental and physical collapse. Retrieving the blueprint from her pocket, Patty guided everyone out of the attic and down the long twisting hallways past hundreds of rooms.

Gradually, youth returned to their faces. Wrinkles and crevices faded. White hair regained natural color. Aches in their backs, knees, and joints vanished.

Simultaneously, the Mansion returned to its rightful old age. Tall spires warped, gingerbread trim chipped, polygonal chimneys crumbled, the paint upon doors and clapboards and stair bannisters peeled away like dead skin, and the roof shingles grew green with lichen and stripped themselves away in sudden gusts.

The survivors descended the rotting staircase. Splinters collected in their palms as they gripped the wobbly banister. Finally, they arrived at the massive foyer.

Here, there were ghosts.

They clustered before the front doors; bodies opaque and translucent as moonbeams.

Thorn, the homeless man, stood among them.

He stepped forth.

Everyone froze at the bottom of the stairs—Anna and Kenny, Jason Hardy and Alice Vandermeer, Patty Keepwell, Darren, Clementine, Sandy, and Sheriff Bradley—all gawked in frank astonishment. Despite witnessing many shocking things tonight, they could never dissuade themselves from marveling at the presence of ghosts.

Thorn beamed with happiness. His hair was trimmed short, his beard was gone, and his face was as smooth and unblemished as a man in his late twenties. He bowed, graciously—then faded into smoke and was gone.

The opaque forms of Officer Dalton, Landis, and Maurice Wainscot took their turn to bow—actors on the final stage of life.

Then they, too, became as smoke.

Sheriff Bradley wept—he couldn't fight back the tears any longer, for the sight of his departed colleagues touched him deeply.

Ted Gable stepped forth now, pressing intangible lips against Sandy's mouth. His smile was radiant, and his body glowed with an aura of gold. He told her that he would miss her dearly, but that there was much to look forward to in the hereafter.

He faded into oblivion.

Sandy palmed her mouth, softly crying.

The old man, Harry Thanatos, and his wife, Elise, held each other's hands—happy as they'd been on their wedding day. All prior slights, offenses, and arguments now long behind them. They kissed, then broke apart like a cloud in a strong wind.

The front doors hung wide open.

In reverent silence, they exited the mansion.

The courtyard jack-o'-lanterns were darkened, their orange flames having winked into smoke. In the blink of an eye, they decayed into puddles of soggy orange rind. For it was well past midnight, and even spirits of the dead must sleep.

Even the moon slipped from its starry summit, sinking into soft sacred ground.

Beyond the rusted iron gates, two police cruisers remained where Bradley had left them, as well as Jason's truck and Elise Thanatos' Buick.

The nine did not know what to say to each other; they had been through so much tonight. Reality seemed more malleable than ever. A great vulnerability had opened them, and they felt susceptible to the greatest of changes. And so they told each other, quite simply: *Goodnight.*

The teenagers filed into the back of one of the cruisers—Bradley insisted as much. Darren, Clementine, and Sandy had the eerie sense they were being hauled to jail. Of course, Bradley simply intended to drive them home. He was beyond exhausted. He longed for bed, whiskey, and the dark nothingness of sleep.

Anna and Kenny sat in the backseat of Jason's truck. Patty squeezed in with them, eager to arrive home, strip away her bloody clothes, and take a long, hot bath. *If I manage to get through tonight without catching pneumonia,* she thought, *I'll be a grateful woman.*

The winding dirt roads led them into Sweet Hollow.

The State Patrol crowded outside the old houses, questioning every resident on the street. Their investigation into the night's bizarre events had only just begun.

Despite the incredibly late hour, countless citizens could not sleep a wink. They daydreamed and fantasized, fretted, and worried. Most of all, they wondered—what, after all was said and done, was the fate of the old dark houses? At very least, the demolition had been forestalled— Bannatyne House, Morton Manor, and Vallancy Mansion were now roped off as official crime scenes.

Meanwhile, within a sterile, brightly lit room at Sweet Hollow Hospital, Deputy Johansen nodded drowsily. She lay slumped in an uncomfortable chair, holding the young girl's hand. The girl's black dress had been exchanged for a hospital gown, and her mouth was stuffed with bandages. She breathed softly through her nostrils, sleeping soundly. Johansen kissed her forehead, intending to stay until the parents arrived.

The exact purpose of the razor-apple had yet to be explained, and, likely, never would be. Many strange things from that night, indeed, would never be comprehended—including the deaths of Ted Gable, Harry and Elise Thanatos, Thorn, and two police officers.

Truly, the sheer gossip and lore this Halloween had wrought

would never fade from Sweet Hollow's social and historical fabric. Men, women, children, and future old-timers would forever tell the story of Charles Vallancy and the old dark houses—or, at least, their own differing versions of it.

Meanwhile, Morton Manor, Bannatyne House, and Vallancy Mansion slept in their dark, hulking structures.

Not a groan to be heard.

Nor the slightest moan of a ghost nor rattle of chains.

Most importantly, not one single beat of some hidden, horrible heart.

Jason parked outside Patty's house on Sowin Street. Everyone wished her a good night's rest, and the cozy warmth she most desperately needed.

Patty Keepwell paused before her front stoop, and watched the truck's taillights fade down the street. Anna and Kenny waved out the back window, and she waved in return, and then they were gone.

October's final chill wind cut her to the bone—and yet she smiled. She did not think of tomorrow, when she would be bombarded with questions from the State Police, questions regarding Vallancy Manse which she would never know quite how to answer.

She listened to the wind. The distant sirens. The voices of neighbors floating on the air. She gazed up at the waning moon, where it brushed the distant treetops. The moon resembled a ghoul's eye, slowly closing; and the whispered word—*Halloween!*—seemed to echo, then fade away entirely. A voice of dead leaves crinkled in the air, then fell to the ground amidst a detritus of chocolate wrappers, cracked plastic masks, and discarded candy bags.

It was the morning of All Saints' Day.

She told herself she ought to turn in for the night, yet didn't. She felt the icy wetness of her hair, the numbness of her toes, and was grateful for it. When she went inside her modest little townhouse, she knew she'd no longer gaze upon the photographs of her parents thinking she'd disappointed them. Nor would she stare longingly at trophies and diplomas of some supposed former greatness. Never again would she feel she'd missed her chance—at last, she began to know that she'd done enough.

Finally, she turned toward the north, the east, then the west—thanking each of the old dark houses.

For being old.

For being dark.

For being dead.

She climbed up the porch steps, kissed the blue-glowing skeleton on its jaw, then closed her door on the night winds.

THE END

About the Author

TYLOR JAMES lives in Sweet Hollow, Wisconsin. He's a writer of the Macabre, and the author of such strange volumes as *Beneath the Jack-O-Lantern Sky: Tales of Sweet Hollow* and *Matters Most Macabre.* His tales and poems have been published in *Cosmic Horror Monthly, Strange Horizons, The Literary Hatchet, Weird House Magazine,* and many other anthologies. He is twenty-nine years old.

About the Artist

LUKE SPOONER is a freelance illustrator from the South East of England. Since graduating from Portsmouth University with a First-Class degree in illustration Luke has gone on to work on a wide variety of projects and commissions, including illustrations and covers for horror, science fiction and fantasy books, magazines, graphic novels, conceptual design, CD packaging and business branding. Luke has also illustrated children's books for authors who aim to promote diversity and mindfulness in younger audiences.

Notable projects for his darker Carrion House style of work have included stories by Neil Gaiman and Clive Barker as part of *Gutted: Beautiful Horror Stories* and *Behold: Oddities Curiosities and Undefinable Wonders,* both from Crystal Lake Publishing. He also provided artwork for two stories by Stephen King; one in *You, Human,* from Dark Regions Press and another in *Gamut Magazine.* Luke also acts as the illustrator for every instalment of Jay Wilburn's ongoing Dead Song series of books.